The
WIDOWER'S
Offering

Gail Lowe

Published by WordPower. September 2023

Print ISBN: 979-8-9890301-0-1
Ebook ISBN: 979-8-9890301-1-8

Book Cover
Original painting by artist
Ellyn Bogdan Olson

Dedication

A heartfelt thanks to everyone who encouraged me to write "The Widower's Offering"—from my editors at the Wakefield Daily Item, Melrose Weekly News, Lynnfield Villager and North Reading Transcript to my family and friends. I dedicate "The Widower's Offering" to my father, Donald Pryor White, one of the best storytellers I have ever known.

The Appalachian Trail

Hopewell ME

Great Barrington MA

Palmerton PA

Damascus VA

Gatlinburg TN

Asheville NC

Springer Mountain GA

FORD

Chapter One

The letter, delivered in a white No. 10 envelope, return address Church of the Blinding Light, 139 Trinity Street, Hopewell, Maine, sits on top of a six-inch stack of mail on the kitchen table in Otis Kingston's five-room bungalow.

If Fern were still alive, she would have torn the letter open the minute she found it in the mailbox. But not Otis. He has ignored the letter from the church along with thirty or so other pieces of mail, all containing bills for utilities, doctor and hospital visits and homeowner's insurance. And there is one other bill he doesn't even want to think about—the one from Serenity Funeral Home.

He has let his mail sit in a pile for the past two weeks unopened, thinking that nothing is so urgent that it can't wait. Actually, if Fern were still alive, she'd wag a finger at Otis and say in a playful way that he was losing his grip on life. Maybe he is.

"What's the matter with you, Otis? You need to get a move on," she would say, giving him a friendly nudge. And in response, he would pick up his fiddle and play *Tennessee Waltz,* her favorite song. And she would sit in her chair while watching him play, a wistful smile on her face. She might even get up and waltz throughout the room with her broom for a partner. How he missed his wife, his best friend.

He had counted on Fern to handle the mail and keep the household humming along for thirty-seven years. And now she is gone. He can almost hear her speaking to him from the grave.

"The house could use a coat of paint, Otis," or "Can you give that toilet a fix? Running water drives me batty." And he would pick up his fiddle and tell her there are more important things in life. Like music. Like a beautiful summer day. A bouquet of flowers. And she would smile that lovely wide smile of hers, the one he fell in love with so long ago.

Yes, he misses Fern, even misses the way she pestered him about the never-ending chores that needed doing. She hadn't nagged the way some wives nag, though. Her prodding had been more like gentle reminders, like whispers in his ear. In some ways, she had kept his heart beating. She watched out for him by seeing to it that he had a hot dinner on the table every night and making sure he had clean underwear in his chest of drawers, even after working all day at the River View Nursing Home. It had been her job to fetch bedpans, help the residents into their wheel chairs, fluff up pillows and a hundred other things.

She'd come home every day at half past three, take off her shoes, fall into her chair by the window and put her feet up on the brown faux leather ottoman. Then she'd tell stories about her day while they were having supper.

"Poor Mr. Dalton has had a terrible time with his bowels, so they gave him a liquid laxative and now he's ringing his buzzer every five minutes. And you know what that means . . ." And Fern would tell Otis it meant that poor Mr. Dalton couldn't make it to the bathroom and she'd had to clean him up and change his sheets at least five times throughout the day.

Then, there was Margaret Stackpole, an elderly woman who, when younger, liked to dress up on Halloween and scare the kids half to death when they came to her door for tricks or treats. Fern once told Otis that Margaret rang the buzzer just so someone would come into her room, and that someone was usually Fern, and when she asked what Margaret needed she would answer, "Nothing, dear. I just wanted a little company."

Though she would have liked to provide it, Fern had had no time to keep anyone company, not even those who were bed-ridden like Margaret.

There was the time a little romance was going on between two residents, both widows. Roy Halliday had had his eye on Helen Reynolds and at night he'd sneak into her room and get in bed with her. One night an aide caught them stark naked under the covers and told Fern she had to pull Roy out of the bed and get him back to his room. She had chuckled at the thought of Roy sitting in a wheel chair naked as a newborn baby under a sheet while being wheeled back to his own bed.

Fern's supervisor, Evelyn Spencer, was always watching her, making sure Fern kept busy every minute. She hardly had time to use the bathroom, she had told Otis.

"There's always something going on in that place," Fern said. "Never a dull moment."

After trying days such as these, Fern talked about quitting her job and retiring, but she never got to do that.

Otis is only fifty-eight years old and will likely live well into old age in spite of his parents' early deaths. He has never smoked tobacco, drank alcohol or used the Lord's name in vain, thanks to his mother's teachings and near-perfect attendance at church over the years. So, he assumes, wrongly or rightly, that he will live well into his eighties or nineties. If Fern were by his side he wouldn't mind living a long life, but now thirty or so years without her seems like a long, lonely road.

Otis sits down at the kitchen table, rubs his eyes and pulls at his chin while staring at the pile of mail in front of him. His unemployment check isn't due until the fifteenth of September, and it is only the sixth day of the month. His wallet holds two dollars; his pants pocket a total of forty-nine cents. Worse, the balance in his checking account shows that it has slipped below the required balance, and that means there will be another fee. When it happened last month, he tried his best to have the fee waived but Kelly, the pretty blonde manager at the bank, scowled and said that as much as she would like to help him it was bank policy to educate customers about managing their money and imposing fees was simply tuition to the school of financial management. Most people, she said, kept a better watch on their spending when they were charged a fee. Otis realized then that though she was pretty on the outside, inside of this good-looking blonde woman named Kelly was a heart of stone. When she saw the look on Otis's face, she softened and said, "I'm sorry, Otis. I don't make the rules." He had to concede then that she was only doing her job.

Otis rubs his chin and feels the wiry brush of silver-white whiskers against the fingers of his right hand. His stomach growls and he thinks about the soup kitchen in Bangor. Today is Labor Day, so most everything is closed. Even the gas station. He will have to make do for today with what's in the fridge and go to Bangor tomorrow, and the days after that if he hopes to eat. Otis has always been cautious about spending, but when Fern came down with cancer two years ago soon after she turned fifty-four the medical expenses far outweighed what they could afford to pay. There was no life insurance, either. That ended when he was let go from his job at the paper mill Logger-Heads off Route 9 six months ago. Now, he is left with thousands of dollars in hospital and medical bills to pay, not to mention funeral expenses. He had requested a modest but decent service when Fern died in June, but it still cost him over $3,000 to bury her. He knows it could have been a lot worse. His neighbor, Ethel Marshall, told him that it cost her four times what Otis paid to bury her husband, Arnold.

Fern had encouraged Otis to find someone new to share his life with after she was gone, but he has no interest. For now, he wants to be alone with his grief.

Chapter Two

Otis reaches for the letter opener, the one Fern gave him for Christmas the year before she was diagnosed with cancer. She'd had the silver handle engraved with his initials. *OK. Otis Kingston.* He has always liked the sound of his name—and his initials—and is grateful his mother and father didn't stick him with something annoying like Claude or Percy. The opener feels light in his hands; it is weightless, like a puff of air.

He opens the bill from Dr. Chase first and lets his eyes roam to the bottom of the statement. The balance due after co-pays is well over $1,200. Fat chance of getting that one paid off anytime soon. The next one is from the company that insures his home. The bottom line shows a nearly three hundred dollar balance. Maybe he should drop the insurance. At least the house is paid for. He is always careful around fire, and what are the chances a tree will fall, leaving a huge hole in the roof? He doesn't have any trees on his property, only a stand of firs out back a hundred feet away from the house.

He opens the next envelope and breathes a sigh of relief. This one isn't a bill but an appeal from the Maine Cancer Foundation. He wishes he could make a donation in Fern's memory, but there is nothing to be done about it. Not with an empty bank account. He sets aside a bunch of envelopes similar to the charity appeal and opens one from Hopewell General Hospital. After Fern's insurance from the nursing home kicked in its portion, he has been left with a balance of more than $10,000. Releasing a long sigh, he then opens the envelope from the Church of the Blinding Light, wondering what the deacons are after this time. Otis is surprised to find that it is a letter from the Pastor himself. It reads:

August 27
Dear Otis,

I am writing to you today because I have not seen you in church lately and you've been missed. I've tried calling, too, but there has been no answer. People have been asking about you, and I don't know what to tell them. Would it be possible for me to drop by some morning? I'd like to speak to you in person.

Homecoming Sunday is at the end of September. Maybe that would be a good time for you to start coming to services again.

Prayers your way,

Pastor Stanley Wright

Otis lays the letter on the table, wonders what Pastor Wright has on his mind. When Fern was alive, they were in church every Sunday. They tithed, too. Giving ten percent to the church was something his mother had always done, no matter how little money she had. She had often talked about the widow's offering, a story told by Jesus. It was his mother's belief that God would provide, no matter how little money a person had in the bank. He gets up, moves away from the table and reaches for Fern's Bible lying on the table next to her chair.

He turns to Luke 21:1-4 and reads:

As Jesus looked up, he saw the rich putting their gifts into the temple treasury. He also saw a poor widow put in two very small copper coins. "Truly I tell you," he said, "this poor widow has put in more than all the others. All these people gave their gifts out of their wealth, but she out of her poverty put in all she had to live on."

Otis thinks about his $2.49. It is all he has to live on until his unemployment check arrives. He will set it aside, invite Pastor Wright to his home and offer the money while telling the Pastor it is all he has to give. Then, he will remind the good Pastor about the widow's offering. What can he say in response? Not much, Otis decides. But maybe Pastor Wright won't ask for money at all. Maybe he just wants a simple visit to say howdy-do.

Otis studies the phone number on the letterhead, picks up the phone and punches in the number. A few moments later, Colleen Johnson answers.

"Church of the Blinding Light. Pastor Wright's office," she says cheerfully in a kittenish voice.

"Hello, Colleen. This is Otis Kingston."

"Oh, hello, Otis. Gosh, we haven't seen you at church all summer. I hope you haven't been sick. You must be missing Fern something terrible."

Otis envisions Colleen sitting at her desk, computer at her side, eyebrows knit together, her dark hair twisted into a knot at the back of her neck. It is likely she has been working on the church newsletter when he called.

"Doing okay. And I'm fit as a fiddle, as the old saying goes," Otis replies, suddenly remembering the fiddle he hasn't played since Fern died. He can't bring himself to pick up the instrument his father once owned. Too many memories.

"We're all so sorry about Fern," Colleen says.

Otis feels himself choking up and mumbles a thank you. He clears his throat and asks Colleen how she has been.

She then tells Otis that her eleven-year-old daughter, Katie, broke her arm at summer camp and that the family dog was hit by a car.

"The vet bill was over the top expensive," Colleen confides. "But pets are family members. You have to take care of them, too."

Otis says he agrees, is sorry to hear, then asks if he can speak to Pastor Wright.

"Oh, sure. Just one moment. I'll put you right through."

While he waits, he listens to a tape recording of a choir singing *How Great Thou Art* before he hears Pastor Wright's voice.

"Hello, Otis. You must be calling about my letter."

"Yes, you're right. So you'd like to pay a visit?"

"Ay-uh. Actually, I was hoping I could call on you sometime this week."

"I'm not going anywhere. Any day will do."

Otis can hear pages turning in the background as Pastor Wright checks his date book. "I have some time tomorrow morning. Shall we say ten o'clock?"

"Ten o'clock, it is. Tomorrow."

For the rest of the day, Otis putters around the house, trying to see it through Fern's eyes. He notices that cobwebs have formed in the corners of some of the windows, and dust has accumulated on the coffee table in front of the couch. There are unwashed dishes in the sink and pots and pans on top of the stove that haven't been put away. He checks the bathroom and sees that the sink and toilet need a good scrubbing, too. He shakes his head. Cleaning the place up will take all morning, and housework isn't something he relishes. But there is nothing else that needs attention, except to figure out how to pay the bills.

After he completes his chores, Otis heats up some tomato soup and eats it with a few saltine crackers. He saves half for supper. He will have the leftover soup with a piece of bread and peanut butter. Tomorrow will be better, he tells himself. The soup kitchen in Bangor always lays out a hearty spread. Rolls and butter. Tossed salad. Fish chowder. Roast beef or pork loin with gravy. Mashed potatoes. Vegetable medley. And there is always a dessert table. Just the thought of all that food puts Otis's saliva glands to work.

He is tired now and needs his afternoon nap. He'll do the rest of the housework later. Instead of going to the bedroom he shared with Fern, he goes to the mud room off the kitchen where there is an old cot. He lies down and soon falls asleep. While sleeping, he dreams.

An image of a harbor springs up in his mind. In the harbor a boat is drifting toward the horizon. Otis is standing on a beach, watching as the boat slips below the waterline. The sun soon fades away, too, and then everything is cloaked in darkness. In the next image, Otis sees himself as the boy he once was. He is with his father and they are picking blueberries. Otis trips over a tree root, and every berry in his quart-sized pail goes flying. He hears his father yell at him. He calls Otis a clumsy ox and says he will never amount to anything. A third image brings more sadness to Otis's mind. This time he dreams Fern is alive. They are walking along a country road when out of nowhere a car speeds by and someone tosses a bag out the window. Otis hears himself crying out for the driver to come back, but he goes around a bend in the road and doesn't return. When Otis opens the bag, he finds weeds inside. Fern tells him she is disappointed and starts crying. It all seems so real that he wakes with a start. His heart is thumping wildly and he calls Fern's name, but there is only the sound of a bird chirping somewhere outside.

Chapter Three

Early the following morning, Otis looks around and thinks Fern would approve of his housekeeping skills. Gone are the cobwebs and dust. The dishes are washed and dried. Pots and pans put away. He has even given the bathroom a good cleaning. "Well, I guess I'm good for something," he says aloud.

At quarter to ten, he looks out the living room window. Anytime now Pastor Wright will pull into the driveway. He has practiced what he will say if the subject turns to why he hasn't been in church lately.

"You know, Pastor Wright, I've been thinking the same thing," Otis will say. "I'll be coming back to church real soon."

He hopes this will bring an end to any talk about where he's been. Then they can move to safer topics like the Red Sox and the World Series or that the region sure could use rain or how prices of everything continue to skyrocket. No, better scratch that one. He doesn't want to talk about money. That might lead Pastor Wright's thoughts to the subject of tithing. Otis doesn't even want to think about that, let alone talk about it.

Since the last week in August, the air has cooled some and Otis knows what that means. Soon, fall will be here, and colder air will start to sweep down from Canada and turn the leaves brilliant shades of scarlet, orange and yellow. Then fall will turn into winter, and with it will come heating bills and the need to chop wood for the fireplace. The arthritis in his right shoulder has been acting up, and he has no idea how he'll manage to swing an axe if it continues to be a problem. He feels the world closing in on him as he contemplates the problems that beset him.

A few moments pass while Otis stands at the window deep in thought. Then he watches as Pastor Wright turns his white Honda into the driveway. He parks behind Otis's black Chevy, exits the car and walks to the front door. When the doorbell rings, Otis opens the door and sees Pastor Wright, a short, stocky man with squinty brown eyes, graying hair and a neatly trimmed mustache, standing on the front porch.

"Good to see you, Pastor Wright. Thanks for the letter. Sometimes I need a kick in the rear to get me going," he says, hoping he sounds genuine.

"Good to see you, too, Otis. It's been a while."

"I guess it has. Well, come on in. Like a cup of coffee?"

"Sure would. I brought some blueberry muffins," Pastor Wright says, holding up a paper bag. "Colleen made them. She's quite the baker."

Otis's stomach growls. He hasn't thought about breakfast. There isn't much in the refrigerator anyway.

"Blueberry muffins. Haven't had any since Fern passed away. She always liked the low-bush berries, not those cultured ones. I miss that woman. I miss my Fern."

"Well, she was a good person, and you were blessed to have each other for so many years," says Pastor Wright. "We all miss her, too. Always willing to work at the church fair, sing in the choir, teach Sunday school . . ." His words trail off.

While Otis heats water in the kettle, Pastor Wright sits in a chair at the kitchen table. When Otis turns back to his visitor, he notices the minister taking in his surroundings. Otis feels shame when he sees that the linoleum floor still needs a good scrubbing and the yellow walls need a fresh coat of paint. And there's that nasty water stain on the ceiling above the refrigerator. But surely Pastor Wright can understand that he has had other things on his mind. He is a widower himself and knows full well that living without a spouse is a lonely, difficult road and can be downright depressing. He notices that Pastor Wright seems to be mulling something over in his mind, and Otis hopes he will get right to the point so they can get the visit over with.

When the kettle starts to whistle, Otis turns away again and shuts off the gas burner.

"I have just a bit of milk left. Or you can take it black. Sugar's on the table. Need to go shopping."

"Black's fine," says Pastor Wright. He pauses, then continues. "I'll get right to the point, Otis. I wanted to visit because you haven't been to any services since Fern died, and we all miss you. I think she'd want you to be with us. Also, the sexton has given notice. He's starting a new job over in Brewer in two weeks. Would you like to fill in for a while?" He takes a sip of coffee before continuing. "The third thing I wanted to talk about is a little more sensitive. It's about the campaign for a new steeple. The one we have now—well, it weakened during that wind storm in April to the point it could topple at any time. You and Fern were always so faithful . . . anyway, I'm asking if you could donate even a small amount. The Bible says . . ."

Otis thinks it is a good thing Pastor Wright is looking at his cup and not at him. The distress on Otis's face would knock the Pastor right out of his chair.

"Excuse me for just a minute," Otis says, remembering the $2.49 in the pocket of his other pants.

When he returns to the kitchen, he says in a tone that he hopes sounds convincing, "I've been meaning to start coming to church again, but when Sunday morning rolls around, I don't have much get up and go. But I would like to make a donation to the steeple." He places the money on the table, and Pastor Wright stares at it.

"Thank you, Otis."

"I know it's not much, but when I remember the story of the widow's offering . . ." Otis says, hoping this will put an end to it.

"No need to explain. It's what's in your heart that counts. As for coming back to church, once you get back in the groove, it'll be the most natural thing in the world. Now, what about the sexton job? Think you could handle it?"

"Depends. If it means heavy lifting, I can't. My shoulder, see. My arthritis has been acting up."

"No heavy lifting involved. It means dusting the woodwork in the sanctuary. Vacuuming the carpeting. Taking out the trash. About fifteen hours a week is all. We'd pay you ten dollars an hour. Think you could manage that?"

"I suppose I could give it a try." Otis suddenly feels lighter. A little income would be good. It'd help pay the bills. But would it interfere with his unemployment benefits? He'd have to find out. God knows, he's looked for work but has found nothing so far. "I guess I could try it on for size." he says.

Chapter Four

A few weeks later, Otis realizes that he isn't up to handling the sexton job, not even on a temporary basis. Though there is no heavy lifting, there are a lot of odd jobs that he simply cannot handle. Jobs like going down on his hands and knees and reaching under pews to sweep up dust and paper airplanes kids made out of their bulletins. He is also in charge of cleaning four bathrooms with industrial strength liquids and sprays that make him cough and sneeze. These chores had not been mentioned when Pastor Wright first talked to him about the job, but here he is, in charge of bathroom duty. With great apologies, he gives his notice at the end of the second week. Pastor Wright encourages him to stay on, but Otis's mind is made up. Someone else will have to fill in.

He sees Pastor Wright's face fall when he gives him the news. "I was hoping you might even replace our sexton permanently," says the Pastor, disappointment on his face. "I met with our treasurer last week, and he had some bad news. The church is hurting in a big way and, well . . . I know what we pay you isn't much, but every penny we can save helps." He pauses before finishing. "Otis, there's a chance the church could close if we can't meet our expenses. I hope you'll stay. I really do. And please come back to Sunday morning services. Things just aren't the same without you."

Otis considers Pastor Wright's words. Fern would want him to help the church she had loved her entire life, but what can he do. He is simply not cut out to keep the church spic and span and is too proud to admit he's broke.

"Let me think about it," Otis replies.

Later that night, he sits at the kitchen table, head in his hands. Worry and loneliness are engulfing him, and the sudden thought that he should end his life suddenly flits through his brain. No. He would never do that, but he is so down in the dumps that he wishes he were lying alongside Fern in a grave of his own. Then, another thought pops into his head—the big bottle of swish sitting on the top shelf in the shed out back. Maybe a little drink would do him good. His old friend, Rodney Bean, brought it with him one day when he was passing through Hopewell while on his way to Vermont. His friend had forgotten to take it with him and Otis had called him about it, but Rodney had told Otis to just keep it.

"Save it for when I stop by again," he had said. "That stuff never goes bad. It only gets better with age. Made it myself, so I know what I'm talking about."

But Rodney wouldn't be passing through Hopewell again. His friend's wife had called a few years ago to let him know that Rodney had passed away. A heart attack. Fell to the kitchen floor one morning and he was gone, just like that.

Liquor has never passed Otis's lips before, but one little glass wouldn't hurt, would it?

Well, yes, it would, according to Pastor Wright.

"The devil is in every mouthful," he was famous for preaching to his congregation. "Take my advice and stay away from liquor. Otherwise, it'll turn into a snake and wrap itself around your neck. Once it's got you in its grip, it'll squeeze the life right out of you."

But Otis is convinced that one drink won't hurt. In fact, he's beginning to think of that bottle of swish as good medicine. He gets up from his chair and goes to the shed. And there, right where he left it on the top shelf, is the bottle.

He takes it down and reads the label hen-scratched by Rodney's own hand. "Rodney's Sauce of Ruination" it reads. The bottle holds about a gallon. Otis walks back to the house and plunks it down on the kitchen table. He takes a glass from the second shelf of the cupboard next to the stove and cracks open the bottle. Immediately, fumes from the rich amber liquid waft to his nostrils. Maybe this isn't such a good idea after all, he thinks.

But then, as if his hand has a mind of its own, he lifts the bottle and pours two inches of the liquid into the glass.

When he brings it to his lips and takes a sip, he shakes his head at the assault of alcohol against his tongue. The second sip is less harsh, and the third even less so. Fifteen minutes later, Otis thinks that he'd like a little more. This time, he fills the glass halfway.

Soon enough, his thoughts become hazy, and his vision blurs. He feels a burst of emotion coming up from deep within, like a volcano ready to spew hot ash, and hears a sob coming from his throat. A second later, he is wailing loud enough to scare a ghost away. With a single sweep of his hand, he sends the stack of mail on the table flying to the floor.

"Why did you leave me, Fern? Why? Why?" he yells into the empty room.

The alcohol is flooding his brain now, and he feels like he might be sick, but the sensation passes. A line of perspiration sprouts on his forehead and slides down onto his cheeks, mixing with his tears. He sits there a while, trying to calm down. Then he pours himself another glass with a wobbly hand. This time, he fills it to the brim and drinks it in three quick gulps.

Minutes later, he feels the room spinning. He tries to stand up, but he cannot get his bearings. Is he still in the kitchen? Yes, the stove is in front of him. And the refrigerator is next to the stove. He staggers across the room but feels disconnected from himself, as if he is a puppet on strings. In the living room, he tries to sit in his recliner but misses the seat and ends up sprawled on the floor. So this is what it's like to be drunk, he thinks, and begins to laugh.

"Come on, snicky-snake. Go ahead and wrap yourself around my neck. My life is over anyway. You might as well finish the job and choke the shit out of me." Otis hears himself laughing again. Not only has alcohol never passed his lips until this day, neither has a swear word.

But his laughter gives way to another sob and again he cries out for Fern. Then, still on the floor, he rolls over, closes his eyes and feels the room spinning round and round.

He lies there for a few minutes before rising to his knees. When he stands up, he stumbles to the left and bumps into the end table where sits a ceramic lamp Fern made in night school. The base is in the shape of a fish and she had given it to Otis for his birthday a few years back. Now it lies in shards all over the floor.

Chapter Five

In the middle of the night, Otis awakens to find himself on the floor. His back aches, and he's sure he has done damage to his left leg. Fortunately, his shoulder feels okay. He glances at the clock on the wall above the TV and thinks it says six-forty, but he can't be sure because his vision is blurry and his head still reels. When he pulls himself up and tries to sit in his recliner, he finds that he is still unsteady on his feet and barrels into a bookcase. He moves toward the bedroom, holding onto the wall for support, and falls into the bed he once shared with Fern. He feels a pounding headache coming on and closes his eyes. Then he sleeps.

It is well past ten on Wednesday morning when Otis opens his eyes again. The room is no longer spinning, but he feels unwell. His stomach is turning over, and he thinks he might be sick. He vows then and there to never take another a sip of alcohol. He will pour what remains down the sink and smash the bottle into a million pieces. And he will pray that the good Lord above will forgive his trespass into the world of sin.

Later that afternoon, Otis is showered and dressed and has eaten left-overs from the soup kitchen. He considers himself lucky he doesn't have a hangover, and his leg no longer hurts. While standing at the front window looking out to the roadway, he sees several cars and trucks pass by, but they are few and far between.

He sighs, recalling his conversation with Pastor Wright. He has to do something, but a part-time job at the church is not the answer. By two o'clock, he decides to get some fresh air. The sun is shining brightly, and the leaves on the trees are moving gently, suggesting a soft breeze. A nice slow walk along SR92 would do him good. It is a flat road, easily navigated on foot, and it will take him past the cemetery where Fern is buried. He'll stop to visit her, ask her what he should do. He needs a peaceful place to amble, a place where he won't encounter anyone. He wants to be alone, to ponder his past and think about his future. SR92 and the cemetery will do nicely.

He wishes Fern could join him, but there's no sense wishing for something he cannot have. She is gone and isn't ever coming back. He turns from the window and heads toward the kitchen where his spring jacket hangs on a hook next to the door. He looks at the thermometer affixed to the kitchen window outside and sees that it is a cool sixty-four degrees. Just right for a walk. He puts on his sneakers, ties up the laces and is out the door.

Otis walks the length of the driveway, then turns right onto SR92. First, he passes Fred Turnbull's home and notices that his RV is up for sale. Otis has always wondered what it would be like to travel in an RV and has often fantasized about where he would go if he had the chance. He imagines himself poring over a road map and getting behind the wheel. He would love to see some of the country. Old Faithful in Wyoming has always fascinated him. Another is Niagara Falls. He'd also like to see the Pacific Ocean. He smiles to himself, thinking what a fool he is. He'll probably never see anything beyond his own backyard.

The road continues around a bend and takes him past a farmhouse, a dilapidated schoolhouse that's been closed since the early 1970s and an unoccupied house and barn that are both caving in. Otis wonders about those two buildings and why the owners, people from upstate New York, have never torn them down or put a FOR SALE sign on the property. Someone in town once told him that the deed was held by a sister and brother, and neither can agree on what to do with the property so the house and barn just sit there, rotting away. What happens in some families is terrible, Otis thinks. Though he is now alone, he is glad in some ways that he and Fern had not had children. At least while they were married. The fact is, they did have a child together, but that was a few years before they married. His mind wanders back to his teenage years when he and Fern were madly in love. He remembers the nights they spent parked in his father's car at the edge of a potato field off SR92. It was plenty dark there, and on a rainy night in July when Fern was fifteen and Otis was seventeen, they both lost their virginity. A baby boy was born nine months later, but they were too young to marry, and Fern's mother and father made her put the baby up for adoption. Over the years, Otis and Fern had wondered about their son and what had become of him, but the adoption people kept all that information private.

When Otis and Fern finally married a few years later and tried to have more children, Fern was unable to conceive. She blamed herself and was convinced that God was punishing her for her sin when she was so young. Otis had tried to tell her otherwise, but she wouldn't listen, and she went to her grave feeling guilty. She never got over giving away their baby boy.

When Otis arrives at the cemetery, he passes through a black wrought iron gate. Fern's grave is on a knoll that faces Machias; it is a restful place, and there is room enough for two. When his time comes, he wants to be buried right next to her. Otis feels intense sorrow when he stands at the foot of Fern's grave. There had been no money for a stone, and now buying one is on his list of things to do so he can memorialize Fern in a proper way.

After asking Fern what he should do about his life and getting no answer, he turns and leaves the cemetery.

He continues for a quarter mile and thinks about Fern and the last year of her life. The year before, she had begun to cough for no apparent reason and it would not go away. She had not had a cold and there were no flu symptoms, so Otis had finally insisted that she see Dr. Chase when she started complaining about pain in her back. But Fern had stubbornly refused to make an appointment. Then, one day while at work Evelyn Spencer had taken Fern aside and told her she must see a doctor out of concern that she could have tuberculosis, a disease that could easily spread to everyone in the nursing home.

After undergoing a series of medical tests, she and Otis met with Dr. Chase a week later to learn the results. How he had hated the doctor when he gave them the news. Lung cancer.

"It can't be," Otis remembers saying. "Fern doesn't smoke and never has."

The doctor then asked Fern if she had been exposed to second-hand smoke at any time in her life. Yes, she had replied. Both of her parents had smoked cigarettes. Fern then mentioned the pain in her back, and a bone scan was ordered. The news wasn't good. The cancer had spread to her spine. There had been chemotherapy and radiation, too, but after six weeks of treatment she had reached her limit.

"The drugs are beating me up, Otis. I can't do this anymore," she had said. After that Fern went downhill. Eventually, the cancer spread to her hip and then her liver. Her appetite gone, she only nibbled at food and lost more than thirty pounds.

One night while they were eating supper, Fern announced that she wanted to die at home, so when the time came a few months later Otis arranged for hospice to deliver a hospital bed. It was set up in the living room, and he slept next to her on the couch every night. During the last two weeks of Fern's life a hospice nurse came in every day to help out. She gave him a kit containing morphine, and Otis used a syringe to squeeze drops into her mouth every few hours. Sometimes she was awake, but mostly she slept. When she did open her eyes, she seemed to look beyond him at the wall. He spoke to her, but she never replied.

"Do you know I'm here with you, Fern?" he asked one night while holding her hand.

But she only stared into space and called out for her dead father. The following morning, she apparently saw her mother because she began to reach out for her. "Mama! Mama! I've missed you . . ." she cried.

Chapter Six

The days seemed long and endless, and Fern's illness kept Otis on edge. Other than sitting next to her and tending to her most basic needs, there was little he could do to make things better.

The hospice nurse had told him that she might rally a final time, and the nurse had been right. The day before she died, she opened her eyes and told Otis to make sure he got her to the train station on time. "I don't want to be late, Otis," she had said.

To help her breathe more easily, Otis set up a small fan next to the hospital bed and turned it toward her face. The next morning, he noticed that there were long stretches of time between breaths, and he knew the end would be coming soon. That afternoon, she slipped into a coma, something Dr. Chase said was a blessing. A few hours later she took her final breath.

On that awful day—the day Fern died—Otis scrubbed the kitchen floor on his hands and knees. Tears spilled from his eyes and mingled with the Pine Sol. When a moment of anger swept over him, he gave the wash bucket a good shove, sending dirty water all over the kitchen. It had taken him an hour to clean up the mess.

Pastor Wright had waived the fee to officiate at Fern's funeral, but Otis had to buy a casket and there were funeral home expenses. Instead of ordering flowers from a florist in town, he had gone to the garden Fern had tended so lovingly and picked the best of the best—red and orange zinnias, day lilies and forget-me-nots. He arranged them in a ruby red vase, the one her flowers had come in when they celebrated their first Valentine's Day as a married couple so many years before. Fern would have thought his gesture sweet. She would have appreciated that Otis was frugal, too.

A few days after the funeral, he went back to the cemetery to get the vase. No sense in letting it sit there and fade under the strong summer sun. Fern would have wanted him to take it home. So he did.

Otis now continues on his walk, grateful for the quiet except for a line of crows perched on telephone lines overhead. Their caw-caw interrupts the silence and Otis wonders what it is they're talking about at this hour of the day. He continues on, enjoying the colors and spicy scent of late summer wildflowers growing along the side of the road. When the driver of a black truck zooms past, he moves onto the shoulder to avoid being struck. "Slow down!" he calls out, but the driver speeds away.

When he rounds the next bend, he spots something lying in the ditch about ten feet away.

As he draws closer, he can see that whatever it is is blue in color. He stops a moment and considers the situation. The ditch is about three feet deep, maybe a little more, and is surrounded by cat o' nine tails and alder shrubs. A recent rain has turned the dirt at the bottom into mud and as he gets closer he sees a road tripper style duffel bag lying there. Curious, he makes his way to the bottom of the ditch to investigate while doing his best to keep his feet out of the mud.

To Otis's surprise, he finds a second duffel bag, this one black, a few feet beyond the first. And then a third a short distance away. This one is army green. Otis pulls at the zipper of the blue bag and looks inside. Astonished, he glances around to see if anyone is watching, but no one is in sight.

He then unzips the second and third bags and discovers that the contents are exactly the same. He quickly zips up all three bags and hefts them out of the ditch. Combined, the bags must weigh at least sixty pounds, probably more. He could leave them there and go home to get his car, but someone else might come along and find them. Instead, he hikes to the edge of a wooded area beyond the ditch and hides two of the bags behind a bush. He will carry the blue one home and drive back to get the others. But why in God's name would anyone abandon the bags? Otis thinks about this as he hurries home, all the while hoping that no one sees him.

He estimates that he needs about twenty minutes to get home. He tries sprinting to shave off some time, but the duffel bag is heavy and it's slowing him down.

As never before, he can't wait to be in the privacy of his own home. He imagines himself sitting at the kitchen table, all three bags in front of him, completely unzipped. But before that can happen, he will lock all the doors and windows. He will pull down all the shades, too, just in case someone is lurking outside. It is unlikely anyone would stop by, but he would never count on that. The way things have been going lately, Pastor Wright or maybe Fred Turnbull would come knocking on his door.

As he continues on his way, Otis's thoughts turn to the contents of the bags. What in the world should he do? Who should he tell? He asks Fern for her opinion, but all he hears in response is birdsong and the whisper of rustling leaves overhead.

A few minutes later, the sound of sirens slices through the air. As Otis continues along, the sirens get louder and louder until not one, but two state police cars come speeding down the road toward him. One cruiser hits the shoulder briefly, and Otis jumps into the ditch, this time not caring about the mud. He watches as the cruisers scream past at a rate of speed he has only seen on TV cop shows like *Hot Pursuit*. Road dust and small pebbles rise up in the air and strike his face and arms. The cruisers are going so fast that he knows the officers probably didn't spot him. He suspects that somewhere along SR92 there's been an accident. If this is so, he hopes no one was badly hurt or killed. Otis clutches the bag while the taste of fear rises up. What if the police *had* seen him? What if they decide to circle back and ask him what he's up to?

When he finally reaches his front porch, he pulls the house key from his jacket pocket and pushes it into the lock. Seconds later, he is standing in the middle of his living room, duffel bag at his feet.

He exhales a long breath and tries to think. First, he needs to hide the bag. Under the bed will do. As soon as the bag is safely hidden, he takes his car keys from the kitchen table and heads for the driveway. Ten minutes later, he pulls to the side of the road where he left the other two bags and jumps across the ditch to get to their hiding place. There they are, behind a bush, just where he left them.

Back at home again, he makes sure all the shades are still lowered and checks that the doors and windows are locked. When he finally returns to the living room, he opens the bags and stares at the contents.

Bundles upon bundles of U.S. currency are inside, each one secured with a paper band. There is so much money inside the bags Otis knows he will need a pencil and paper to count it all. Soon, he finds that whoever banded the money purposely placed a $50 bill on top of $100 bills. He begins counting: $150, $250, $350, all the way to $5,050. He licks his lips and lets out a low whistle when he begins to comprehend how much money is in the bags. Could be $1 million or more sitting right in front of him. Every bundle he counts has the same amount as the first. When he opens the third bag, he finds a small notebook on top of the money. Curious, he pulls it out and reads what is written on the pages. Slowly, he begins to understand what he has stumbled upon. Drug money. He lets this sink in before continuing to count. Maybe he should call the police, he thinks. Let them take over. But he's not ready to do that just yet.

After more than an hour, he takes a break and goes to a kitchen drawer to get the little calculator his bank gave him for opening a new account a few years ago. The entire counting job and double checking takes nearly two hours, and by the time he finishes he has counted well over $4 million. Otis feels a drop of sweat trickling down his neck; he notices, too, that his legs feel weak.

Otis knows he has a problem, a moral dilemma he never expected to encounter in a million years. He looks at the phone on the table next to his chair. Should he call the police? Pastor Wright? He laughs aloud when he thinks of the good Pastor. He imagines what he would tell him over the phone.

"Pastor Wright, I've been thinking about our little talk . . . I've decided to make a donation to the church. How does a cool $50,000 sound?"

He imagines that the Pastor would bluster and stammer while searching for words. Otis would play him along, ask if he is still at the other end of the line. He chuckles at the very thought.

He decides the best thing to do is to sleep on it and not make any decisions for at least a day. By tomorrow he'll be able to think more clearly. He'll know what to do then, even if it is nothing.

Otis suddenly recalls reading a story in the newspaper about a couple who tried to hide a huge inheritance. Millions of dollars. The Internal Revenue Service finally caught up with them, and they had to pay a big tax and fines, too. Not only that, both had to spend time under house arrest. Otis thinks it was about six months. He realizes that he will have to open accounts in lots of different banks if he ends up keeping the money. But what is he thinking? The money isn't his to keep. Or is it?

He goes to each window and door to make sure they're still locked. Then he puts the money back inside the bags and carries them to the bedroom. He shoves the bags under the bed and checks to see if they can be seen from any angle in the room. No, they can't. The Vault, as he has come to think of the bags, is safe from prying eyes.

Next, he pours himself a glass of Moxie and sits at the kitchen table to think. If he keeps the money, he'll have enough to last the rest of his life plus ten lifetimes more. If he calls the police, they might take the money and keep it for themselves. He isn't sure what to do and can't think about it right now. It's all too much and he's exhausted from last night's drinking binge.

He goes to the living room and turns on the TV. And when he does, he catches the words of a newscaster.

"The drugs are believed to have been valued at more than $4 million," says a young man wearing a navy blue jacket and paisley tie. "Police are now looking for two men who were driving a black truck with a Florida license plate."

Otis puts down his drink, turns up the volume and leans in to listen.

"The drugs are thought to have originated from a Mexican cartel and police have reason to believe that the drug dealers distributed heroin, cocaine, ecstasy and fentanyl along the East Coast, from Key West to several points in Maine. Anyone with knowledge of this crime is urged to call their local police."

The newscaster goes on to report another story about a five-car pile-up on a bridge in Bangor before circling back to an update on the drug dealers.

"We have breaking news," the newscaster says. "Police now think the two suspects involved in the drug case were traveling along SR92 earlier in the day. There was a police chase after the driver was stopped for questioning, but the driver sped away and two officers were unable to catch up with them. There's a possibility that the suspects traveled across Route 9, and border patrol agents at the U.S.-Canada border in Calais have been asked to be on the lookout for the pair. We take you now to the scene with Seth McKenna. . ."

Otis recalls the black truck and state police cars speeding past him when he was out walking and now knows he had witnessed something extraordinary. He decides to stay up for the 11 o'clock news in case there's another update.

The evening passes slowly as Otis tries to think about anything but the money and two suspects, but he can't stay focused. He can't even concentrate on "Wheel of Fortune," let alone admire Vanna White in one of her fancy dresses.

Chapter Seven

As the clock ticks toward eleven o'clock, Otis checks the bags to make sure they're still under the bed. Satisfied, he returns to the living room and tunes in to the news.

A newscaster says, "A few minutes ago, state police headquarters confirmed that two men police believe were involved in dealing drugs were spotted by a resident of Brewer who heard about the chase on a scanner. The pair were traveling in a black 2010 GMC Sierra. The vehicle has a Florida license plate, number HWVL26. Anyone with information concerning the case is asked to notify police."

Otis turns off the news and sits on the couch in silence, stunned to know that he is now mixed up in a crime.

The black truck that sped by him while he was walking SR92 has to be the same one the newscaster was talking about. And then the state police cars zoomed past soon after. The drug money is under his bed. About that, there is no doubt in his mind. But what is he going to do now? If he reports that he found the money, the police might ask why he waited so long to turn it in. They might think he had intentions to keep it. Maybe they'd put him in handcuffs and arrest him. In a flash, Otis knows he has to do something. Hide the money? Bank it? Burn it? Any second now the police could arrive at his front door. The state police officers might have seen him jump into the ditch. Maybe they had even glimpsed the blue bag.

Otis further realizes he is in a pot of boiling hot water, and no matter what he does he might have to answer a lot of questions if the state cops show up. He could even end up in jail. But as the clock continues to tick, no one comes knocking at his door and he allows himself to relax just a little.

At one o'clock Thursday morning, Otis goes to bed. But sleep won't come, not while The Vault is only inches away. He is tempted to get up and check to see if the bags are really there, and temptation finally gets the best of him. He gets out of bed and pulls the blue bag out from under. Then, he hauls it into bed with him and pulls the sheet and blanket over it. He cuddles it the way he once cuddled Fern and squeezes it a few times. He laughs aloud then, wondering what Fern would think if she knew she'd been replaced by a bag of money. Maybe he's in the middle of a dream. Maybe there is no money at all. But he quickly dismisses that thought when he recalls what the newscaster said during the news report. Yes, there is money and it is right in bed with him. A vast sum of money that he now has the fortune or misfortune to deal with, depending on how you look at it.

Otis prays for divine intervention. He prays that this is all a nightmare and that in the morning he'll wake up and find that there is nothing in or under his bed. But then he remembers his dire financial straits and thanks God for the unexpected gift.

He apologizes for what might appear to be greed or even theft. He asks for forgiveness that he has become so focused on money he can think of little else. The unpaid stack of bills tempts him to keep the loot. He prays that God will forgive him for not trusting in His abundance.

Around four in the morning, Otis finally falls into a restless sleep but wakes with a start an hour later when he hears a car pull into the driveway. Before getting up, he puts the blue bag back under the bed and makes sure it's hidden. Then he walks to the front window, moves the shade an inch and peers outside. Whoever is out there has had a change of heart. Otis sees the driver back up and head east on SR92 in what looks like a small white sedan. His heart is thumping wildly as he breathes a sigh of relief. He has never seen anyone do that before. Or, if it has happened, he has been sound asleep and had not known about it. Now, because of the money, even while sleeping he is on high alert for anything out of the ordinary. The phrase "A guilty conscience is an alert sentinel" comes to mind.

If peace of mind eluded him before, it eludes him even more now. The money has become a source of anxiety and worry, like a boil ready to burst.

He laughs when this reality hits him. He worried when he didn't have money. Now he has it and worries even more.

He recalls the Bible verse about not storing up wealth while on Earth but instead storing up treasures in heaven. Treasures like loving and helping your neighbors if they are hungry, naked and poor. Treasures like living an honest and moral life. The longer he sits there, the more these thoughts tumble through his head like wet laundry in the spin cycle.

He thinks about taking the money to his bank for safekeeping just long enough until he can figure out what to do with it. But he can't make a deposit that large. All that cash. It boggles Otis's mind. Kelly, the bank manager would come to Wanda's teller window when called over.

He could hear Wanda, a tall, buxom redhead, say, "Mr. Kingston wants to make a rather large deposit."

And Kelly would look at Otis with a mixture of scorn and incredulity. "And where did you get such a large sum of money, Mr. Kingston? Just last week you were complaining about a bank fee." He could envision her mouth going into a pout while waiting for Otis's answer.

Where indeed? No, he will have to divvy it up in small amounts and make deposits at multiple banks. But maybe there's another way. Maybe he can put it in plastic Zip-Loc bags and bury it in the backyard. Or in Fern's flower garden at the side of the house. He could buy the Zip-Locs at the dollar store and place the currency inside and dig up the money as he needs it to buy groceries or pay a month's worth of utility bills. He could peck away at the medical and funeral bills. Deposit a little at a time in his account. No one would be the wiser. He wonders how long it would take to spend all that money if he only used it for paying bills and buying necessities. He'll probably be dead and buried by the time he spends even $50,000. It would be a shame to just let The Vault sit there, buried under a pile of dirt. And he wouldn't be able to tell anyone about it. Maybe on his death bed, he would call for Pastor Wright and make his confession. Then, it would be Pastor Wright's problem, wouldn't it? He wonders what the minister would do with the money then. Keep it? Turn it over to police? Build a new church? He wonders just how much anyone can trust a clergyman. They are, first and foremost, members of the human race. And hasn't he heard often enough that the human heart is, above all, wicked and deceitful? That would include Pastor Wright, right?

⇒⇒⇒⇒ ⇐⇐⇐⇐

While Otis is trying to sleep, Detective Craig Larson is seated with his partner, Brian Wheaton, in a first floor conference room at the Bangor Police Station. Also at the table are Lieutenant Dan Pelletier and Sergeant Maureen Williams along with Bob Rossi and Pete Burgess from the state police.

The two detectives are giving the others a full report about the drug dealers who swept through the area the day before and led police on a wild chase.

Police had received an All Points Bulletin from officers in southern Maine about two suspects allegedly carrying not only a huge stash of narcotics but millions of dollars.

They were last spotted driving a black GMC Sierra on Route 95 north in the vicinity of Augusta. Police set up surveillance from Augusta to Bangor in order to capture the pair, but the driver had apparently taken an exit before the starting point and continued on back roads.

Police in Brewer knew about the surveillance and were on the lookout while Detectives Larson and Wheaton were dispatched along with Rossi and Burgess to search the area. Forty-five minutes later, the two state police officers spotted a vehicle that answered the description of the one the drug dealers were driving. The driver took a right onto SR92, and a chase began.

Rossi and Burgess are now telling the others about the chase and how it took them over Route 9 all the way to the Canadian border in Calais. A flat tire delayed the officers, but the border patrol agents had been notified to be on the lookout. When the suspects were questioned at the border, police arrived at the scene to investigate. A brawl broke out, and both suspects were killed during a shoot-out.

The GMC they were traveling in was impounded and towed to the barracks in Calais. Police searched high and low for the drugs and drug money, but nothing was found in the hide or anywhere else in the vehicle.

Now Rossi and Burgess, along with the other officers, have been instructed to hold a brief search along Route 95 in Bangor and the back roads stretching to SR92 to see if the missing drugs and money can be found. Police fear that drugs left out in the open could fall into the wrong hands and possibly cause someone's death. The search will last for only a few days before it is suspended.

The officers glance at each other. They know a lot of work faces them, but if The Vault is found, it could eventually find its way to the police department's bottom line. Meanwhile, any drugs found will be destroyed.

"Meeting adjourned," says Pelletier. "Search starts at 7 a.m. sharp. All hands on deck."

Chapter Eight

When Otis wakes up the next morning, he turns on the TV to see if there's a news update about the drug dealers.

A pretty, dark-haired newscaster is just finishing up a report. "As more news comes in, we'll inform our viewers. Once again, the two men alleged to have been involved in a major drug deal were killed during a shoot-out at the Calais-St. Stephen, New Brunswick U.S.-Canada border last night. The drugs and more than $4 million are reportedly missing . . ."

Both suspects were killed. So, he didn't imagine what he heard last night. It takes a minute or so for the news to sink in. If they're dead, then they won't be telling police where they dumped the money. If they're dead, the police might launch a search along the route where they think the suspects traveled, but in the end they'll probably close the case. Or, they might continue to look for the money and not give up until they've turned over every stone and every speck of dirt. They could look, but they will never find the money if Otis sticks with his plan. But what if the police show up at people's doors to ask about anything they might have seen and someone had noticed Otis walking along the road with the blue bag slung over his shoulder. Did it mean the authorities would have the right to search his house? Even worse, what if the drug lords from Mexico come to Hopewell looking for the loot?

First thing he needs to do is bury the money in case the police do come with a search warrant. He will go beyond the tree line out back, dig a hole and bury it, but good. Then, he'll spread pine needles over the hole. Doing that will help him rest easier if the police come nosing around. Otis is so excited over his sudden wealth that he jumps up and down in the living room.

"Whoopee!" he shouts.

An hour later, the money is buried three feet deep inside the duffel bags and Otis is back inside his house. While out yesterday, he went to the grocery store and is now eating a bowl of Cheerios with sliced banana and milk. He hears a car door slam and a few seconds later a knock on the door. He freezes. Surely, it is the police, come to question him.

He takes a few deep breaths and goes to the door to see who's out there. Just as he suspected, two police officers are standing on the front porch. Otis does his best to appear unshaken and friendly.

"Good morning, officers," he says. "Great day, isn't it? What brings you out this way?"

"Mind if we have a few words?" The first officer flashes his badge while Otis stands there with shaking hands. He shoves them into his pockets so the officers won't notice. "Sure. Come on in. I'll put on a pot of coffee."

"There's no need. We can conduct our business right here," says the officer on the left. He is a tall, burly man with a ruddy face and striking blue eyes. He stares at Otis and waits for his response.

"Sure. Suit yourself," Otis replies.

"You live here alone?" asks the officer.

"That I do. My wife died a few months ago. Why do you ask?" Otis feels perspiration break out under the collar of his shirt. He's sure his face must be as red as a tomato.

"There's been trouble in these parts. Drug runners passing through. Two suspects are dead. Killed at the Canadian border in Calais. But the money and drugs they were transporting are missing. Have you seen anything out of the ordinary in the past few days?"

Otis pauses a moment, looks at his shoes, then says, "Can't say that I have . . . except for state police cars speeding down SR92 yesterday."

"Mr. Kingston—that's your name?"

Otis nods. So the officers know who he is. How would they know unless they did some digging around at Town Hall?

The officer looks at Otis as if to size him up.

"You're sure now. Any suspicious activity? Anything at all would help our investigation."

Otis looks toward the driveway, tightens his brows and pretends to think. He studies his car, one end to the other, in mock concentration.

"I wish I could help you—what did you say your name was?"

"I didn't. I'm Officer Mark Curtis. This is Officer Glenn Keating. We're with the state police."

"I'll tell you the truth, Officer Curtis. Since my wife died, I haven't gone out much. I'm pretty much a homebody these days, except when I need groceries, that is. I sure do miss Fern . . . ," he says, his voice trailing off.

"All right, then. We may stop by again if we have any further questions. You have a good day now."

"You, too. Who should I call if I think of something?"

Officer Curtis hands Otis a business card, then turns to walk down the stairs toward the cruiser.

"I hope what you're looking for turns up," Otis calls out.

"We hope so, too," the officer replies.

After Otis goes back inside, he watches out the window for a few minutes until he's sure the officers are gone. They'll never find that money, not while it's buried behind the tree line. His own private vault. The Bank of Otis. He laughs at the very thought.

>>>>> <<<<<

When Fern approached him about buying a home computer, Otis had resisted at first, saying they would never use it, but she was determined to have her way.

"We're living in the 21st century, for Pete's sake," she had said. "It's time we joined in."

Fern had taken a night course at the local community college where she learned how to use e-mail and surf the Internet. One night when she told Otis about search engines and what they could do, his curiosity finally kicked in. She taught him everything she knew, and soon they were using the computer to educate themselves about the world. Not long after, they each got a cell phone.

"You never know when you might need one," Fern had said. "What if I got a flat tire on the way home from work? I'd need a phone to call you." Otis had to admit she was right, and the following weekend they visited a T-Mobile store to buy phones.

Now he's glad Fern had insisted they buy a computer. He has an encyclopedia at his fingertips and can look up anything he wants, whenever he wants. He knows that burying the money under a pile of dirt probably wasn't the best idea and thinks that instead he should put it in some kind of storage boxes that lock. Carrying the money around in those duffel bags would be out of the question. Having multiple bank accounts would be time consuming and record keeping complicated, but he has few other choices.

Rather than use his computer, he goes to the local library and uses one there so what he Googles cannot be linked to him. On the Google search line, he types "how to hide money so it can't be traced." Google then takes him to a list of sites that explain how it's done. One site says that money is often deposited in Grand Cayman Island banks. But there's a $15,000 limit.

Once he has read through some of the sites, he wonders what it would be like to take a cruise to Grand Cayman, maybe from Key West. But the more he thinks about it, the less appealing it is. For one thing, he won't fly and if he were to drive to the Keys he'd have to buy another car. His Malibu has well over 200,000 miles on it. Then again, so what? He has the money to buy a new vehicle.

Otis likes the idea of a road trip. He could stop in various places and do a little sightseeing. He is finding it hard to focus on what he should do, so he asks the librarian for a pencil and paper to make a list. First thing in the morning, he'll go to Keane's Hardware to look for storage boxes to stash the money. He'll need long, deep, narrow boxes he can lock and store under the bed. At night he would sleep more soundly, knowing the money is under lock and key and within reach.

Just as he makes this decision, something else comes to mind. Tomorrow, he can go for a drive down to Kittery where his favorite restaurant serves turkey dinners. Otis loves turkey and all the fixings and thinks nothing could be more in line with finding wads of cash than to eat at Turkey Lurkey where Thanksgiving is celebrated nearly every day of the year. Otis has a lot to be thankful for. Those bags full of money tell the tale.

Just as Otis is about to leave for the hardware store the following morning, he hears a knock on the door.

This time when Otis opens it, he sees two different police officers. He steps onto the porch and looks from one to the other. "I suppose you're here about the drug case," he says. "State police came by yesterday."

"You're right," the older of the two officers says. "We're going door to door to see if anyone noticed anything out of the ordinary in the past few days," says the older officer. Otis wonders why the state and local police aren't on the same page, why they're not sharing information.

Otis says no, that he hasn't been out much lately and hasn't been paying attention to much of anything—except for the incident when the police cruisers sped down the road.

Otis asks about the suspects, and the younger officer tells him that the two men were brothers. He goes on to say that they were from Mexico and were carrying a load of money and drugs.

"How do you know this?" Otis asks.

"We found the drugs," says the older officer. "Where there are drugs, there's always money, and our intelligence officers know the ballpark figure."

Otis looks the older officer in the eye, "No wonder we have a drug problem in this country. With the likes of those two . . ."

The younger officer replies, "This is just the tip of the iceberg, sir. It's why we're doing everything we can to put these characters out of business."

"Well, I'd like to help you, but I don't have anything to add. Except, of course, that I'm sorry you have to work so hard. And I'm sorry for people who buy these drugs. Must be a terrible thing to be addicted." Otis suddenly remembers Rodney's Sauce of Ruination and what it did to him.

"If you see anything, anything at all, or remember something, please give us a call," says the older officer. He hands Otis his business card. Police Officer Jon Gentile it reads. Next thing, the FBI will come calling.

"What happens now?" Otis asks.

"Nothing," says the younger officer, who tells Otis his name is Jim Leland. "Just remember to call if you think of anything, no matter how minor you think it is. We're asking the same of everyone who lives on this road."

Otis nods, then breathes a sigh of relief. His mind starts spinning. Now what?

Worry clouds all logical thought. What if someone stumbles across the buried money? An animal even. Maybe he was too hasty, burying it out back. After weighing his options, he decides to dig it up and take it with him to the hardware store. He can transfer the money into gun safes if the store has any. Then, while he's at Turkey Lurkey he'll park where he can keep an eye on his car. That will mean no visits to the men's room. No problem. He'll bring an old milk carton with him. That way he won't have to use the men's room. Unless his innards start acting up, that is. He sighs, goes to the bathroom and sits on the pot. Fifteen minutes later, he's ready to go. He makes a mental note to buy some Milk of Magnesia. It's something he can afford now.

Chapter Nine

Otis feels so free he is nearly giddy. The realization that he is now a rich man sweeps over him like a swift wind. He begins to think about what he'll do with all that cash. He wonders, also, if there's a law regarding finders-keepers. He'll have to look that up next time he goes to the library.

First, he'll pay down his bills a little at a time so no one gets suspicious. Next, he'll make an appointment to have work done on his teeth. Then, he'll visit Pastor Wright and give him a cash donation. He'll explain that there was a mix-up at the bank and that it was easier to just give cash to the church. Pastor Wright might wonder where Otis got the money, but it's none of his business, and he doubts the man would have the gall to ask. And if he does? Well, there are always inheritances. He could say that his elderly uncle in Kentucky died and left him some money. Sure, why not? Things like that happen all the time. Except for one thing. It would mean that Otis would have to lie, and if there's one thing he hates it's lying.

He'll have to think of something else. Maybe he should just tell the truth but stretch it a bit. He could tell Pastor Wright that he found an old account that had been overlooked. An account that Fern opened and made him beneficiary but never told him about. That would work, wouldn't it? It's still a lie, but Otis knows he'll have to concoct some kind of story to cover his tracks. He has read about husbands and wives who've hidden money from each other. It isn't the right thing to do, but people do it anyway. But then, if he tells this story to Pastor Wright, it will make Fern look deceitful. He shakes his head as if to clear cobwebs from his brain. No matter what he does, it will involve sinful behavior.

Otis glances at the clock on the wall above the TV. Five minutes past ten. He should be ready to leave by eleven or so. He'll take a nice leisurely drive over to Keane's Hardware first, get onto Route 95 and then make his way down to Kittery. It'll take about three hours to get to Turkey Lurkey. He should be back home by early evening.

Otis returns to the shed to get his shovel and heads out to the stand of firs. Fifteen minutes later, he hauls the duffel bags out of the hole, drags them back to the house and cleans them off.

Once he is showered and shaved, he puts on a clean pair of jeans, a long-sleeved red plaid shirt and his comfortable old Jack Purcells. While he's in Kittery, maybe he'll stop at one of the shoe outlets to see about getting a new pair. The ones he has are at least a dozen years old. It's high time he got new ones.

He takes his jacket, the one Fern bought him, picks up his keys and heads for his car with one duffel bag at a time. He figures the best place to put them is in the trunk. That way, no one will see them if they look inside his car. Once the bags are tucked inside the trunk under a blanket, he gets inside the car and puts the key in the ignition. A few moments later, he is at the end of his driveway and turning left onto SR92.

He turns on the radio to see if there are any news updates about the drug deal gone wrong, but there is only music playing so he shuts it off. When he arrives at Keane's, he sees the owner sweeping the sidewalk. He likes Aubrey Keane, considers him a friend. In the past, the old man extended him credit, like the time he had to replace the lawn mower. He paid it off over time, all $198 plus tax. Otis pulls into a parking spot and shuts off the engine. He opens the car door, steps out and locks up.

"Say there, Aubrey. Sure is a nice day."

"Ay-uh. We've got a nice string of days coming. Might close for a few and take Grace to see her sister down east. The leaves are starting to turn already." Otis smiles to himself. Pastor Wright and Aubrey Keane still have the "ay-uh" habit. Fern had insisted that Otis stop saying it long ago when someone at the nursing home told her it made people in Maine sound like country bumpkins.

"That'd be nice," says Otis. "Everyone needs a few days off now and then."

"You can say that again. Time to take a little 'leaf' of absence." He laughs at his pun.

"Sure thing."

Aubrey stops sweeping long enough to take a good look at Otis. "Now, son, I know you didn't stop by to pass the time of day. What can this old fella do for you?"

"I need a gun case. More like three. With locks."

"Three gun cases? You got three guns, Otis?"

"No. Only one. But I need two more for ammo."

"You don't need a gun case to store ammo."

Otis hadn't counted on a debate with Aubrey, but he's becoming good at thinking on his feet. "They're not for me. Going hunting with a couple of friends. The cases are for them."

Aubrey gives Otis a funny look. "I thought you said you wanted them for ammo. And since when have you enjoyed huntin'? You're too much of a softie."

"I'd never shoot anything, but I'm not about to tell my friends that." There. That should shut Aubrey up. But it doesn't.

"Then what's the point of havin' a gun?"

"The point is I need to get going. Got a lot of errands to do. Now, about those gun cases."

Aubrey sighs. "All right. Come on. They're out back."

While Otis is waiting for Aubrey at the front of the store, he looks out the window. A state police car is parked across from the store. Officers are probably questioning business owners and shoppers. He hopes they don't come into Keane's while he's there.

A few minutes later, Aubrey returns with the gun cases. "Grace almost wouldn't let me order these this year. Ever since she got on that PETA mailing list . . . ay-uh."

"How much for the three?"

"Let's see . . ." Aubrey uses a pocket calculator to tally it up. ". . . $420 will do the trick. Plus tax."

Otis hands Aubrey $500 and tells him to keep the change. "Take Grace to lunch," he says.

Aubrey looks at Otis, his mouth dangling open. "What? All of a sudden you've got money to burn?"

Otis's face turns hot. He has to think fast. "Birthday money. From Fern. Last gift she gave me. The extra is for all the credit you've given me over the years." There. He did it. Lied to Aubrey Keane. He feels miserable. Like he has just killed someone. But what could he do? Maybe he should have waited until he got to Kittery to buy the gun cases. No one knows him there. He could kick himself for thinking Aubrey wouldn't ask questions.

Aubrey's face softens. "Say, Otis. How you makin' out these days? Without Fern, I mean."

Otis pauses, then says, "Better than I expected. I miss my wife. I sure do. But I have to live. That's what she'd want, and that's what I'm doing."

"Yes, well, you have a good day. And remember to tell your friends that anything they can get at Reny's they can get right here at just about the same price—probably less."

Otis thanks Aubrey, gives him a friendly cuff on the shoulder and leaves with the new gun cases tucked under his arm.

After leaving the hardware store, Otis places his new gun cases in the back seat and heads home. Once the money is stored and locked away, he'll go to Kittery for his turkey dinner.

Aubrey Keane was right. The leaves are starting to turn. Such a pretty time of year, thinks Otis. No time better than the fall to become a man of great wealth. He corrects himself. Any time is a good time for that to happen.

The drive to Turkey Lurkey is uneventful, and when he arrives the parking lot is nearly empty. He moves into a spot about thirty feet from the entrance, and that makes him happy because he can see his car from anywhere he sits inside. But no sooner is he seated than a bus full of tourists pulls in. He had forgotten that it's the time of year when seniors from the South and Midwest head to New England to leaf peep.

Soon enough, a crowd of senior citizens get off the bus and stand around in small clusters. A few minutes later, the restaurant starts filling up and this takes Otis's attention away from his car. As soon as he remembers, he looks out at the parking lot, only to discover that two men are pointing at the front end of his Malibu and are talking about something. Otis wonders what's so interesting.

"May I get you anything from the bar, sir?" a waiter asks politely when he appears at Otis's table. The man is about fifty and is wearing a red shirt and black bow tie.

"Um . . . no. I'm driving, see. Can't take the chance. If I'm stopped . . ."

"Very well, then. I understand. How about a soft drink? Or a hot beverage? Water?"

"Ice water will be fine. And I'm ready to order. I've got someplace to be in a little while."

"Very well, then. If you're ready to place your order . . ."

Otis wishes the waiter would stop saying "very well." Everything is not very well as long as those two men are hanging around his car.

The waiter notices Otis's distress and asks if everything is all right.

"Everything is fine. Tell you what. I'd like a turkey dinner. Mashed potatoes, butternut squash, gravy, cranberry sauce, stuffing, the works. But I need to go check on my car. I'll be right back."

"Very well, sir. The turkey dinner is always good. We just received a fresh supply of birds. We don't have butternut squash today, but we do have Brussels sprouts and spinach, whichever is your preference."

Otis wants to crown the man. "Spinach? Since when does spinach go with turkey?"

The waiter shrugs. "I don't plan the menu, sir."

He tells the waiter he doesn't have a preference. It could be rutabaga for all he cares.

"Spinach then," he says testily. He hates spinach, but he hates Brussels sprouts even more.

"Very well, sir. I'll put your order in post-haste. Would you like an appetizer?"

"No, I would not like an appetizer," Otis says, clearly annoyed. What did Turkey Lurkey do? Import this guy from Boston? "Just get me my dinner!"

"Very well, sir."

Otis lets out a long sigh, throws down his napkin and leaves the table. He moves toward the front door, only to find that most of the senior citizens are now gathered at the entrance and blocking his way.

"Excuse me," he says to an elderly gentleman wearing a black Kangol cap. "I need to get through."

"Ow! You just stepped on my foot!" cries a woman with a tidy silver perm. She stares directly into Otis's face.

"Sorry, ma'am."

"And don't call me ma'am!"

Otis moves through the mob until he is at the end of the line. Once he rounds the corner of the building, his car comes into view. The men are still there, pointing and talking.

When he gets closer to them, he gives a cheerful greeting and asks if anything is wrong.

"No," says the taller of the two. The man has a huge paunch, a bald head and a David Niven mustache. He reminds Otis of Humpty-Dumpty. "I own an auto body shop in Iowa. I was just pointing out what would need to be done to get this old girl back in shape."

Old girl? Back in shape? Otis doesn't see anything wrong with his Chevy until he looks at it from the vantage point of the body shop owner. There is rust near the tire wells on the driver's side and a noticeable dent and scratch in the door where a woman's shopping cart crashed into it last winter.

"I haven't seen one of these for a long time. Does she run well?" asks the shorter man. He has a head full of stiff, wavy gray hair, and Otis thinks he can smell hair spray, the kind that Fern used.

"Yes, and that's why I still drive it," replies Otis. "I haven't had the body fixed yet, but one of these days I'll get around to it."

"Mind if I look it all over? The interior, too?"

Interior? Would he mind? Of course he'd mind, but Otis decides to be cool about it.

"I'd be happy to let you have a look, but I can't take the time right now. The dinner I ordered is probably sitting on my table right this very minute. I have to get back inside."

"Well, how about after you eat? We're just stopping for a quick sandwich. Probably be done before you are," says Mr. Auto Body. "In fact, I'd like to take her for a quick spin if we have time. Just around the parking lot, of course. Would you mind? Used to own one just like it."

This time Otis is more firm. "Actually, I would mind. I never let anyone get behind the wheel of my car. Not even my wife." There. He has now allowed another lie to slide out of his mouth. Otis has to think quickly. "Anyway, I've got an appointment to see my doctor in an hour."

"Give me your address then. We'll be in the area a few days. I'll give you a call."

"You sure are persistent," says Otis. He is happy that he doesn't live in the area. "I'm not from around here. Just on a little day trip."

"Day trip? I thought you said you have an appointment with your doctor," says Mr. Auto Body.

"I do. Now if you'll excuse me, my food is getting cold. Good talking to you."

Chapter Ten

By the time Otis gets back to his table he is tied in knots. First, there is the worry about leaving his car unattended with all that money in the trunk. Then, Mr. Auto Body had wanted access to his car. He looks at his plate, loaded with everything he loves, except for the spinach, and suddenly doesn't feel hungry. He takes a sip of water, pulls out his wallet, throws down a $20 bill plus another $10 for a tip and leaves without so much as having taken a single bite.

Back in his car, he decides instead to stop at a fast food place. There's one only minutes down the highway. When he finishes eating, he'll go to the outlet stores to see about buying new sneakers. And something else is poking at his mind all of a sudden. Maybe he should stop at an auto dealership to look at new cars.

After enjoying a double cheeseburger and jumbo bag of French fries and downing a diet Coke—Fern had always insisted they not drink plain Coke due to the sugar content—Otis pulls into the lot of a shoe outlet and sees in his rear view mirror that a tour bus is following behind. Maybe it's the same one from Turkey Lurkey. Otis hopes not. If Mr. Auto Body is on that bus and sees him he'll know that he lied.

Otis gets out of his car and hurries through the door. Right away, a sales clerk with dark curly hair pounces on him like a cat on a mouse. "What can I help you find today?" she chirps.

"Sneakers," Otis says. "And I'm in a bit of a hurry, if you don't mind."

"Of course. Aisle six. That's where you'll find them. Everything is on sale," she says.

"Well, that's good. I'm on a fixed income." At this, Otis chuckles. He is becoming quite good at lying. He notices that the woman has a look of compassion on her face.

"If you don't find your size, let me know. We have more stock out back."

Otis thanks her and takes off for aisle six. Just what he is looking for is on the bottom shelf. In his size, too. He takes the sneakers and the box and rushes to the front of the store to pay for them. He glances out the window to check on his car. Everything seems to be okay this time. No one is hovering around his vehicle. Then he sees another tour bus parked out there, and the first person to step off is Mr. Auto Body. Otis is beside himself when he sees him come through the door. A moment later while Otis is paying for his sneakers, Mr. Auto Body calls out, "Hey, this isn't a doctor's office."

"I know. On my way now. Have a good trip," Otis replies and off he goes.

Otis has had just about enough for one day. He hurries to his car, gets inside, slumps onto the seat and leans his head against the steering wheel. He'd like to go home, but he has one more errand. He drives out of the parking lot and onto the highway.

When he turns on the radio, he hears a newscaster giving a weather report. Sunny skies will prevail for the rest of the week, Otis learns. This bit of information cheers him, and he feels a little more calm. September sometimes brings overcast, rainy weather, but not this year. He dreads the cold winter months, and they'll be here before anyone can say Jack Robinson.

The newscaster finishes the weather report and announces that word has just been received about the recent drug case that left two men dead in Calais. Otis turns up the volume and listens.

"Police have called off the hunt for the missing money but are asking Bangor area residents to be on the lookout for anything that might look suspicious," the newscaster says. "It is estimated that the suspects were carrying about $4 million. Anyone finding the money is asked to turn it in to police. Stay tuned now for an update on the recent product safety scandal at . . ."

Otis lowers the volume. As if anyone who found the cash would hand it over. He certainly has no intention of doing that. But then, he hears two little voices inside his head. One is Fern's; the other is Pastor Wright's. "What would Jesus do?" Fern says.

Well, Jesus was never down and out, he thinks. This time he hears only Pastor Wright's voice in response. "Jesus was never down and out, Otis? What Bible have you been reading all these years?"

Otis sighs, turns off the radio and thinks that maybe he should turn in the money. But then he thinks about the busload of tourists. He and Fern had never gone anywhere, and now he regrets it because he has so few memories of their marriage to keep him company. His recollections are limited to shopping for plants for the garden, helping her around the house, attending church services, hearing the click-clack of her knitting needles and spending nights in front of the TV. They didn't eat out much, either. Once in a blue moon they'd take a ride down to Turkey Lurkey, but that was the long and short of it. Now and then, Otis would stop in at the Moose to see his friend, Steve Pierce, but even those visits were few and far between.

Now he needs to set up bank accounts. He can start that process in another day or so, but something else is on his mind. He wants to find a bookstore. A few miles down the highway, he spots a mall just off the exit. The first store he comes to is a Barnes & Noble.

Just beyond the front door is the customer service desk, and Otis asks a woman seated there where the travel section is located. She points a finger, and Otis notices the red nail polish. Her fingertips look like bloody arrows. "Two aisles down to your left. It's in the middle of aisle four," she says. She smiles at Otis, and he notices her teeth are big and white, like Chiclets. She a bush of blonde hair and is wearing red lipstick to match her nail color.

He goes to aisle four where he finds the travel section, just as the woman said. The books are all arranged according to destination and interest. "Backpacking for Beginners." "How to Discover Europe on Pennies a Day." "The Best Restaurants in the World." "Martha and Me — Hiking through Appalachia." "The Rand McNally Atlas Large Scale: United States."

The last two books intrigue him. He'd seen a TV documentary about a man who backpacked his way across the country a few years ago. When he came home, he wrote a book about his adventures and was a featured guest on one of the talk shows. Otis pulls this book off the shelf and studies the cover. The hiker is standing in front of a raging river with a mountainous background and is shown smiling into the lens of a camera. He is sporting an army green cap and is carrying a backpack. There is something else besides. A dog. The animal looks like a Golden Retriever, but it could be a mix of some kind.

Martha must be the dog, Otis supposes. When he opens the book and turns the pages he sees other photos of the author and the dog. Martha. What a name for a dog. But it's better than Barker or, worse, Bimbo.

He looks at the back cover and sees that the book is priced at $24.95. He sets it aside and picks up the Rand McNally. This one is $29.95. While thumbing through the pages, Otis notices that it lists all the national parks, including two along the Appalachian Trail. Another TV show he saw recently focused on people who live along the Trail, some so poor their homes are nothing but shacks. Otis had wondered how they were able to find any joy in life, living as they do. They probably have to make their own happiness, not knowing any other way of life.

He decides to buy the two books and heads to the check-out counter. On the way, he hears a woman with frizzy silver hair ask the man standing beside her what he thinks about the missing money from the drug case.

"All that money," the man says. "Whoever finds it . . ."

Otis wants to say, "I already did, and tough luck for you." Tough luck? As soon as he thinks this thought, he realizes how mean it would sound if he had spoken the words aloud. Otis doesn't like that he has told lies, was rude to Aubrey Keane and short with the Turkey Lurkey waiter, not to mention Mr. Auto Body. Now, he's given himself over to thinking a mean comment? It's not like him at all to act this way, and he knows it. What would Fern think? What would she say? She'd most likely tell him that his love for the money has got the best of him. "It's the *love* of money that's the root of all evil, not the money itself," she had always claimed.

Otis rushes to get in line, only to find the man ahead of him is buying a stack of books and the cashier is taking her time ringing them up.

A few minutes later, the cashier hands the man his receipt and puts the books in a plastic bag bearing the store's name and logo. "Hope you enjoy your reading," she says politely. The man assures her he will and goes on his way.

Otis steps up to the counter and lays down his books. "Going on a trip, are you?" she asks, while casually eyeing the titles. "Your credit card, please?"

He adjusts his attitude and tries harder to be nice. "I'm thinking about it, but no plans yet," he says. "Oh, I have cash."

"Now that's rare. No one seems to want to carry cash anymore," she says.

"Isn't that the truth," Otis replies, handing her a $100 bill. Ha! If only she knew. He's been nice to her, but he doesn't want to get into a big long conversation about money, so he says nothing more.

"Here you go," she says, handing Otis his receipt and change. "Enjoy your day."

"You, too," he says. "And by the way, that's a pretty sweater you're wearing. I like the color."

"Got it at Marshalls. It's called pink shrimp."

"If you'll excuse me, sir, there's a line of people here," the customer behind him says.

"Just trying to make the lady's day," Otis says, adding to himself that he's damned if he does and damned if he doesn't.

Chapter Eleven

On the drive back to Hopewell, Otis makes a plan.

When he gets home, he'll take a look at his new books, first the Rand McNally. The book contains maps and information about famous sites in the United States, and he wants to read up on them. And before he goes to bed, he'll make a list of banks and addresses where he can set up his new accounts. That has to be done this coming week.

A new life for Otis is beginning to take shape, and he congratulates himself for taking his fate into his own hands. He thinks of Fern again and thanks her for being by his side for so many years. Aloud, he says, "I'll always love you, darlin', and I'll never forget you, but just as you said I have to go on living. We'll be together again someday. You weren't right about everything, but I believe you were right about that."

>>>>>> <<<<<<

Later, while studying the map of Maine, he sees that the state has an irregular coastline with plenty of coves and harbors north to south. He wonders why he and Fern had never bothered to visit any of them.

Well, maybe it's no wonder at all. Fern, the homebody. Always content with nothing more than a quick trip to town. He had asked her over the years if she wanted to take a drive down to Camden or over to Bar Harbor, but she had always said no, she'd rather stay home and bake a loaf of bread or work on her knitting projects. Now that Otis thinks about it, he realizes he has never explored his own state, and that's a shame because from what he sees on the map there's a lot of ground to cover.

Otis has always loved being near the water. When he was a boy, he and his family lived near the Penobscot River, and before his father died he would take him and Otis's brother, Carl, out in a canoe to paddle around. He thinks back to the time when he was eleven years old. Carl had been about thirteen, just around the time his father died of a heart attack. His father's death had put an end to their days on the river, and he, Carl and his mother moved to an old, run-down cottage in Aurora out on Route 9. The house had four rooms and was owned by a man from the church where the Kingston family attended services. The two boys had shared a room while his mother slept on the living room couch.

Like his father, Carl is dead now and so is his mother. They had lived hand to mouth when they were kids, and they got by because of the kindness and charity extended by neighbors and the pastor of a tiny white Baptist church smack in the middle of the hundred-mile hilly Airline road. His mother made ends meet by waiting tables at a breakfast place in Brewer. She walked the three miles to and from work every day, regardless of the weather, and Otis can still remember his mother coming home and putting up her feet. "There's gotta be a better way to make a living," she would say.

Fortunately for the boys, the owner of the one-pump gas station half a mile from where they lived taught them about the mechanics of a car. It wasn't long before Otis and Carl were changing tires, oil and spark plugs and replacing fluids and fixing brakes. Eventually, Carl left the state when he married Florence Douglas and settled in Keene, New Hampshire. Carl opened up his own gas station and invited Otis to join him in business, but Fern didn't want to leave Hopewell. Instead, Otis applied for a job at Logger-Heads, the local paper mill, and worked there for more than thirty years before being laid off in January. The owner of the mill said he had to cut his staff because the demand for newsprint and other paper products was in decline. He and Fern only had a few months together after he lost his job. Soon after the calendar page turned to June she was gone.

Otis now has a chance to continue living but in a new and different way. He continues to study the map and notices that the Appalachian Trail begins at Mount Katahdin about twenty-five miles northeast of Millinocket. Or maybe it starts in Georgia and ends in Maine. Either way, he feels excitement building when he thinks about driving along the Trail. Otis recalls a TV show about a group of hikers making the trek all the way to Georgia. He opens the atlas to the page showing the state of Georgia to see where the Trail ends and finds it at Springer Mountain. So that piece of information is now clear in Otis's head.

He reaches back into his memory to recall details of the TV show, but all he can remember is that one of the men on the trek had an encounter with a bear and survived to tell the tale.

As Otis continues to study the map, he notices the number of small towns surrounding the Trail. He wonders what it would be like to drive parallel to it and talk to people who live in the area. Maybe he could stay in motels or bed and breakfast places. The more he thinks about it, the more memories of the show pop into his head. The hikers had said they enjoyed the fresh air and exercise while on the Trail. One said it motivated him to get into shape both physically and mentally before they left, and the others joined in agreement. One said there was a spiritual quality to the trek. In fact, Otis now recalls his exact words: "I never felt closer to God. When I came home, I enrolled in seminary and became a pastor."

Otis stands up to stretch and goes to the living room. The evening sky has darkened and rain is threatening. So much for the weather forecast earlier in the day. He remembers he left his car window open and goes out to close it.

The more he thinks about a drive along the Appalachian Trail, the more he wonders if he could ever do such a thing. He'd definitely need a decent car to drive, not his old Malibu. He'd have to trade it in for something new, maybe even a car that has four-wheel drive. He has no idea what the terrain is like along the Trail, but surely there would be hills and mountains to navigate. Four-wheel drive would come in handy on a journey like that.

Otis comes back inside and sits at the kitchen table to continue his studies. He turns to the page that displays the eastern side of the United States and sees that the Appalachian Trail winds its way through Maine, New Hampshire, Vermont, Massachusetts, Connecticut, New York, New Jersey, Pennsylvania, Maryland, West Virginia, Virginia, Tennessee and North Carolina before ending in Georgia.

He then looks at the pages dedicated to each state and studies photographs showcasing their individual natural beauty. In his mind's eye,

Otis sees himself driving his new car. A convertible maybe. He has the money now. He doesn't have to settle for something old and beat up. Next week, he will set up his new bank accounts and deposit just enough to pay for a car and leave a balance in each one to keep the accounts open. He'll dress in his Sunday best to make a good impression on the banking people, and if anyone questions why he has so much cash on hand, he will say that he has not been satisfied with the service at his previous bank and kept the cash at home until he could find a bank he liked. He will admit how dangerous it is to keep cash at home, but he will make a point of putting on a confident air. Doing that will help convince the bankers that he is on the up and up.

Otis shakes his head and forces himself to move back into the moment. What is he thinking? Why has he become so deceitful all of a sudden? Besides, he would never go on a road trip by himself. Or would he?

His thoughts turn to Fern. She should be alive to go with him. A fresh wave of anger wells up, and he pounds the table with his closed fist. If only she had not been exposed to second-hand smoke. If only she hadn't died and left him alone. What was life, anyway, but a series of disappointments and problems to be solved, one after the other. At that moment, Otis doesn't care whether he lives or dies. He misses Fern. Misses her terribly.

"What should I do, Fernie? Should I just sit here and rot? Or should I do something with my life? Tell me what to do!" He cries out the words in desperation. Then, his anger begins to subside and he takes in a long, slow breath. As if in response, he hears a voice inside his head saying, "Go. Live. We'll be together again one day. Forget the past. Live!"

The words are so clear, it is as if Fern were sitting right there speaking to him. But she is a mile from where he now sits, buried under a mound of dirt. Maybe the words he heard were from God Himself. In spite of his grief, he suddenly feels better, thinking that both God and his beloved Fern have reached out from the great divide between heaven and earth and the living and the dead.

Chapter Twelve

Otis returns to the kitchen table, picks up the Rand McNally and goes to the living room to sit in his recliner, the one Fern bought him for his fiftieth birthday. He turns on the floor lamp behind the chair, raises the footrest, puts on his glasses and settles in.

According to what is written about Appalachia, the Trail originated with a forester named Benton MacKay. Otis reads that MacKay's idea was to create a grand trail that would connect a series of farms and wilderness camps for people who lived in the city. His idea made its way to a story in the *New York Evening Post,* and as soon as it was published the idea was adopted by the Palisades Interstate Park Trail Conference as their main project.

Otis pauses before he continues to read. He looks through the chapter listings to see if there are any that talk about the people who live along the trail, wildlife, plants and flowers. When he finds what he's looking for, he learns about black bears, rattlesnakes, copperheads, white oak, hemlock, poplar, ash, various firs, mountain laurel and rhododendron. He thinks the region must be beautiful and is probably why John Denver wrote *Take Me Home, Country Roads.*

Otis envisions himself seated behind the wheel of a new car, luggage in the trunk along with The Vault. If he decides to drive the Appalachian Trail, he'll pack only what he needs: Jeans, T-shirts, a few flannel shirts in case it gets cold at night, a jacket, a pair of sneakers, hiking boots, socks, shorts, sandals and a pair of gloves. And a hat. Can't forget that. Otis wonders what time of year is best for traveling the Trail and decides that late spring—around May—might be a good option when it's neither too hot nor too cold. Yes, there'll be bugs, but he'd bring tick and insect repellant to keep them away.

He closes the Rand McNally, reaches for the TV remote and presses the ON button. The news is in progress, and a young blonde meteorologist named Kira Murphy is talking about the extended weather forecast. Otis listens while she updates viewers on what they can expect in the next few days. Rain is coming but not until next weekend. And a hurricane is brewing in the Atlantic. Kira says the region can expect warmer than usual temperatures and sunny blue skies through Friday. When she is finished, she turns to newscaster Tom Cullen. He thanks Kira and gives an update on the two drug dealers killed in Calais.

The men, Otis learns, were traced to a drug cartel from the West Coast of Mexico, and they had a criminal record to rival Al Capone's. He doesn't mention the missing drugs or money. Tom Cullen doesn't reveal the names of the two men, either.

Otis feels uneasy, knowing The Vault is under his bed. Who knows if the drug lords are lurking nearby and looking for the lost money.

He decides to drive to Ellsworth on Monday morning to open a new bank account. He hopes no one will question him about where the money came from, but then why would they? Otis wonders if he's becoming paranoid. No one knows him in Ellsworth.

While in deep thought, he looks up when a TV commercial about a Volkswagen dealership appears on the screen. Nice vehicles, but Otis is patriotic. He wants "made in America," something he would be proud to drive. Sure, Volkswagens are great cars, but he doesn't want to drive anything even remotely connected to Adolf Hitler.

Just before "Wheel of Fortune" starts, another ad comes on, this time for a truck. He listens to the sales pitch. It's for a Ford F-150 in that nice Velocity Blue. The phrase "extreme off-road handling" captures his attention. Just what he'd need if he were to travel the Trail. Otis has never owned a truck before, but he sure would like one. While in Ellsworth he'll try to find a Ford dealership. By this time tomorrow night, he might be the owner of a new vehicle. Anything is possible now that he's a man of means. He laughs aloud at the very idea. What would Fern say if she were alive? What would she think?

Otis clicks his tongue when he realizes that Fern would say that he should turn the money over to the authorities. He would try to convince her that there would be no harm in keeping it, but she would insist that if he kept the money it would be the same thing as stealing, and heaven forbid she should be married to a thief. Lying was enough to set her teeth on edge, never mind thieving. No, if Fern were alive, she would not want anything to do with what Otis has hidden under the bed.

He can hear her now. "You keep that money, and it'll do nothing but bring us grief. God has His eyes on everyone, including us, Otis. Mark my words. He does. Don't let money become your idol."

Fern sure did have her ways. She was a virtuous woman, plain and simple, but sometimes she took things to the extreme. Even so, he knew he could always count on her to tell the truth. Nothing dishonest about her.

Otis considers another angle. What if he doesn't keep all the money for himself? What if he gives it away? Already, he has made up his mind to give a big donation to the church, but what about the rest of it? There's no way he'll spend all that money during his lifetime. And if he keeps most of it hidden under the bed and suddenly has to go to the hospital, he might have to give the key to Colleen or Fred Turnbull in case he needs something from the house. And what if one of them finds The Vault and opens it? What then?

Otis knows he has to open more bank accounts than just one in Ellsworth. On Monday, he'll go to Hampden, Orono and Hermon, too. Maybe even Bucksport. Maybe even as far as Bar Harbor.

His thoughts turn once again to the people who live along the Appalachian Trail and he turns off the TV. There's not much information about the population in the Rand McNally, so he boots up his computer and finds several sites that give statistics. There are reports about some people who lack basic indoor plumbing and electrical power. He reads that Kentucky was a hub for coal mining and some folks still live in squalor. Another site shows a dog eating out of an old milk jug, a young boy wearing ragged clothes and running barefoot in a yard and an old man sitting on his front porch, a look of despair etched into the lines of his face.

Something rises within Otis, a feeling that he should do something to relieve their suffering. He has the money. Why not share the wealth?

He heats up some canned beans and fries some hot dogs for supper. Later, while eating, he thinks about the route he'll take if he decides to travel south and what towns he'll stop in. Maybe he could eat at diners and talk to people and hear their stories. People who own diners usually know everyone in town. They'd be the ones to tell him about the neediest. As thoughts about such a trip tumble through Otis's mind, he grows more and more excited over the prospect. By the time he shuts off the lights and goes to bed, his mind is in spin cycle.

He cannot stop thinking about going on the road.

Finally, around midnight, he falls into a dreamless but restless sleep. He has kicked off the blankets, and the chill in the room wakes him up. He needs to use the toilet, so he gets up and walks to the bathroom while half asleep. Before he goes back to bed, he looks at himself in the mirror. His hair is sticking up all over the place, there are huge bags under his eyes and the corners of his mouth are drooping. He shakes his head, knowing that the loss of Fern has taken an appalling toll on him. If he doesn't make his plans now, he knows he never will. Life is speeding by at breakneck speed, and any time now he could be joining his wife in that eternal bed under the ground. If he doesn't act now, he knows he never will.

Chapter Thirteen

On Monday morning, Otis wakes up later than usual. He turns over and looks at the clock. Five minutes past eight. He has a lot of business to take care of so he has to get moving. He makes himself a cup of coffee and eats a bowl of Cheerios and sliced banana before showering and getting dressed.

After breakfast, he unlocks The Vault and counts out $30,000. Then, as an afterthought, he counts out another $30,000 plus a few $100 bills. Oh, heck, what's another $10,000. He counts that out, too, and places the banded money in a big manila envelope. He will take the envelope and The Vault with him to Ellsworth.

On the highway, Otis notices two tour buses passing him. Come next May, he'll be on his own tour but instead of heading north he'll be heading south.

When he arrives in downtown Ellsworth, he heads to Main Street to look for a bank. A block ahead, on the left is one with a no-nonsense, straightforward name: The Savings Bank.

Otis squeezes into a tight space and hopes his errand won't take long. While inside the bank, he'll ask someone about auto dealerships in the area, Ford being his first choice, Chevrolet his second. He'll take his time and shop around, but he'll try to make a purchase sometime this week.

He makes sure the Malibu is locked before he goes inside the bank. He doesn't trust anyone around his car, not since that incident with Mr. Auto Body at Turkey Lurkey. Otis squares his shoulders and tightens his grip on the manila envelope before stepping inside the bank's lobby. To his left are the tellers, to his right a rack of deposit and withdrawal slips and bank brochures describing various checking and savings accounts, retirement accounts and investments. Private offices are lined up at the back wall. He

the room and reads a nameplate on one of the doors—"Nancy
Burke, New Accounts."

Otis knocks twice before he hears a woman's voice. "Just one moment," she says.

He waits patiently, wondering what's going on inside her office.
Someone else might be in there, maybe her boss or another customer.
A few minutes pass before he hears her say it's okay to enter.

The woman, presumably Miss or Mrs. Burke, looks up when Otis
steps into her office. She is wearing a black sweater, a double strand of
red beads, purple-framed glasses and orange lipstick. A cloud of silver
hair is swept away from her face. Otis guesses she is about his age or a
little older. She eyes him with a bit of nonchalance before inviting him
to have a seat.

"Sorry. Just finishing up a letter that has to be hand-delivered today,"
she says. "I'll be right with you."

Otis mumbles something under his breath, clears his throat and sits
across from her. He waits for what seems like an entire lunch hour
before she finally turns to him.

"I'm really sorry. Had to take care of some business for a client. It
couldn't wait. At The Savings Bank, we take customer service to the
highest level. Now, what can I do for you?"

The highest level? Then why did she make him wait so long? "I need
to open a checking account," he says, making sure his tone of voice is
calm and confident.

"Of course. Here's my business card. I'm Nancy Burke," she says,
handing him the card. "What type of account would you like to open?
Did you say a checking account?"

A short attention span, too. "Yes. I'll be buying a vehicle soon."

"Oh, in that case, you might want to speak to one of our loan
officers," she says with a bit more animation. Presumptuous, too.

"I won't be needing a loan," he tells her. "I have the cash."

"I see. In the envelope?"

"Yes. Quite a bit of cash. I'd like to deposit $9,500."

"For goodness' sake, why are you carrying all that money around?
It's dangerous, don't you think?"

His mother died long ago, and now here she is, a woman just like her, sitting across from him.

"Yes, I suppose. But no matter how you look at it, there's danger everywhere. Identity thieves, for instance. My neighbor got ripped off for more than $50,000 when someone stole his identity. Whoever it was went on a shopping spree. It was fraud so he didn't have to pay for what was stolen, but still." Another lie. He doesn't know anyone whose identity was stolen. Otis knows he is on shaky ground with God but doesn't seem to be able to stop himself.

"Yes, identity theft is a terrible thing. But it isn't safe to carry a lot of money around, either," Nancy Burke says in a haughty manner. She is scowling now, as if talking to a naughty child.

Okay, Mama. You think I'm bad? You don't know the half of it. "Well, I'm here now, and once I give you the money it'll be safe in an account, won't it? Let's talk about paperwork. What do I have to fill out?" Otis knows he sounds crotchety and tells himself to chill or she'll start in on him again.

Nancy Burke looks at Otis for a long moment before opening the drawer at the side of her desk and pulling out forms for him to sign. She shuts the drawer with a slam, shoves the paperwork across her desk and asks Otis in a crisp tone if he has a beneficiary in mind. He thinks a moment before answering. "I guess I could name my church, but there won't be much left. As I mentioned, I plan to use it to buy a vehicle." That should chap her . . .

She interrupts Otis's thoughts and says, "Your church?" She says this as if he had suggested he leave his money to the devil.

"Yes, my church. Is that illegal?"

"No, it's just . . . unusual."

Otis is becoming exasperated. Why would she care who he leaves his money to? He isn't asking her to marry him. He only wants to open a damned checking account.

"I see. Well, you fill out these two cards, sign your name on both and I'll do the rest," she says.

Otis takes a pen from a cup perched at the edge of her desk and fills in the blanks before signing his name. Then he places the envelope on top of the desk and fiddles with the metal clasp.

He waits for her to finish her computer work, and when she does Otis opens the envelope and pulls out the cash. She begins counting and arranges the $100 bills in neat stacks. While she works, she uses a calculator with a paper tape to help her keep track of the money.

In a minute or so, she says, "Well, all righty, then. I counted $9,500. Wait here while I ask one of the tellers to take it to the vault. We can't have that kind of money floating around. Just last month we were robbed and lost more than $20,000."

From one vault to another? Otis tries hard not to laugh.

His business finished, Nancy Burke hands him a block of starter checks and tells him he can expect to receive a package of checks bearing his name, address and account number in about a week. The starter checks, she says, will see him through until they arrive in the mail. Now, how would she know that, Otis wonders. She seems to be assuming an awful lot. Nancy Burke asks if he would like an ATM card but he declines. The checks will be enough. Otis thanks her and turns to leave.

"What kind of vehicle are you planning to buy?" she asks.

"I'm not sure yet. A truck most likely." Otis wonders why she is asking. "Do I need your approval?"

She gives him a hard stare. "You might want to take a drive to the dealership where my husband works," she says feigning friendliness. "Young's. Just off Route 95 in Carmel. They sell Fords and Chryslers."

Now Otis is wondering if she and her husband are in cahoots. Maybe she gets some kind of kickback for sending bank customers there. Mr. and Mrs. Cahoots.

"Thanks. I'll take a ride over. Ford is at the top of my list."

"Mine, too," she says, softening even more. "I drive a Ford Fusion. Love my car. Ask for Phil Burke."

"Okay, Mrs. Cahoots. I mean Mrs. Burke."

"Mrs. Cahoots? Where did that come from?"

"I'm sorry. I was thinking about my neighbor, the woman who lives next door. You remind me of her." Otis is sure he's headed for hell.

He turns and leaves the office, gently closing Nancy Burke's door behind him. There's no doubt in his mind that something shady is going on at the home of Nancy and Phil Burke.

Back in his car, he heads to Prospect. He lingers near the Fort Knox Historic Site until a teenage boy approaches. Otis asks the boy to take a picture of him in front of the sign. When he has a chance, he'll ask Jeff at the little shop in Hopewell to enlarge and frame it. He thinks it'll make an interesting conversation piece. Fort Knox and Otis Kingston. It'll give him something to smile about.

Chapter Fourteen

After his Fort Knox photo op, Otis drives to Bucksport to open another account. When he finishes, he continues on to Hampden, Orono and Hermon to set up three more accounts.

While driving along, a Ford F-150 passes him on the left. It's a good looking truck in that Velocity Blue, and it has ample cargo space. Just the sight of it makes Otis think it's an omen and that he should own one himself. The sign for Young's auto dealership comes into view, just as Nancy Burke had told him, so he takes the next exit.

Otis drives onto the lot and passes new Ford coupes and sedans in all the latest models and colors. There are also a few new trucks parked alongside a wide lane leading to the rear of the building. He looks forward to test driving an F-150.

He parks in a visitor space and exits his old Malibu, hoping that no one will bother his car while he's inside the showroom.

As soon as he opens the door, a man wearing a crisp gray suit approaches. "A good morning to you, sir. What can we show you today?" he says in a deep, resonant voice. The salesman could easily pass for Steve Harvey.

"Might be interested in one of your F-150s," says Otis.

"We just got a few in," the salesman replies, extending his hand. He introduces himself as The Bishop.

"The Bishop? People call you that?"

"They sure do.

"Why?"

"Because . . . Mr. . . . ."

"Otis."

"Because, Mr. Otis, this is my second job. On weekends, I'm a preacher."

A preacher and a car salesman? In Otis's mind, the two occupations are miles apart. "Sorry for the confusion. Otis is my first name."

"Had an uncle whose name was Otis. Well, then, Otis, what can I show you today?"

"Thinking about buying a truck. Like I said, an F-150."

"New or used?"

Otis can hardly believe it when he says "new." He has never owned a new vehicle in his entire life.

The Bishop pauses, turns his eyes skyward, raises his arms and says, "Lord, help me to lead Otis here to the truck of his dreams . . ."

He's funny like Steve Harvey, too. Otis chuckles and waits for what else The Bishop has to say.

"Come with me. I think I know just what you're looking for. Velocity blue. That's what you want, right?"

"How did you know?"

"They don't call me The Bishop for nothing," he says, pointing to the sky.

"I guess not."

"You ever own a truck?" The Bishop says.

"No. This would be my first one. I lost my wife a few months ago, and now I've got time on my hands so figure I might as well take in some of the country before I kick the bucket, too . . . I mean, before my time comes." Otis is embarrassed to have used that slang term in front of a man of the cloth, but The Bishop takes it in stride.

"Couldn't agree more. Come along. Let's take a look at what we've got."

The Bishop leads the way to the rear of the lot where a pair of brand-new F-150s are parked. One is Velocity Blue. The other is Silver Spruce.

"Here you go," says The Professor. "A pair of beauties, in my most humble opinion. Wouldn't mind owning one myself."

The Bishop goes on to tell Otis that the F-150 is good on gas and gives a smooth ride.

"Can't find better handling than one of these babies," he says. "Let's step inside and have a closer look." The Bishop pulls a key fob from his pants pocket and hands it to Otis. "Showed this one to another customer a couple of hours ago."

Otis steps onto the running board and swings himself into the driver's seat. He glances around and sees that the dashboard has lots of gauges, controls and indicators. The seats are leather, and they give off that new vehicle smell.

When Otis presses the ignition button, the entire dashboard lights up in bright red, green and blue. "Just like an airplane cockpit," he says to The Bishop, now seated beside him. "Not that I've ever flown in a plane."

"This one has all the bells and whistles. Deluxe speakers for the audio system, navigation, back-up camera, air bags, SRS. Towing package. Leather interior. Seats that fold flat. The works."

Just what Otis was hoping for. He steps outside and takes a look at the sticker sheet—$48,900.

When Otis steps back inside, the Bishop waits for his reaction. "In your price range?" he finally says.

In response, Otis gives a little shrug.

The Bishop points out the other features, including the 375 HP engine. He tells Otis the truck will make it through all kinds of weather.

"Everything you could ask for under one roof," The Bishop says. "You can even use the seats for beds. And speaking of that, let me show you the cargo area."

The two step outside again, and The Bishop shows Otis the spacious bed. While Otis is thinking about filling the space, he wonders if he could install a secret safe big enough to hold all the money. He'll look online later to see what he can find.

Otis looks at his watch. Nearly four o'clock.

"What time do you close?"

"Eight o'clock. You in a hurry?"

"Not at all. I'd like to buy something today but don't want to rush into anything, either."

"Want to take this little beauty for a spin?"

"Sure. Love to."

"You know, if you buy this truck today I could probably get you a good deal."

"Really? Why is that?"

"I'm an honest man, and I'll be honest with you. More are coming in at the end of the week. We have to move them off the lot quickly. Now, I have to let my sales manager know we're going for a ride. You wait here, and I'll be right back."

The Bishop leaves Otis standing next to the truck while he goes back to the showroom. He runs his hand along the sparkling blue finish and pictures himself driving along the highway. The truck is a solid machine, and the more he thinks about buying it, the more convinced he is that his name is written all over it.

A few minutes later, The Bishop returns. "Here you go," he says, handing Otis a promotional brochure. Otis gets into the driver's seat again and starts the engine. The Bishop tells him to go straight ahead and take a left at the end of the building. "That'll get us onto 95," he says, "Let's go for a little ride."

Otis does as The Bishop tells him and takes off. Already, he likes the way the truck handles.

"Seems like there's a lot to learn. My old Malibu doesn't have all these gauges."

"I wouldn't worry about that. It's easy when you know what they're for. If you decide to buy, I'll give you some lessons before you take it home. Go on, now. Pull onto the highway. Let's get rocking!"

His foot on the brake pedal, Otis checks for traffic behind him before taking off. He notices that the engine purrs like a contented little kitten.

"Go ahead and give it the gas," says The Bishop.

Otis likes the quick pick-up when he presses the gas pedal. When he comes to the next exit, he slows but The Bishop tells him to continue on to the next one.

"I want you to get a good feel for what this truck is all about," he says.

Otis settles in for what he is beginning to think of as the ride of his life. The truck's reputation for extreme handling is absolutely true, and he is thinking that it already belongs to him.

He tries out the windshield wipers and activates the lights, then looks at the odometer. Only eight miles.

"Like it?" The Bishop asks.

"Oh, yeah. Handles real well. Brakes are nice and tight. Mileage is low enough," Otis jokes. He smiles at The Bishop and gets back an even bigger smile in return. Otis notices that he has perfect white teeth just like Steve Harvey's.

"I'll go back to the lot now," says Otis. "Maybe we can do some business. And speaking of business, a woman at the bank told me her husband works here. Burke is the last name."

"Burke? Odd you should mention him."

"Why's that?"

"Boss fired him right after lunch today."

"Really? What'd he do?"

"No one knows, but we all think he might have been involved in some kind of shady sales practices."

"You mean he might have been in cahoots with someone?"

"That's exactly what I mean. As a preacher, I always try to see the good in people, but there was something about this guy Burke. Never could figure him out. There are rumors he was involved in some kind of monkey business, but no one really knows what went down. Just between us, okay?"

Otis thinks about Nancy Burke and his suspicions. He knows what went down but keeps what he thinks to himself. "I won't breathe a word," he says, "and that's a promise."

After his test drive with The Bishop, Otis heads for home in his old Malibu. Tomorrow, he'll go back to the dealership and hand over $45,500 plus tax. He was thrilled to learn that The Bishop got him such a good deal. Otis is sorry to say goodbye to his old car, but there's no sense in keeping it.

He wishes he had jotted down the name and number of the man who had shown an interest in it while he was at Turkey Lurkey. Maybe Mr. Auto Body would have wanted it for reconditioning. Or a kid who loves old cars would probably enjoy tinkering with it. Too late now.

He loves how the F-150 handles, loves the sleek, modern interior, the navigation system built into the dashboard and the lockable glove box where he can keep some of The Vault. No one will be able to get inside but him. He'll also figure out a way to install a compartment at the rear of the truck to hide The Vault.

His thoughts turn to Fern and he wonders if she would approve of the truck. Of course she would. For one thing, she always loved blue vehicles, and the metallic paint dazzles in the sun. She would also say that the ride is smooth and takes bumps in the road well, and now Otis won't have to worry about getting stuck on snow-covered roads during the winter months because the truck goes in all kinds of weather.

Hungry now, Otis stops for Chinese takeout. Peking ravioli, egg roll, spare ribs, chicken chow mein and pork fried rice. He can't wait to celebrate the purchase of his new truck, even if no one else celebrates with him. Maybe he should invite his work buddy, Jack Colby. On second thought, no. Too much going on.

Chapter Fifteen

After supper, he puts the leftovers in plastic containers, places his dishes in the sink and settles at the kitchen table to continue his map studies. He runs his finger down the length of the Appalachian Trail and thinks about what he will need for the trip.

He'll probably shop in the spring for some new clothes. And he should make an appointment with his dentist because one of his molars is giving him trouble. As he ponders what he'll need, he thinks about nailing down a departure date. If his boss at Logger-Heads calls him back to work, Otis will tell him that he isn't coming back, that he's decided to take early retirement. He figures a two- or three-month trip will be enough time for him to see all the sights and give away some of his newfound wealth.

He wonders if there should be a limit to what he will give. If someone needs a wheel chair, for instance, the cash outlay wouldn't be much. But suppose someone needs a motorized wheel chair or one of those big scooters. That would be a horse of a different color, wouldn't it?

Otis brushes aside this concern. So what if he has to buy a motorized wheel chair or scooter. His frugal days are over. He reaches for a writing tablet and pencil from the kitchen counter and begins to write:

Otis Kingston — Appalachian Trail Trip — Departure May 1

There. It's settled. The very fact that he has written a headline for his adventure and departure date shows that he's serious about going. He feels his heart rate kick up a notch just thinking about it. He begins to make a list:

UTILITY — Flashlight, batteries, maps, camera, Swiss army knife, compass, cell phone, Coleman stove, propane tank, folding chair, collapsible table, cooler. He has already ordered a secret stash box on the Internet he can install easily under the truck's bed. No one will know it's there but him.

He continues writing: Insect spray. Tool box. Bungee cords. Tarp. Dog.

Dog? Did he just write d-o-g? Otis gives a little chuckle. Where did that come from? The last thing he needs is a dog. But then again maybe a canine companion would be good for him. He'd have someone to talk to, someone who would come along for the adventure. He'd had two dogs when he was a boy—both black Labs named Walter and Pepper. Otis has to admit that they weren't actually *his* dogs. Walter and Pepper had belonged to a neighbor, but Otis had loved those dogs is if they were his own. Yes, a black Lab would do nicely. Not too big, not too small. Walter and Pepper had loved a pat on the head or scratch around the ears. They never asked for much.

⇝⇝⟩ ⟨⫷⫷

On Tuesday, Otis gets up early, makes himself a cup of coffee and continues his list. He starts with clothing and ends with bottled water. He reviews what he has written and is satisfied that he has not forgotten anything. If he has, it will come to him and he'll add it later. Goodness knows, he has enough time to plan over the next eight months. This year, fall and winter won't seem so long and dreary, not when he has this magnificent adventure coming next spring.

Once again, his thoughts circle around to getting a dog and where he might find one. Probably an animal shelter would be a good place to start. There's a vet and shelter in Bangor, and he decides to visit later in the day. First, though, he wants to read more about his new truck. He takes the owner's manual to his recliner and sits down. While reading, he's reminded that the back seat is bench style, a comfy place for a dog. An hour later, he calls the dealership to ask if the F-150 is ready for pick-up. He's told he can come and get it now if he wants.

By mid-afternoon, Otis has opened three more accounts: One in Bangor, one in Brewer and another in Holden. When he arrives at the dealership and meets with The Bishop and sales manager. He hands over the check and he and The Bishop walk to the side of the lot where Otis's new truck is parked.

"Hope you enjoy it and have some fun," says The Bishop. "Had one of these myself about ten years ago," he adds wistfully. "My wife and I went everywhere in that truck. Sort of miss it now. Maybe one of these days I'll get another one."

Otis nods. Tells him he's sure he'll enjoy it. Thanks him for his time and trouble and the good deal.

"No trouble at all. Glad to be of help. Stop in and let me know where you're going. I might have some tips for you."

"Thanks for the offer. I might do that."

Before he leaves the dealership, The Bishop teaches him what the gauges and indicators are for and shows him how to use the navigation system.

Otis's happiness meter hasn't registered this high since before Fern got sick. Now he wonders what he'll find at the animal shelter over in Bangor.

The dogs are making an awful racket with all their barking and yipping when Otis arrives at the shelter. These are dogs and cats with a past that may have included abuse. The very thought tugs at his heart.

When he opens the front door to the shelter, a woman and golden retriever on a leash are heading his way. She smiles and tells Otis he might need ear plugs. He laughs and reaches down to pat the dog's head.

"What's this good looking guy's name?"

"Einstein. Suits him, too. He's whip smart," she says.

Otis nods and smiles as the dog licks his hand. "Friendly, too."

"I watched you get out of that truck. Is it new?" she asks, as if to prolong the conversation.

"Right off the lot."

"Wow. When my husband was alive, we did a lot of traveling in an F-150."

"No kidding . . . I'm planning to drive the Appalachian Trail next year."

"Really? That's the last place we visited. Now isn't that the strangest thing, meeting someone who's going there. I always say . . ."

Something tells Otis that this is going to be a long, drawn-out story so he cuts her off politely. "I'm really sorry," he says, "I've got a load of errands to do, and I really need to take a look at the dogs."

"Well, I hope you find what you want," she says. "Come on, Einstein. We need to get you home so you can have a treat." And then the woman and her dog are gone.

Inside, the shelter has a musky smell mixed with some kind of cleaning agent. A stout middle-aged woman with a double chin, short brown hair and frameless glasses looks up from her desk when Otis approaches. According to her badge, her name is Harriet.

"Hi there," she says. "Looking for a dog, cat . . . a pig?"

Otis laughs at her joke.

"Thought I'd stop by to take a look at the dogs," he answers.

Harriet smiles. "You picked a good day. Four new dogs and five cats arrived yesterday. Poor things. All bent out of shape from being penned up. But they seem healthy in spite of some hard knocks. Are you looking for anything in particular?"

"I'd love a black Lab," Otis says. "What are my chances? Have you got one?"

Chapter Sixteen

Otis doesn't dare to hope that Harriet will tell him there's a black Lab in one of the cages.

But then he hears her say, "Well, I'll be a monkey's mother . . . a young female black Lab came in last night. She's with Dr. Dalton right now getting checked out."

Otis can't believe the good news. First the money. Then the truck. Now a dog. What next?

"Can I see her?" Otis asks. Hope fills his heart.

"Sure. Wait here. I'll see if the doctor is finished," Harriet says as she leaves her desk and disappears behind a door that leads to the vet's exam room.

While Otis waits, he looks at the posters tacked to a bulletin board. One warns about the dangers of heartworm. Another tells how to get rid of fleas. Yet another is an advertisement for some kind of scientific food claiming to be good for a cat's urinary tract. The fourth one warns pet owners to protect their animals from predators like coyotes and fisher cats.

When Harriet returns, there's a smile on her face. "Dr. Dalton is finished," she says. "We're calling her Blackie, but we don't really know her name. She's in good health. Teeth are fine. She's been spayed, too, and he's guessing she's about two years old." Harriet sits down at her desk and pulls an adoption form out of a drawer.

"Where'd she come from?" Otis asks.

"The street. No collar, no microchip. Someone probably couldn't afford to keep her."

Otis supposes that her previous owner dropped her off in the middle of nowhere. He knows all too well that people have all kinds of sad stories and hardships. He only hopes the dog wasn't abused.

"You said I could see her."

"My goodness, you're an eager beaver. Miss Blackie must be in the kennel by now. Come with me," she says.

Otis follows Harriet through another door that leads to an adjacent kennel where the dogs are held. Otis follows her along the row until they come to the last cage. "Here she is. Meet Blackie, our new black Lab," says Harriet.

Otis goes on one knee to have a look. The dog is lying in the cage on its belly, head resting on its front paws. "Poor little girl," Otis says. "You need a home?"

Harriet opens the door to the cage and coaxes Blackie to come out, but the dog only lies there, listless. "Don't worry. She'll come around. She obviously hasn't had much human contact in a while. Come on, girl. This nice man wants to meet you."

Harriet and Otis take turns encouraging the dog until, a few minutes later, she stands and moves slowly toward the door of the cage. She looks at Otis with sad brown eyes while he beckons her with an outstretched hand. She moves closer to the door while letting out a soft murmur, and when she licks Otis's hand, he falls instantly in love.

Harriet tells Otis that under Maine law people who adopt from a shelter must have two character references. He gives her the names and phone numbers for Colleen and Jack Colby, fills out the adoption form and a few days later Harriet calls to tell him he's been approved.

"You can come get her today if you want," she says. "And by the way, have you chosen a name for her? We like to note that in our records."

In fact, Otis has decided to call her Sadie. When he tells Harriet, she pauses, then says, "That was my mother's name. How did you know?"

Otis tells her he didn't know, that he just picked the name out of thin air. "I hope you're not upset."

"Not at all. I'm actually touched by it. Like it was a gift from heaven."

"Probably was," he says. "That's been happening a lot lately."

While Otis was waiting for approval to adopt Sadie, he bought her a soft bed, two dishes (one for water, the other for food), a big bag of kibble (the scientific kind) and a red collar and leash. He also found a book on black Labs and bought that, too, figuring he should learn about the breed. Now that he's brought her home, Otis can't imagine life without her.

"You and I are going to have the time of our lives when we go on our trip," he tells her. She looks up at her new master with those same sad brown eyes he fell in love with and nudges his hand with her nose.

"Wanna go for a walk?"

Sadie murmurs and wags her tail. She moves toward the back door and looks at the red leash hanging on a hook, signaling to Otis that she's ready and willing. Otis hitches it to her collar and takes his new canine friend out for a walk.

"I want to introduce you to someone," he says. "Fern would have loved you, and you would have loved her. We had an orange cat one time—Hector—but we had to give him up because Fern was allergic to his fur."

When Otis and Sadie arrive at the wrought iron cemetery gates, they go inside and begin the climb to Fern's grave. Up on the knoll, the view to Brewer is a stunning blend of blue sky, puffy white clouds and a grassy expanse of emerald green. All that's missing is Fern. Though she is no longer with him, Otis carries her in his heart. It is his way of keeping her close to him. He kneels down and places his hand on Sadie's shoulders. And then Otis prays.

Dear Lord, thank you for bringing Fern and me together all those years ago. She was a good wife and an even better friend, and I miss her. Thank you, also, for Sadie. Please let Fern know that Sadie is my new girlfriend, but I'll always love her best. Amen. And to Fern, he says, *"Fern, this is Sadie. I wish you could come with us on our trip."* Somewhere in his mind, he hears the old song by the Skyliners *Since I Don't Have You.* When he recalls the lyrics, he cries and Sadie licks away his tears.

Chapter Seventeen

September turns into October, then November and December. When the calendar page turns to the new year, Otis feels a little adrenaline rush in anticipation of what lies ahead. Since early fall, he has spent his nights working on an itinerary for the trip and learning as much as he can about each destination. Sadie has been right beside him, lying at his feet.

So far, his travels will take him to Rangeley, Maine; Great Barrington, Massachusetts; Palmerton, Pennsylvania; Damascus, Virginia; Gatlinburg, Tennessee and Asheville, North Carolina. His final stop will be Springer Mountain in Georgia.

Two days ago, Otis visited the local bookstore and added another book about Appalachia. This one is about the people of Appalachia. He finds their history fascinating and depressing at the same time because so many of them have lived in poverty all their lives. They are, in fact, indigent to such a degree that most people lack the capacity to even imagine that kind of poverty. Otis thinks about the money in The Vault and the good it will do by bringing a bit of happiness to them, especially children.

He knows only too well what it's like to be a child who doesn't have much. Otis remembers, for instance, finding an old bicycle wheel lying by the side of the road when he was nine or ten.

The wheel was in good enough shape to roll all the way home. He played with that wheel all summer and took great care to make sure he didn't leave it out in the rain or where it could be stolen. No matter where he went, the wheel went with him until one night he forgot to put it away and when he went to his front yard the next morning, it was gone. He accused his brother, Carl, of being jealous and hiding the wheel or hurling it into the pond in back of their home so Otis would have nothing to play with. But Carl swore up and down he had nothing to do with the wheel's disappearance. Carl, in turn, pointed the finger at Alfred, a neighbor boy known for being a bully.

"You go on over to his house, and I guarantee you'll find your wheel. I'll bet he's the one who stole it. It wasn't me," Carl had insisted.

And then, sure enough, one day on the way to town with his mother, Otis spotted Alfred in his front yard playing with a wheel just like the one that went missing. He thought about confronting the boy, but Alfred was much bigger than Otis and had a reputation for beating up younger boys. Otis decided not to pursue the matter but instead scoured the road every day to see if he could find another wheel. In the fall, he did find one but it had probably come from a tricycle. It was the size of a Frisbee and not much fun to play with.

Yes, Otis has a heart for the poor, and the people of Appalachia need a helping hand. Many were coal miners who lost their lives in mining disasters. Just as many others came down with black lung from breathing in coal dust. It didn't seem fair that these people should be stricken with such misery just because they were born in a certain geographical location. When he thinks about it for any length of time, Otis always comes back to one simple truth: That no matter how you slice the pie, life isn't always fair. It just is, and it's best to be grateful for whatever good comes your way.

⇛⇛ ⇚⇚

The thermometer outside the kitchen window of Otis's bungalow registers two degrees above zero on this mid-January Sunday morning. When he wakes up and opens his eyes, he sees Sadie staring at him. He smiles, rubs the dog's head and says, "How long you been sitting there, girl? You hungry? Come on. Let's get you fed."

Before heading to the kitchen, Otis uses the bathroom and looks at himself in the mirror on the way out.

Since Fern's death, he hasn't given much thought to his appearance, but as he regards his reflection now, he notices that there's more gray in his dark hair. He also sees lines at the corner of his mouth that weren't there six months ago. His green eyes have not changed, and for that he is grateful. Fern had once told him that she fell in love with his eyes before she fell in love with him. Overall, he thinks he looks okay for his age. He has kept his weight at 165 pounds, easily borne by his nearly six-foot frame, and he attributes this to the daily walks that help him stay fit. Otis opens his mouth and looks at his teeth. He is now grateful that Fern kept after him about his dental health. He will see Dr. Benoit in March for a cleaning and while he's there, he'll ask the dentist to check the molar that's been bothering him.

Outside, fresh snow covers the ground and it sparkles like a field of crushed diamonds when the sun hits it just right. He hopes it warms up so he and Sadie can take a walk. He hums now as he goes to the kitchen, the dog at his heels. When Otis breaks into song, Sadie whines.

"You want to sing, too, girl?" In answer, Sadie nuzzles her master's hand.

After he feeds her, he lets her out but she comes right back in as soon as she has finished her business. A band of cold air comes in with her, causing Otis to shiver. He starts a fire in the fireplace, and soon the logs are crackling and the room is warming up.

After breakfast, Otis picks up his fiddle and plays a Scott Woods tune. Otis had taken Fern to see Woods in person a few years before her death, one of the few times she had agreed to attend a live performance. He had never heard such fiddling in all his life, except for maybe Natalie MacMaster and her husband, Donnell Leahy. Otis had watched Woods closely while he and his band played all the old fiddle tunes. The following morning, he tried to copy Woods's techniques and eventually mastered them. He had also watched in awe when Woods stepped on top of a barrel tipped on its side and roll-walked it across the stage while playing *Roll Out the Barrel*. When Otis tried it at home, he fell off the barrel, broke his wrist and couldn't play for three months. Fern had told him his name was not Scott Woods and made him promise to never try that trick again.

In the afternoon, the outdoor temperature reaches twenty degrees. When Otis takes Sadie for a walk, they stop at the place where he found the money last September and on the way home, they visit Fern's grave. Like everything else, Otis finds it covered with eight inches of snow.

On March 14, Otis's birthday, his friend Jack Colby stops by to say hello. Like Otis, he's still out of work but is now helping to stock the shelves at Aubrey Keane's hardware store. Jack asks Otis about the gun cases and wants to know what he plans to do with them.

"I didn't even know you owned a gun," Jack says, scowling. "Didn't know you hunted, either."

Otis wishes Aubrey had kept his mouth shut about those gun cases. It's none of Jack's business, and Otis is dismayed to think he was a topic of discussion when he wasn't even there.

Otis has to think quick. What lie had he told Aubrey? "Oh, those," says Otis, now recalling his conversation with Aubrey. "Thought I might be going hunting with a few guys, but they backed out. I might keep them. Or return them to Aubrey."

"I could always put 'em on e-Bay for you," says Jack.

"Thanks. I'll remember that," Otis says, glad to end the matter. He then asks Jack to check on the installation of The Vault and the pair go to Otis's driveway to have a look. Jack admires the F-150 and tells Otis he wouldn't mind owning one himself, but first he has to find a full-time job.

Jack is mechanically inclined and Otis trusts his friend when he tells him he did a good job with the installation. Otis can tell The Vault intrigues Jack, and he's probably curious to know why Otis installed it in the first place. Instead of waiting for Jack to ask, Otis takes the lead and tells him a cock and bull story about needing The Vault for his father's antique tools—that he can't take the risk that they'd be stolen while he's away. He realizes too late that Jack knows his father never owned anything beyond a screwdriver.

When Jack pulls a face, Otis quickly adds, "I found the tools after he died. Probably belonged to my grandfather." His explanation seems to satisfy Jack.

When he is ready to leave, Otis asks Jack about buying a weapon for the trip. "Get yourself some mace," he says. "Easy to carry in your pocket. Walmart has it."

Chapter Eighteen

A computer class at the senior center is keeping Otis busy during April, and he's learned more about the power of the Internet. He also has a new cell phone he bought at the Apple store and is now up to speed on how to use it.

The third week in April brings warmer than usual weather, and Otis thinks it's time to shop at Walmart.

All the prep for his trip is taking up most of his time, but when he crosses off something on his list, he becomes more and more anxious to get on the road. He can't wait to meet new people and see places he's only read about. His only regret is having to leave Fern behind. But he has Sadie, and Fern will be with him in spirit. Just then, his heart gladdens when he hears Sadie's claws on the hardwood floor. As she approaches, she is practically telling him with each step that she will be his loyal companion. He hopes she'll enjoy the ride, and he hopes the same for himself. That night he goes to bed with a sense of optimism he hasn't felt since before he lost his job and Fern got sick.

❧❧❧ ❧❧❧

A few days before May 1, Otis visits Pastor Wright at the church. Before he leaves, he hands the Pastor a check for $10,000. Pastor Wright stares at it for a long moment before responding. "Otis, is this for real? If it is, a miracle has just happened. Now we can replace the steeple. Thank you!"

Otis nods, shrugs and says, "Can't take it with me." He doesn't mention anything about the fictional uncle in Kentucky who left him money. In fact, Otis is determined to break his new habit of telling falsehoods.

On his way out of the church, he runs into Colleen and asks if she would mind checking on his house now and then to make sure no one has broken in. She says she'd be happy to help out and offers to take in his mail, but he has already made arrangements with the Post Office to hold it until he returns.

On Sunday night, April 30, Otis goes to bed early, but he's so worked up about leaving in the morning that he tosses and turns until midnight. Then he falls into an agitated sleep that interferes with his rest. Around two in the morning, he wakes up suddenly and realizes there is one thing he forgot to buy. Dog food. Otis sighs and turns over. He'll stop at PetLuv in the morning before he leaves. As if to read his thoughts, he hears Sadie let out a deep sigh. Otis decides he'll sleep a little later and leave at ten o'clock instead of nine. Better to delay his time of departure, come to think of it. He'll be more rested and avoid traffic.

He'd like to stop for lunch at Turkey Lurkey, but it's out of the way. Maybe he'll have lunch or supper there on the way back to Maine. It would make a good ending to the story of his trip.

⟫⟫⟫⟶ ⟵⟪⟪⟪

Otis had planned to sleep in but opens his eyes a few minutes past six. Outside, the birds are quiet, and he hears a hard rain lashing his bedroom window. He hadn't counted on that. Last night's weather forecast had called for nothing more than a cloudy day.

Otis is relieved that the truck is packed and ready to go. All that's left to do is lock the house and drive away with Sadie. But first he'll take a hot shower to limber up his muscles for the drive to Rangeley Lakes, his first stop on the Trail.

After a quick errand at PetLuv (Otis apologizes to Sadie for forgetting to buy her food), he drives onto I-91 south and heads east. Otis bought himself a new Canon 50-megapixel EOS 5DS (he took a course in photography after finishing his computer classes in February) and plans to use it along the way to take pictures. The lakes region of Rangeley is beautiful, according to what he has read, and he'll start there. There are campgrounds in the area, and he plans to stay a few nights before heading south to Great Barrington.

Otis loves this time of year more than any other. The trees have sprouted leaves the color of limes, the magnolias and dogwoods will soon be in full bloom with their pink powder puff flowers and the perennials are coming along nicely. While driving along the open road, Otis's thoughts wander back to his bungalow in Hopewell where Fern had planted phlox, peonies, gay feather, daffodils, crocus and tulips. He recalls how Fern had fussed over her flowers as if they were her children. He had even heard her talk to them while she worked in her garden. Maybe that's what made them grow so beautifully. All of Fern's attention had paid off. Colleen will water the plants while he's away, and Otis will reward her for it.

He switches on the radio but then turns it right off, remembering that he has brought with him a dozen CDs of his favorite music. There's jazz pianist Bill Evans, Old Crow Medicine Show, The Blues Brothers, Willie Nelson, Spanky and Our Gang, The Doors, a 1950s album and his all-time favorite hymns.

He fishes out a CD and pops it into the CD player. Instantly, the strains of The Doors' seven-minute version of *Light My Fire* fills the cab. Sadie perks up her ears at the enthralling blend of organ and guitar and Jim Morrison's vocals. She's been resting on her soft doggie bed just behind the cab, but now she's on her feet and rubbing her muzzle against Otis's arm.

"I know. You like music, too. Well, Sadie, there's a lot more where that comes from. I wish you could play piano. We'd make a great duo," Otis tells her.

By early afternoon, Otis arrives in Rangeley. Signs are posted along the roadway for campgrounds, motels and inns. He's looking forward to settling in, meeting other campers and hearing stories about their adventures. It's not camping season yet, but there might be some early birds who just had to get a move on. Up ahead, a sign for Whispering Pines campground looms into view.

Otis pulls the truck to the side of the road to have a better look. The smaller print says . . . *Sites and RVs Available—Toilets and Showers—Boat Rentals—Inquire Within.* Just what Otis is looking for. As he follows the

arrows and continues along the road leading to the campground, he begins
to see tents, pop-up campers, self-contained RVs and truck bed campers,
about a dozen in all.

A guard shack is up ahead and a man pokes his head out the open
window. Otis approaches the shack slowly and comes to a stop.

"Looking to stay with us, are you?" asks a man about twenty years older
than Otis. He notices that the man is wearing a red plaid shirt and has a
head full of curly silver hair. When the man leans his upper body out the
window, Otis also notices that he has the hands of a working man, a man
who knows how to chop wood and change the oil in a car.

"Just for a few nights," says Otis. "I'd like a Class B if you have one."

"There are rentals out back near the tree line. It's off season, so the price
is $40 a night," the man says, handing Otis a map of the campground.
"This is where we are now, right where that X is, see? Lot 18 is available.
Nice little unit, fully equipped. There's a dining hall and chapel off to
the right. We have a swimming pool, but it's too cold yet to open it. You
traveling alone?"

"Yes and no. I have my dog with me." Otis pauses, thinking that the
campground might not allow pets.

The man strains his neck to see inside Otis's truck. "Well, how about
that. I see you've got yourself a black Lab. I've got one, too. Nothing' like
'em, in my opinion."

"I'm partial to them myself," says Otis.

"I'm on my third," the man tells Otis. "A male this time. Four years old
now. Name's Fred."

"Nice to meet you, Fred."

"No, no . . . Fred is my dog's name. I'm Lloyd. Last name's MacNeill."

"Well, good to meet you, Lloyd."

"Like I said, the rate is $40 a night for a Class B. Credit cards and checks
but no cash. Too risky having money lying around."

Otis smiles. The Vault is only a few feet away.

"Right," says Otis. "The Class B will do. One night." Otis hands Lloyd
his credit card and takes it back when the transaction is complete.

"Enjoy your stay," says Lloyd. "Just park your truck next to the lot."

"Will do," says Otis.

The phone inside the shack rings then, and Lloyd takes the call. "Whispering Pines," Otis hears him say as he begins the slow drive down the dirt road ahead.

Chapter Nineteen

Otis finds Lot 18 and parks the F-150. He steps inside the RV to check it out. Everything he needs is right there, even towels and linens.

It is no longer raining, so Otis and Sadie take a walk around the campground. While out, he meets a few fellow campers from Florida, upstate New York and Ohio. They all seem friendly and willing to talk about life on the road. Otis finds out that the people from New York and Ohio are taking in the highlights of New England. The couple from Florida started their trip in January, and their travels will take them to Quebec City before they turn around and go home.

Before suppertime, Otis takes a drive through the area to have a look at the scenery. As he passes the guard shack, he gives Lloyd a little wave. A few minutes later, he is driving along Route 4 and begins to see signs for swimming and hiking areas and billboards featuring pictures of waterfalls, blue lakes and trout jumping through plumes of water. He drives past signs for Angel Falls, Coos Canyon and the Wilhelm Reich Museum. Small homes dot the roadside, some hidden behind skyscraping pines and possibly owned by people who spend summer and winter vacations here. It reminds Otis of home in some ways, except for the lakes. Back in Hopewell, there's the Penobscot River and a few ponds but nothing like this. Off to the right, he comes upon Webb Lake. He shakes his head in wonder. Never before has he seen such blue water. And Mount Blue in the background creates a striking scene. Otis stops the truck for a few minutes and gazes at what looks like a work of art. He takes out his camera and snaps some pictures.

Maybe he'll stay a day or two longer than he planned to take in more of the stunning scenery. There's no agenda for him to follow, so why not?

Though it's still chilly, he decides to rent one of Lloyd's boats in the afternoon and visit Angel Falls and the Reich Museum tomorrow. He also wants to stick around long enough to meet more people before getting back on the Trail.

Later that night, Otis checks on The Vault. Still locked and tightly mounted, just as Jack Colby said.

He thinks about Jack now and wonders what might have been going through his mind when he saw the F-150. Was that a look of jealousy that crossed Jack's face? Yes, Otis is certain it was. He now recalls Jack's parting words. "Must have been one big payout from the life insurance people when Fern died."

Otis had not responded. Jack had always had a bad habit of not thinking before he opened his mouth. That comment about life insurance—why did he have to say that? Bad enough he has lost Fern. Jack needed to mind his own business and not speculate about anyone else's, especially when it comes to money. Something Fern had complained about Jack suddenly springs to Otis's mind. "He talks too much, and he doesn't care what he says," Fern had said. Otis thinks that his wife had been right. He also thinks it's time to make some new friends.

⇒⇒⇒⇒⇒ ⇐⇐⇐⇐⇐

When Otis returns to the campground, he sets up the portable grill he bought at Walmart and starts cooking a hamburger. While rummaging through the cooler for a bun, cheese, pickles and chips, he looks up and sees Fred approaching. Lloyd is with him. Or is Fred the dog? Otis has forgotten who's who.

"Hey," Otis says. "Wanna join me?"

"Smells great," Lloyd replies as he approaches. "Just wanted to make sure you have everything you need."

"Sadie and I are doing fine." The dog has been lying under the collapsible table but is now on her feet and sniffing Lloyd's dog.

"Fred, say hello to your new friend," says Lloyd, giving the dog a rub around the ears.

"It's Lloyd, right?" Otis hopes he got the man's name right.

"Ah-uh. Lloyd MacNeill. I brought coffee, plenty enough to share if you want some," he says, holding up a thermos.

"Sure. I'd love the company. Should I put a hamburger on for you?"

"Thanks, but I brought a chicken sandwich," Lloyd says, now holding up a paper bag. "But wouldn't mind a chip or two and a pickle."

"Help yourself." While setting up a chair for Lloyd, Otis asks him who's minding the guard shack.

"My son. Lloyd Jr. He and I run this place together. He went off to college to study accounting but came back after graduation. Missed the place too much, I guess," says Lloyd. "One day it'll be his. Right now, he helps me keep the books. Real convenient having an accountant for a son. Handles my taxes, too. A good kid." Otis smiles when Lloyd refers to his son as a kid. He must be around Otis's age. He also thinks about his own son, the one he never got to know.

Lloyd takes his sandwich out of the bag, then hands Otis a cup of coffee before placing small containers of cream and sugar packets on the little table.

His burger cooked, Otis plops it onto a sliced bun and adds cheese and ketchup. While they eat, Otis asks Lloyd if he's married.

Lloyd looks away, sadness etched into his face, and Otis is sorry he asked. "My wife died three years ago. My father left the place to me and my brother," he says. "Co-owning was one major ordeal, let me tell you."

"Ordeal?"

"Well . . . you know how it is in families. Someone always wants the upper hand. One wants to keep the property; the other wants to sell it. One doesn't mind spending a few dollars to keep it up; the other pinches pennies till they bleed."

Otis nods vigorously as if he understands, as if he has been through the same thing a thousand times.

"Did it happen to you, too?" Lloyd asks, taking a hard look at Otis.

"No, can't say I went through anything like that. Heard enough stories, though. Seems to be common."

"I suppose so."

Otis pauses for a long moment, then looks at Lloyd. "Push comes to shove, most people would rather fight over a nickel than try to get along. Real world. The long and short of it is that money rules."

"Hmm. Never gave it much thought," says Lloyd. "You could be right."

"You still in touch with your brother?" Otis asks.

"Matter of fact, we haven't spoken since I took over ownership. He's got his life. I've got mine. He's got his troubles. I've got mine. Aren't those the lyrics of some song?"

"The Fortunes. 1965. *You've Got Your Troubles (I've Got Mine).*"

"What about you? Married? Divorced? Single?" Lloyd asks.

"Lost my wife a year ago. Fern died right after Memorial Day weekend. June 6. Life hasn't been the same since." Otis's thoughts now turn to The Vault.

"Sorry to hear. What happened to her, if you don't mind my asking?"

"Cancer. Of the lung. It spread to her spine. Suffered with it for about a year. There's a lot of it nowadays. Probably more since cell phone towers are everywhere."

"Think that has something to do with it?" Lloyd pours more coffee into Otis's cup.

"No idea. Just seems strange that all of a sudden we're hearing a lot more about it. Radiation coming from those towers. It can't be good."

"Well, cancer's always been around. Could be the environment. Could be our food and water. Could be in our genes. Even the experts don't know what causes it, except maybe for smoking." says Lloyd.

The two men slip into a companionable silence while they eat.

Otis then says. "You know many people in the Rangeley area?"

Lloyd lets out a little chuckle. "I know just about everyone," he says between bites. "Good people, mostly. But now and then, someone goes off half-cocked. Just the other day news broke that a teacher at the high school got caught with his hand down a sophomore's pants."

"Poor girl. Just a kid."

"The teacher is a woman. And it wasn't a girl." Lloyd says, helping himself to a pickle.

The two men look at each other. "Oh," says Otis. "What a lousy thing to do, preying on a young kid. What else is goin' on?"

"Lots of people are out of work around here. That recession in '08 really took a toll. Then, there's a man who lost his wife and daughter in a drowning accident and now he has to raise five kids by himself. He's out of work, too, but how can he work and take care of his family at the same time?"

"Terrible situation," says Otis, curious to know more.

"Ah-uh. You never know what's gonna happen next."

"Five kids and no mother. How does he manage that?"

"No idea. No family around to help him out, either. I wouldn't wanna be in John Penewait's shoes."

"Penewait? Interesting last name."

"Native American. His people were from the Penobscot Tribe."

"Huh."

"Ay-uh. His mother was Molly. His father, Louis. Molly made fancy baskets out of ash and birch bark. She used whatever was left over from Louis's canoes. That was his trade. Canoe making."

"You say his wife and daughter drowned. What happened?"

"Nell—that would be John's wife—and their six kids were at one of the lakes down yonder a mile or two. Beautiful summer day. Louise was about four at the time. She went into the water by herself. There was a drop-off, and she went under. Nell must have seen it happen and jumped in even though she couldn't swim. Guess everyone on the beach was having a good time of their own to notice."

"Then what?"

"Eventually the five older kids noticed their mum and sister were missing and ran home to tell their dad. Meanwhile, people on the beach were looking all over for them. John called the police and fire, and they went running to the scene. They figured Nell had no reason to leave the area with only one kid, so they started dragging the lake. And that's when they found Nell and little Louise. Sad, sad story. A nice bunch. Good church people. Nell always cooking for church suppers, visiting the sick, taking care of other people's kids when their parents weren't home. Lord almighty, the things that happen to good people. Life ain't fair sometimes. It can be downright cruel, you want the truth of my opinion."

Otis nods, thinks about the family's situation. "So, what does the father do for money? Does he work at all?"

"He can't work because there's no one to take care of the kids. Lately, word is that the state authorities have been nosing around. Some people think the kids will end up fostered out. The church can only help so much, you see. John Penewait—he was one of seven himself—wanted to be a teacher and put himself through three years of college. But then both of his folks passed away within six months of each other. His brothers took off for Canada, and his sister lives out West. Nevada, I think. He had to call it quits for his education. Ended up logging for a while, then he opened a little breakfast place at the edge of town. Did okay for a long while, then the economy tanked and so did the restaurant. Last I heard, he was trying to find a job, but in these parts it's pretty hard."

"I'll bet it is . . ."

"And pulling up roots with five kids? How would he do that?" Lloyd continues with his train of thought. "Poor guy doesn't know whether he's coming or going half the time."

"Maybe the kids would be better off in foster homes," Otis replies, knowing full well that they wouldn't. Lloyd has no idea that he is feeding Otis an idea.

"Maybe. Maybe not. Like I said before, life can be downright cruel. People who know him have pitched in some, but we've all got our own troubles, our own responsibilities, you understand."

Otis is quiet while thinking about John Penewait. Not only has he lost his wife but his little girl, too. It just doesn't seem right. He thinks about his own loss, which pales in comparison. In fact, Otis has to admit that Mr. Penewait has an impossible situation on his hands.

Chapter Twenty

Otis thinks that if John Penewait had the chance to finish his final year of college, he could become a teacher as he had hoped and stay home with his kids during school vacations and the summer months. It would be a perfect set-up for a man in his situation. Otis mulls over these thoughts while he and Lloyd continue to talk.

"Where'd he go to school?"

"John? Might've been the University of Maine."

"Where's he live?"

"That's another sad part of the story. The family lived in an eight-room cottage down near the center of town, but John had to give it up when the recession hit. His finances crashed when that happened. He didn't know which way to turn and ended up selling the house at a loss and moving to a summer rental near the state park."

"Does he live in the rental year round?"

"That he does. There's no insulation to keep them warm in winter, though. I have it on good authority that they rely on space heaters, and those can cause fires, don't you know. I'd hate to think that John and his family could be wiped out if the place went up in flames."

Otis now wonders what he can do for John Penewait. A family that big would need a lot of money, and he has it to give. He could provide a new start for the man. He wants to meet John Penewait and find out more about him. Otis now realizes he'll have to stay in the Rangeley area longer than a night or two if he wants to meet the Penewait clan.

"I'd like to meet this man," Otis says. "Any chance for that?"

"Why do you want to meet him?" Lloyd asks, giving Otis a side glance.

"Just interested in people and their stories. I'm keeping a notebook about them. Might want to take some pictures for a photo album, too. We all have a story, right? Some are just more interesting than others."

"I suppose I could give you his address, but let me give him a call first. People around here don't mind visitors just dropping in, but they're a little wary of strangers. Still, he'd probably be glad to have adult company for a change. But why are you so interested in people's stories?"

Otis hesitates. He doesn't want to tell Lloyd about his mission. He'd learned long ago at his mother's knee, and in church, too, that no one should ever let their left hand know what their right hand is doing. "Here's the thing . . . I've got time on my hands now. Before my wife died I was always busy working. Never paid much mind to anyone else other than Fern and the people at church plus a friend or two. Now I regret it. Guess I just want to give John Penewait a little encouragement, a little sympathy. We all need it at times."

"Ain't that the truth." Lloyd thinks a moment, takes a sip of his coffee, then tells Otis where he can find John Penewait. Otis writes the directions on his napkin. "Don't know what his days are like, but my guess is he probably stays close to home most of the time," says Lloyd.

"Thanks. I'll look him up sometime this week."

"Okay, but let me give him a heads up," says Lloyd.

"Sure. You can let me know."

Before he falls asleep that night, Otis thinks about John Penewait and wonders how the man copes with his situation. He has a tough row to hoe, and Otis wants to meet this unsung hero.

He wonders what a year's tuition and books would cost at the University of Maine. If John Penewait could complete his education and become a teacher, his life would be much more manageable. But if Otis pays for his education, he'll have to come up with a plan for child care while John is in school. Maybe there's someone local who'd be willing to take care of the kids for a year. Lloyd would probably know someone, and Otis has the money to pay a decent salary. Then there's transportation to think about. Maybe he can take classes online. But then the man would need a computer if he doesn't already have one. Otis turns on the light beside his bed and makes notes on a piece of paper. He can hardly wait to meet John Penewait, his first possible beneficiary. Maybe he can also arrange for the summer cottage to be insulated. Or buy him a home of his own. Then, at least the family would be warm during the cold winter months, and John would be able to study in comfort.

➳➳➳⟩ ⟨≪≪≪⟩

In the morning, Otis looks at the map of Maine and sees that he'll have to backtrack to Orono where the University of Maine's primary campus is located. The drive will take more than two hours, but it'll give him a chance to give the truck a good run. So far, it's been a pleasure to drive. It handles well, seems easier on gas than he expected and there's plenty of room for both him and Sadie, not to mention their provisions, including The Vault.

He and Sadie set out right after a breakfast of coffee, scrambled eggs and toast. Sadie looks at Otis with her sad eyes, and his heart melts at the sight of her. He thanks his lucky stars—well, God, actually—that she needed a home, and he was the one to claim her as his own. He isn't concerned about the time it will take to get to Orono. He has all the time in the world and all the money he'll ever need.

According to a Google map, the University of Maine is situated on a leafy campus near the Stillwater and Penobscot rivers. He's anxious to state his case to the person he speaks to, can hardly wait to tell him or her he is prepared to pay for someone's tuition. He wonders about the person's reaction. He will soon find out.

When Otis arrives at the Orono campus, he parks in the visitor's lot and double-checks the locks when he exits the truck. Before setting off with Sadie, he also checks to make sure The Vault is still secure.

A sign for Heritage House Admissions is in front of an old brick building a short walk away. Otis moves quickly and when he steps through the front door, he finds that the admissions office is on the first floor.

Once inside the foyer, he approaches a reception desk and asks a young dark-haired woman wearing a sweatshirt with the university's name printed across the front if he could have a word with the person in charge of admissions. Otis also thinks about Sadie. "Okay, if I keep my dog with me?"

"Sure. Just one moment," she says. "I'll see if Mrs. Rogers is free."

A woman then. All the better, Otis thinks. The receptionist presses a few buttons on her phone and announces that Otis is here to see her.

She takes the phone away from her ear for a moment. "Who should I say is calling?" she asks.

"Otis Kingston. I want to check on some courses. Please tell her I'm not selling anything."

The young woman laughs and takes up the phone again to pass along Otis's information.

"You can go on in," she says. "Second door on your right down that corridor." She points the way for Otis.

Otis nods and turns to go. "Good luck," he hears her say.

He stops and tells the receptionist that there's no such thing as luck, but she only stares at him with a blank look on her face.

⇝⇝⇝ ⇜⇜⇜

The meeting goes well with Mrs. Rogers, a tall gray-haired woman dressed in a black pant suit and white shell. She is wearing a half dozen dangly silver bracelets on her right wrist and when she waves Otis into her office, they jingle. He notices her friendly manner and likes Mrs. Rogers right away. When she hears what Otis has to say, she leans toward him and hangs on to his every word.

"So, what you're proposing is to fund the education of a perfect stranger? I can't recall anyone ever doing that."

"Yes, I'd like to pay for this man's final year. You might not understand what it's like to be poor, but I do. I grew up in a poor family and I never had much, including a father. He died young. So did my mother. My brother went into business for himself, wanted me to join him, but I met my wife and married her instead. Please don't misunderstand me. We had a good life, Fern and I. We worked hard all the years we were married. But she's gone now, and what am I supposed to do? I think Fern would want me to share what I have left. I don't have kids to leave anything to, but there are people in the world who need a lot of help. And the gentleman I have in mind needs it more than either of us could ever imagine."

Chapter Twenty-One

"Well, Mr. Kingston, I can see that you're serious about wanting to help this man. What can we do to make it happen?" Mrs. Rogers plays with her pen while waiting to hear what Otis has to say.

He thinks a moment, then says, "The man is a Native American. Would that make any difference? A scholarship, maybe?"

Mrs. Rogers raises an eyebrow. "I should say it would. He'd be entitled to a free education."

"He probably didn't know that when he was a student here," Otis replies. "Someone who knows him well told me he couldn't finish his final year because of financial problems. He had to leave school."

Mrs. Rogers takes off her glasses and lays them on her desk. "His tuition and fees would be absorbed by the government as well as room and board."

"He wouldn't live on campus, but what about books and other supplies?" Otis asks as he tries to sort out in his mind the financial end of things.

"He would be responsible for his books, fees and any other learning materials. He could also take classes online or at one of our satellites. There's one not far from Rangeley, in fact. You mentioned that's where he lives?"

"Yes. In a summer rental with no insulation."

"What a shame," she says, shaking her head. "And he has five children?"

"Yes, he does."

Mrs. Rogers stands up and moves toward a file cabinet in back of her desk. "I'll give you one of our booklets. All our courses are listed inside. What field of study was he pursuing?"

"He was hoping to get a degree in teaching. How would I pay for his books and other needs? Set up an account?"

"You can speak to our bursar. David Hammersmith. He'll know how to handle things. In fact, I'll call him right now to see if he can meet with you."

Otis looks into her eyes and says, "I want to make sure that what I'm doing will be kept confidential. I don't want to draw attention to myself in any way. I need you to understand that this has nothing to do with my generosity. It's about humility, about sharing with someone in need."

Mrs. Rogers nods, smiles at Otis and says, "Of course." She calls David Hammersmith's office and tells him that Otis is in her office. "Mr. Kingston wants to fund the cost of books for a student who is not currently enrolled. Could I send him over to see you?" She listens and nods her head.

"Excellent. He's on his way." After ending the call, she hands her business card to Otis and tells him to call her if there's anything else she can do to help.

Otis thanks her, steps outside her office and walks toward the reception desk and, beyond that, into the brilliant sunshine. His spirits are soaring; he feels as light as dandelion fluff.

⟫⟫⟫⟩ ⟨⟨⟨⟨⟨

Otis finds his way to David Hammersmith's office in another brick building on the left side of the campus only a short distance away.

Once inside, he approaches the reception desk where a young man wearing a blue Oxford shirt is seated. Otis wonders if he is a student and working part-time to earn his way through school.

"May I help you?" the young man asks. "I'm Justin."

"Yes. I'd like a word with the bursar. David Hammersmith."

"Is he expecting you?"

"Yes. I'm Otis Kingston."

The young man uses the intercom to announce Otis's arrival. While waiting, he thumbs through the brochure Mrs. Rogers gave him. There are pictures of students laughing while walking across a grassy quad and professors standing at podiums. If all goes well, he'll write a check today and leave it in the bursar's hands.

While Otis is lost in thought, a man with a bald head and silver goatee opens an office door and looks around the room.

"Mr. Kingston?" he asks when he sees that no one else is waiting. "Come on in so we can chat."

Otis follows Hammersmith inside his office and sits across from him. "Do you mind if I close the door?" Otis asks.

"Not at all." Hammersmith uses the intercom and asks Justin to hold his calls.

"Justin is here on scholarship. A brilliant young man headed for great things. Math and chemistry are his interests. Wants to be an engineer. He'll be able to name his salary someday," the bursar tells Otis.

"Fortunate for him," he says.

"Very. Sad story, though. His father died when he was just nine. His mother has had to do housekeeping jobs to keep the family afloat. That's what the lack of a good education will do to you. Assign you to a life of servitude. Such a shame," he says, shaking his head. "Now, what can I do for you, Mr. Kingston?"

"Please call me Otis."

"Otis, then. Tell me what's on your mind." Hammersmith rests his elbows on his desk and stares into Otis's eyes.

"I'd like to set up an account for a possible student."

Mr. Hammersmith pauses for a moment, then says, "A possible student? And who might that be?"

"I'd rather not say until I'm sure this can be done. I've learned about his plight, and I'd like to help him out."

"Plight?"

"Yes. He lost both his wife and young daughter in a terrible drowning accident last summer, and now he has to support his other five children without any help."

"Phew. Now that's a tragedy. Seems to me I read something about that in the news." The bursar clears his throat before he speaks again. "Now that I think about it, well . . . never mind. Please continue."

"I only heard about his story a day or so ago. You see, I'm on a mission of sorts. Along the Appalachian Trail. I'm wealthy, and I want to find people in Appalachia who can use my help."

"This man you're talking about—he's a student here?"

"Not right now. He was a student some time ago, but he left after his junior year. He has one year left, and I'd like to help him. He's Native American, so his tuition would be paid for by the government. But he'll still need books and learning materials. I would pay for them."

Hammersmith is taken aback momentarily, but he quickly recovers and says, "Well, this is most extraordinary. Of course, I know that secret benefactors sometimes pay for a person's education if there's a lack of money, but I've never come across anyone who's actually done it."

"Well, I plan to."

"First off, if you present a check to the university stating that it is to be used for items specific to the man's education, we would set up an account for him and oversee it. We would keep you informed of what is spent on a monthly or quarterly basis. You said he was a student here?"

"Yes, he was." Now that Otis knows an account can be set up, he finds himself relaxing and more willing to talk about John Penewait.

"Would you be comfortable giving me his name?"

"As long as you promise you'll set up an account for him."

"Yes, we can do that. We will hold your money in trust. I'm just wondering if I would remember him if I knew his name."

"John Penewait."

Mr. Hammersmith looks off into the distance and bites his lower lip. "Sounds familiar."

He swivels around in his chair until he faces a bookcase. He pulls a box from the bottom shelf and rummages through a stack of folders until he finds what he's looking for. When he does, he lays a folder on his desk and opens it. A thick sheaf of papers is inside, and he rifles through them. He stops when he comes to a paper that looks like a list of grades.

"Just what I was looking for," he says. "The contents of this folder were headed for the shredder this very week. Odd that you would come in before that happened."

Hammersmith shows Otis John Penewait's last academic report.

"As you can see, he excelled in his classes. There's a note here that says he withdrew due to the death of his parents. And look, here's a newspaper clipping about Mr. Penewait's tragedy."

Hammersmith says nothing more for a few moments while Otis skims the news story. Hammersmith then says, "Some people have it tough. It seems that this man's situation takes the cake."

Otis nods his head. "And the frosting, too. What would you suggest for an amount to cover his books and anything else he'll need?"

"I'd estimate that $2,000 would cover his final year. Books and learning materials. Lab fees, if there are any. He could withdraw money as needed as long as it pertains to his studies."

"Can I write a check to get the process started? And would you be the one to notify him that someone has offered to fund a portion of his education?"

"Yes and yes. He would receive a letter of offer from me."

"Could you arrange to send the letter a few weeks from now?"

"Why would you want to wait?"

"I'll be gone by then. I don't want him to suspect that it was me who provided the money."

"We can arrange that. And should Mr. Penewait decide not to pursue his final year, we will notify you and reimburse you."

Otis gives Hammersmith his contact information and writes a check for two thousand. "Thank you," he says, handing him the check. "This means a lot to me." He then pauses and tears off another check and writes the words *one hundred thousand and no/dollars.*" When he finishes, he hands the check to Hammersmith.

"What's this?"

When Otis tells him what it should be used for, the bursar covers his face with his hands. "I can't believe this. Are you sure? That's an awful lot of money."

"I'm sure. And I know it will be put to good use."

"God bless you. I can't wait to share the good news!"

"Thank you," Otis says, shaking Hammersmith's hand.

He leaves the office then and heads toward Justin's desk. Before Otis makes his exit, he hears Hammersmith say in an excited tone of voice, "Justin, please come into my office right now. I need to talk to you about something!"

Otis tries to imagine the young man's surprise when the bursar tells him that all his educational expenses have been paid. Maybe Justin won't believe what Hammersmith is telling him. Maybe he will jump for joy. Or it could be that he breaks down and cries.

Chapter Twenty-Two

While driving back to Rangeley, Otis thinks about David Hammersmith. Maybe the man had anticipated a dull and boring day. Now he might be looking forward to going home to his wife and telling her the interesting story about the man who stopped by to help pay for the education of two complete strangers. Otis also thinks about visiting John Penewait and talking to him. He wants to meet his kids, too.

Later that afternoon, Otis asks Lloyd if he knows how to play cribbage.

"Sure do," says Lloyd.

"Stop by after supper then if you have the time," says Otis. "I've got the cards and brought my board along."

"Love to. See you tonight."

While they play, he will ask Lloyd more about John. He reflects on the day's events and thinks that staying at Whispering Pines and meeting Lloyd MacNeill was meant to be.

"Anyone home?" Lloyd calls out a little after six o'clock.

"Inside here cleaning up a bit. Be right out."

Otis cuts two pieces of chocolate cake and places them on paper plates. After adding a scoop of vanilla ice cream to each one, he heads for the door to the RV, the cribbage board tucked under his arm and two decks of cards in his pockets.

Lloyd licks his lips when he sees the cake and comments that chocolate is his favorite. "Don't have it often. Have to watch my waistline or my doctor will kick my butt all the way to Texas," Lloyd says with a chuckle.

With Otis's collapsible table between them, the two men sit opposite each other and begin their game. While they play, they chat casually until Otis gets around to mentioning John Penewait.

"So, Lloyd, did you give John Penewait a call?" he says.

"Sorry. Meant to tell you first thing. He said he'd welcome a visit from you. Just as I thought, he said he'd like some adult company for a change."

Otis is elated to hear the news. "Think I could stop by to see him tomorrow morning?"

"Don't see why not. He said he'd be home all week."

Good. In the morning, as soon as he cleans up from breakfast, he and Sadie will visit John. Now that it's settled in his mind, he concentrates on the game.

⋙⋙ ⋘⋘

At ten o'clock the following morning, Lloyd shows up at Otis's door and tells him that John had a last-minute errand to run and would be home around one o'clock. "That'll give you about an hour of quiet before the kids come home from school," Lloyd says.

By twelve-thirty, Otis has tidied up the RV, fed Sadie, taken her for a walk, cleaned himself up and put on his finest shirt. He's looking forward to his chat with John Penewait. In fact, he can hardly wait.

At twelve-forty-five, he puts Sadie in the truck, buckles up, starts the engine, pulls out of the campground and takes a right-hand turn onto the main road. He passes the dirt road where John lives and continues on, not wanting to be too early. The man has his hands full raising five kids. Probably has to make every minute count.

Otis drives five minutes down the road, passing a paddock where horses are grazing and a farm where small Christmas trees are growing in straight rows. He then makes a U-turn and heads back to the dirt road where the Penewait family lives.

A minute later, he comes upon a house with a stone front, sloping roof and farmer's porch. An older model Chevrolet is parked in the driveway.

Otis parks behind the car, picks up his camera and walks to the front door with Sadie at his side.

John is at the door before Otis can knock even once.

"Been lookin' forward to meeting you," John says in an easy and friendly manner. Otis first notices the man's straight dark hair and tanned skin. Then he takes in the high cheekbones, almond shaped eyes and heavy lids. He figures John might be in his mid-thirties, give or take a few years. "Would you rather sit out here or come inside?"

The weather is good, and a soft breeze is rustling the leaves on the trees. "Outside is fine," Otis says, introducing himself. "Happy to meet you, John." He sits down on an old kitchen chair painted bright yellow. "I don't want to take up too much of your time."

"Don't worry about that," says John. "I've got all my work done for the day. Just put together a stew for tonight's supper." He pauses and then asks Otis what's on his mind.

"Nothing important," says Otis. "I just thought we could sit and talk a while. Would you mind if I stay until your kids come home from school? I'd like to meet them, too. Lloyd probably told you about the photo album I'm making. I'll be traveling all summer, and I'd like to get to know some people because I'm planning to write a book."

A book? Where did *that* come from? Otis has a hard time writing a shopping list, never mind a book. He needs to stop all this lying. Oh, yes, he sure does.

"That right," says John, letting his eyes fall over the length of Otis's frame. "Well, I've got quite a story to tell."

"So I hear. You're raising your children alone, are you?"

"I am. Ever since two loves of my life passed away last July. It's been a tough road, but there's nothing I can do about it," he says, softly. "Just do my best and teach the kids things my wife probably would have taught them." John looks down at his shoes. Otis sees his chin tremble a bit.

"If you'd rather not . . ."

"No. It's okay. Sometimes talking about a hard thing does the soul good."

A long moment of silence follows, and then Otis asks him what he thinks his wife would have taught their children.

"Well, you know. Respecting people, keeping promises, telling the truth, not spreading litter all over the place. I want my kids to grow up to be decent citizens."

"Yes, I would want that, too." Without knowing it, John has just reminded Otis to always tell the truth. He promises himself he will from now on.

John glances at Otis. "You have kids?"

"No, my wife—Fern was her name—she couldn't have children. We never missed what we didn't have, though. She died last June, a month before you lost your wife and daughter."

"Sorry to hear. So, I guess we have something in common."

"I guess we do."

"I can tell you this. I miss Nell and little Louise. It's been tough sledding ever since the accident."

"Both drowned, did they?"

"Yes. A terrible day I would never wish on anyone."

"What do you do for a living?"

"Started out as a logger, but that didn't suit me, so I bought a diner, but when the economy tanked so did my place. And then last year happened and I've been trying to get my life back on track ever since." He pauses a moment, examines the nail on his index finger. "At one time I wanted to teach American history. It's always been my favorite subject. Finished three years of college, but had to quit."

"Why's that?"

"One word. Money. I was three years finished when my mother died of pneumonia. My father died a few years before her. Managed to get through those three years, but I had to leave school. Logging and owning a restaurant, even a diner, are tough ways to make a living, and to tell the truth people from the state came around a few weeks ago to ask questions about my kids. I don't know what they have in mind, but when the state gets involved in your business, it's never good."

Otis nods, listens intently to what John is saying.

"You have a computer?"

John chuckles. "An old one. Why do you ask?"

"Just curious. My wife insisted we get one a few years ago, and I'm glad she did."

"Mine works when it wants. I make do."

When Otis doesn't respond, John fills in the silence. "My wife—she was a good woman. True blue. A good mother. Loved people. Great sense of humor. I miss her like nobody's business."

As John continues to talk about his wife, Otis takes mental notes. He can tell that he is genuine and honest. The man has suffered two terrible losses, and when Otis hears him talk about his wife's virtues he is convinced even more that he has to help him with his education.

"Ever think about going back to school?" Otis ventures. He hopes the question comes across as casual. He doesn't want to tip his hand.

"Sure, but what's the good of thinking about it? Can't afford it."

"I don't mean to pry, but could I ask you a question?"

"Sure."

"Your last name . . . are you Native American?"

"Yeah. Why?"

"Because Native Americans qualify for a free education."

"Is that so? How do you know that?"

"Read it somewhere."

"Huh. Had no idea. You sure?"

"Pretty sure. You should check into it."

Otis notices the beginning of a little smile playing at the corners of John's mouth. Otis also sees that the man is doing some thinking and maybe even feeling a bit of hope.

⤞⤞⤞⤞ ⤝⤝⤝⤝

An hour later, a yellow school bus stops at the end of the dirt road and lets off five children of various ages.

"That would be my tribe, pardon the pun," says John, giving Otis a hint of a smile. "There's Sam, 13; James, 10; Mary, 9; Josie, 7; and Jonathan, 6."

Three boys, two girls. A handful for anyone, yet their father seems to take it all in stride, thinks Otis. "The five-year-old. Her name was Louise. Nell was my wife."

"Yes, so you said. Beautiful names," says Otis, and John nods his head.

The children, now on the porch, run to their father and look warily at Otis, no doubt wondering who the visitor is come to call.

"What's your name?" asks the youngest boy.

"Otis Kingston. What's yours?"

"Jonathan Penewait. I can count to 100," he says excitedly.

"Smart boy. You take after your Dad, then."

"I guess. What are you good at?"

"Well, I'd have to think about that a bit. But I like to play the fiddle. Oh, and I take pictures, so I guess I'd have to say photography." Otis holds up his new Canon to emphasize the point.

"Are you going to take our picture?" Josie asks.

"If you want me to."

"We want you to!" says the little girl. "Is your camera the kind that makes pictures come out right away?"

"You mean a Polaroid camera? No. But I can send you the best ones in the mail."

The girl jumps up and down at the news and smiles broadly, revealing a gap where her top two front teeth are growing in.

Otis notices for the first time that the children are wearing worn-out clothes, perhaps bought at a thrift shop. Jonathan's pants are well above his ankles.

He arranges the children, the tallest one in the middle, the shorter ones on each side, with John standing behind them. When he adjusts everyone just so, he begins to snap pictures. Jonathan plays the fool, making faces at the camera and sticking out his tongue. When his father catches him and gives him a look, the boy resumes a natural pose and gives Otis a big grin.

"That's about it," Otis says after taking a dozen or more shots. "I'll get them printed and mail them to you." He'll frame them, too, when he considers that John Penewait is in no position to buy even a cheap plastic frame from the dollar store.

The children disperse, the three older ones going inside the house, the younger two heading for a swing made from an old tire hanging from a tree branch on the opposite side of the driveway.

"Careful now," John warns. "Don't swing too high. We don't want any broken bones."

"We won't, Papa," Josie replies. She runs off, her ponytail swinging from side to side.

John turns his attention back to Otis. "Would you like to stay for supper?"

Otis is humbled by the man's generous offer. "I'd love to, but I promised Lloyd a game of cribbage. Maybe another night. But I would like to hear more of your story."

John leans forward in his chair, drops his hands between his knees and becomes pensive. "Well, there's more to tell, starting with my mother," he says. "She was a saint—my father was another story."

"Hmm . . . tell me about them," Otis says.

"My mother grew up hardscrabble. She loved to read and escaped all the drama around her by getting inside her books. She once told me books were her salvation. She avoided reality by getting caught up in the characters and the stories. I guess I inherited my love of reading from my mother. My father, though. He was . . . difficult"

"How so?"

"In a word, alcohol. He drank himself to death."

"A terrible thing, alcohol is when it's abused," Otis says, recalling Rodney's Sauce of Ruination. "Drugs, too. And when you come right down to it, they're pretty much the same thing."

"Never thought of it that way."

"What happened to him?"

"It was a hot summer day. My mother was a church woman. Lived her life according to the Bible. She was working at the church fair that day. Meanwhile, my father was home with nothing to do. His friend, Charlie, gave him a call. Said his wife was out of town and he asked my father to join him that afternoon for a few drinks—of homemade brew."

"Hmm . . . I know something about that."

"I'm not a drinker myself, but I can tell you this. That stuff is poison and it's potent enough to kill a horse. It's made in a barrel, and when it's rolled this way and that and turned upside down and then you take a drink of it, it's like playing Russian roulette. You don't know if you're getting the good stuff or the poison."

Otis shakes his head, realizing that he may have been playing Russian roulette when he got into that swish. "Let me guess. Your father got the poison."

"That's the long and short of it."

"And your mother?"

"She waited at the church for him to pick her up. The man was like clockwork. You could set your watch by him. Never late for anything. But not that day."

Otis waits for John Penewait to continue. After a long pause, he says. "My mother sat with the minister's wife for forty-five minutes. Alma offered to take my mother home, but she was sure my old man was just stuck somewhere with a flat tire and would be along any minute. He was stuck, all right. Lying face down in Charlie's yard. Dead of alcohol poisoning. Alma ended up taking her home after more than an hour."

He then tells Otis the rest of the story—that his mother had walked the floor for three hours, watching for her husband to come up the driveway, hoping against hope that he had not met a bad end.

"Never knew what hit him."

"Must have been awful for her, for all of you."

"Sure was. Dad didn't have any life insurance, and my mother never had any education to back her up if something like that happened. She had to go to the state for help. The church pitched in some, too, but it was never enough. And when it came time for me to figure out what to do after high school, I knew I wanted to go to college, and I went for three years. Paid for it myself. But then my mother died of pneumonia, and that left me and my brothers and my younger sister. My brothers took off for parts unknown. I had to take care of my sister and leave school. I didn't know anything about a free education."

"Where's your sister now?" Otis asks, curious about the rest of the story.

"Charlotte met a long distance trucker when she was eighteen. Lives in Nevada, not far from the Arizona border. I hear from her now and then, but she's got her own life to live. She's a busy woman. Looks after her twin girls and works for the town where she lives. I've often thought about visiting her—Nevada has those wide open spaces I think the kids would love—but where would the money come from? I would never be able to afford that."

Otis shakes his head but sees an opportunity. His excitement is building over the possibilities, and the ideas begin tumbling through his brain, one after the other. John Penewait has no idea that his future will now include not only a college degree but a trip to the Southwest. And his kids? Won't they be surprised when they find out that after the school year ends they'll be going to a dude ranch with their father where they can ride horses, go to rodeos, try white water rafting, eat by campfire, visit the Grand Canyon and have the time of their lives. If Otis has any say in the matter, they'll be on their way by July.

Chapter Twenty-Three

The following day, Otis orders a computer, software, printer and six reams of paper for delivery to the Penewait home a few weeks after he leaves Rangeley. He also talks to an online travel agent about booking a trip for one adult and five children to a dude ranch in Arizona. Then, he visits a department store where he opens an account funded with enough money for backpacks, shoes and clothing for when the children go back to school in the fall. Next, he goes to an auto dealership where he purchases a new Subaru Forester for the Penewait family, also to be delivered a few weeks after he leaves. He sets up a pre-paid account at Staples for supplies the kids will need and goes to Walmart to buy six new bicycles, including one for John. His last call is to the man who owns John's rental house. Now, a contractor will install insulation inside the walls so the Penewaits will be warm next winter. He'll see about buying a house for them later.

Otis can't recall ever being this happy, this euphoric. He was thrilled when he got his first bike. Joyful the day he graduated from high school. And the day he and Fern got married he was beyond happy. But none of those things can compare with the feeling he has this very minute—a feeling of overwhelming love and peace, knowing that he has lightened the load for a man he has only just met, knowing his investment will reap many rewards that will trickle down through the generations. Now, he can hardly wait to meet his next beneficiary.

After his visit with the Penewaits, Otis and Lloyd play their final game of cribbage after supper. He will leave Whispering Pines in the morning and tells Lloyd that he'll call to check in while he's on the road. When he talks to Lloyd, he'll work John Penewait into the conversation somehow. He'll be curious to know if Lloyd has seen John and whether he said anything about returning to school.

That night, Otis sleeps like a bear in hibernation. His dreams are sweet for once, and he wakes up refreshed and contented as never before. Now that he has tied up all the loose ends, he'll take a drive around Rangeley and enjoy the scenery one more time before he leaves. Maybe he'll invite Lloyd to go along. After showering, he takes a walk down to the guard shack with Sadie to see what's what. But when he approaches, there are a half dozen cars lined up waiting to get into the campground. There's no way Lloyd will be able to go for a ride.

Minutes later, Otis drives past one of Rangeley's lakes, and once again he is in awe of their beauty. The weather forecast promised that the sun would break through the clouds around noontime. As the calendar inches toward June, the air temperature is rising and more flowers are in bloom.

When Otis returns to the campground to pack up, he takes Sadie for a walk to say goodbye to the people they've met. Staying at Whispering Pines turned out to be a good decision. Not only did he make a new friend, he found a man desperate for financial help.

Otis wants to say so long to Lloyd and thank him for such an enjoyable stay. When he finds Lloyd in the dining hall moving a broom across the floor, he taps him on the shoulder.

Lloyd spins around and sees Otis standing there. "You startled me," Lloyd says. "I thought I was alone here."

"You were," says Otis. "Until I came in. Just wanted you to know I appreciate all you've done for me. I'll do some advertising for you while I'm on the Trail. Anyone would love this place."

Lloyd waves his hand in the air, dismissing Otis's gratitude. "I didn't do anything special," he says. "Just doing my job is how I see it. But I'd appreciate the advertising."

"Well, without you, I wouldn't have played any cribbage, and I wouldn't have taken some good pictures for my photo album." Otis stops there. He won't tell Lloyd anything about what he has done for John Penewait and his family.

He glances at the clock on the far wall of the dining hall. "Time for me to hit the road," he says. "Maybe I'll stay with you again in September on my way back to Maine."

"Leaving now, you'll have the road to yourself. And you know, you're always welcome to stay here. You've been good company, Otis. A real shot in the arm."

"And I'd have to say the same about you."

Otis then asks Lloyd for the bill, but his new friend shakes his head slowly. "No. No bill. You should be billing me, not the other way around."

"No, I can't accept. What you charge is more than fair."

"That may well be, but you gave me far more than I gave you. Why don't we just call it an even swap. My accommodations in exchange for your company. Plus, I learned a few new things about cribbage."

Otis nods. "Fair enough," he says. Though he doesn't say anything to Lloyd, he'll find ways to repay him. There's the big coffee urn in the dining hall that needs replacing. The guard shack and other areas that need a fresh coat of paint. Bushes and trees that need thinning out. As time passes, he'll think of other things and arrange for Lloyd's needs to be taken care of.

"Remember that promise you made. Keep in touch, son," Lloyd says. "I'm gonna miss you."

"Likewise. Maybe I'll send you a postcard from a few of my stops. Go back to your sweeping now. Time's a-wastin'. Campers will be here in no time flat looking for their second cup of joe."

Lloyd laughs and Otis walks away after giving his friend a quick hug. He knows he'll miss Lloyd even though he's only known him for a brief time. But Otis also knows there are some people in the world you never forget, and Lloyd is one of them. He'll miss Lloyd, but he needs to move on. There are other people out there who need his help.

When he and Sadie drive away from Whispering Pines, Otis pops in a Willie Nelson CD and starts singing. *"On the road again . . . just can't wait to get on the road again . . ."*

Later in the day, Otis stops at The Gypsy Joynt Cafe in Great Barrington, Massachusetts where he wants to sample Bayou bacon and big cinnamon buns he read so much about when he checked the online reviews. The restaurant also serves beer in Mason jars, but Otis thinks he won't sample any because he's never been a drinking man—except for that one night when he got into Rodney's Sauce of Ruination—and he isn't about to start now. He has also read that the wait staff wear all kinds of flowing garments and when delivering food to the tables they show off their tattoos and piercings. He also read that the place has a certain hippie charm. There's an American flag flying inside near the bar and beads and streamers hanging from the ceiling all the way to the floor.

After being seated, he orders a hamburger loaded with jalapeno peppers and caramelized onions with a side of creamy macaroni and cheese and thinks it's possibly the best meal he has eaten in months. He orders a half dozen cinnamon buns and another burger with the Bayou bacon, which he'll heat up for tomorrow night's supper. Otis walks back to his truck, convinced that in the one hour he has been at The Gypsy Joynt Cafe he has added ten pounds to his slender frame. He worries that he'll have indigestion later and stops at the local pharmacy to get some Rolaids. He buys two packages, just in case.

He wants to go to bed early tonight because his plan is to rise at dawn and get on the road as soon as possible. Before he calls it a night, though, he studies the map and thinks about his next stop—Palmerton, Pennsylvania.

>>>>>> <<<<<<

According to what Otis has read online about Palmerton, the borough sits in the shadow of Blue Mountain and was once a depository for the New Jersey Zinc Company. The owners apparently left thirty-three million tons of slag in Palmerton, creating a cinder bank over two miles long, a hundred feet high and between five hundred and a thousand feet wide. Otis envisions it to be a small mountain.

It concerns him that the company's operations let off huge quantities of heavy metals, including lead, throughout the valley. As a result, about two thousand acres of trees on Blue Mountain, adjacent to the former smelters, have been stripped of their foliage, leaving a barren mountainside. Rain water and run-off carry contaminants into the Aquashicola Creek and Lehigh River that run on either side of town.

About eight hundred and fifty people live within one mile of the site of the cinder bank and have been exposed to the heavy metals, and the total population in Palmerton is only five thousand. When Otis thinks about it now, he does a quick calculation in his head. He lets out a low whistle when he figures out that about twenty percent of the population has breathed in these toxins. Operations ceased around 1980, and now some of the effects of toxic inhalation is beginning to show up in people's health.

Otis wonders if it's a safe place to stop off for a few nights. If he does, he'll be extra cautious and buy bottled water and stick to the basics. He won't buy any fruits or vegetables because they might be contaminated. After thinking it over, he decides that a few days in the area won't be enough to make him sick. Still, he doesn't want to take any chances. He has read news reports about the high levels of lead and their negative effects on human and animal health and wants to remain healthy to complete his mission and not fall ill. No needless risks for Otis.

He figures that the drive from Great Barrington to Palmerton will take just under four hours, according to the truck's navigation system. He's in no hurry—he has all summer—so he swings north, with the idea that he'll stop for a few nights in Stockbridge first. He wants to find out if Alice's Restaurant ever existed. He thinks Arlo Guthrie wrote his famous song about a real place, but he's not sure. The folk singer might have made it up for all Otis knows. He could have checked Wiki, but going to Stockbridge and finding out will be more fun.

When he arrives, he stops for gas at the edge of town and rolls down the window to ask the attendant.

A man who appears to be in his thirties sidles over to the driver's side of the truck, looks up at Otis and gives him a lopsided smile.

"What can I get you?" the attendant asks. Otis notices that he has a bit of a southern drawl and wonders if he might have migrated north from below the Mason-Dixon.

"Filler-up, regular," Otis says, pulling his wallet from the console. "And by the way, do you know if Alice's Restaurant is a real place or did Arlo Guthrie make it up?"

Chapter Twenty-Four

The gas station attendant tells Otis to hang on, that he'll tell him all about Alice's Restaurant when he finishes pumping his gas.

When he returns, the attendant tells Otis that Alice May Brock was born in the early 1940s and went to a fancy college in New York. Sarah something. He can't remember the rest of it. Her mother then gave Alice two grand, which she used to buy a "dead church" in Great Barrington. At this news, Otis wishes he had known about it when he was there. He would have liked to see the church the attendant is talking about.

"She bought the church to live in with her husband Ray," he continues. "They had dinner there one Thanksgiving and Arlo made up a song about it. The thing is, Alice had better things to do than run a restaurant. She was a painter and designer, see, and Ray was an architect and woodworker, and they both worked at the Stockbridge School right here in town. It's some kind of fancy arts academy. I do believe Arlo might have graduated from that school."

The attendant continues, telling Otis that she only owned the restaurant for a short while before she broke up with Ray and divorced him in 1968. After that, she opened two bigger restaurants in Housatonic and Lenox, he tells Otis.

"She quit the business in 1979. Lives in Provincetown now. Might have preferred women to men. Maybe that's why she divorced Ray. Who knows?"

"But what about the restaurant in the song?" Otis asks.

"That? The original one was called The Back Room. It was on Main Street right here in Stockbridge. Down the road a piece. Situated behind a grocery store and would you believe it? It's right below Norman Rockwell's studio. Some woman named Theresa went into the location and opened up a new place. There's a sign that says the place was once occupied by Alice." He gives a laugh and says, "Ain't life funny?"

Otis agrees with the attendant, pays for the gas and continues on his way. He decides to return to Great Barrington now. As long as he's in the area he might as well stop at the church Alice and Ray once owned to see Officer Obie's chair and the Guthrie Center, which was turned into a folk music spot. After scouring the Internet, Otis finds out that the center once hosted hootenannies and concerts featuring Tom Paxton, Tom Rush, The Highwaymen and Guthrie himself.

Otis realizes, with a great deal of satisfaction, that his truck has become a classroom. He wonders what else he'll learn on his journey along the Trail. He'll find out soon enough, he tells himself. Soon enough.

As he drives along, he reaches out to give Sadie a pat on the head. The dog licks his hand, her way of telling Otis that she's enjoying the trip as much as he is.

After seeing the church and other sights in Great Barrington, Otis gets onto the Taconic State Parkway and I-84 through New York state. He glances at the clock on the dashboard. Twelve-thirty. He has allowed himself four hours to get to his destination, factoring in a little extra time for traffic. The terrain is pretty, Otis notices, and includes winding rivers, valleys, mountains and forest land. As he gets closer to the Pennsylvania border, the region changes to a vista of low rise mountains and there are signs announcing state parks and side trails. He passes Fitzgerald Falls, Bear Mountain and Hudson Highlands where the route follows a ridge over several low elevation peaks. But when he arrives at Lehigh Valley Gap, he notices something else, something appalling. All the trees—from beech to maple to black hickory—are dead. So this is the effect heavy metals has had on forest land. Otis had read that the animal population was affected and that there are no longer squirrels, chipmunks and deer in the area. But he also read that American kestrels, once on the endangered species list, have made a comeback in recent years. At least there's that.

By mid-afternoon, Otis begins to see signs for Palmerton and notices a slight change in the air, as if something permeates it, something repugnant and unpleasant, something so metallic he can almost taste it. Fern would say it smells like rotten eggs. Otis thinks it smells like something from the pit of hell. Though the weather is bright and sunny and the air temperature is in the low seventies, Otis closes the driver's side window and turns on the air conditioner, concerned that whatever is in the air will be toxic to his health and Sadie's, too. Or, maybe he's overreacting and has nothing to worry about.

After driving for a few hours, he pulls to the side of the road and checks his cooler to see if there's anything for lunch. While in Great Barrington, he decided not to stop at the local grocery to stock up. Now the drive has made him hungry, and he's thirsty, too. Peering inside the cooler, he sees a jar of strawberry jam and a plastic container of tuna already mixed with mayonnaise and diced red onion, but he's low on bread, bottled water, milk, and, yes, potato chips. Then he remembers the burger he ordered at the Gypsy Joynt that's tucked away in the smaller cooler. He takes it out and, though cold, eats it with gusto. He shares a few bites with Sadie.

Otis continues on for a few miles before coming to the Entering Palmerton sign and then sees DPW Grocery on the left side of the road. There's a gas pump, too, at the front of the building but at a higher price per gallon than what he last paid. He laughs at himself over his automatic response to being a penny pincher. He no longer has to worry about the price of gas or anything else, but Otis knows that old habits die a slow death. All his life he has had to be frugal, and The Vault has done nothing to change his mindset.

He pulls into the paved parking lot and shuts off the engine. If the gas price is high, then the store's food prices will probably be inflated, too. Even so, he needs to replenish the cooler. He looks over at Sadie settled in the passenger seat. She looks up at Otis. "I know. You're hungry and thirsty, too," he says. "Don't worry, I'll fix that up right away."

On his way into the store, Otis notices a man dressed in denim overalls, red plaid shirt and work boots. He is seated on an old wooden bench near the front door and is smoking a cigarette. When the man sees Otis, he flicks the cigarette into the air, and the butt lands in a small puddle left over from a recent rain. He gives Otis a little wave and says, "Howdy." Otis returns the greeting by giving a salute and nod of his head.

When he steps inside the store, he sees a woman he guesses is in her eighties standing at the end of one of the check-out lanes. She can't weigh much more than a hundred pounds. The woman must sense Otis's presence because she turns, glances his way and gives him a smile while placing a customer's groceries inside a paper bag. The customer stands there watching the woman without offering any help.

"A nice day out there," she says to Otis when he walks by.

"Sure is. We've had a whole string of 'em."

"Hope we have even more. Got some good sales going. Check out the meat."

The woman has Otis's full attention now, and he notices that she's wearing a blue flowered dress that's seen better days. She has a cloud of white hair and big brown eyes that probably captured many a man's heart in her younger days. He watches as she packs groceries with a blue-veined hand that's been deeply wrinkled by the sun and old age. He wonders if she is bagging groceries because she has to work or if she just likes to keep busy. Maybe she's a relative of the owner. His mother, even. Otis will get around to asking eventually, but right now he needs to shop.

But the woman wants to continue talking. "You don't look familiar," she says. "You're not from Palmerton, are you?" The woman looks into Otis's face and studies him as if he were a puzzle.

"No. I'm from Maine. Been doing some traveling lately. Thought I'd stop here to check out the town. But I have to ask—what's that awful smell in the air?"

"You're not the first to ask. It's from the zinc." The woman shakes her head slowly and says, "You've heard that old saying 'take zinc, don't stink'? Ha! Everyone who lives here knows that's not true. I'm Edith, by the way." She pauses, then says, "You don't look familiar."

"Otis Kingston. Nice to meet you, Edith. I don't look familiar because I live in Maine," he says. "See that truck out there? I'm driving down the Appalachian Trail all the way to Georgia. At the end of summer, I'll head for home." Edith glances out of the store's big plate glass window and sees Otis's truck.

"Maine? You don't say. My great-grandparents came from Maine. Somewhere near Millinocket, I think. Never been there myself, but the stories got passed down through the generations. I was born and raised here in Palmerton. My father came to work in the mines."

Otis nods and says, "So that smell is coming from zinc then."

Edith sighs and nods her head. "Sure is. We live with it day in, day out, not that we have any choice. There was some kind of fund set up by the government that was supposed to clean it all up. A lot of good that did. Maybe the money was spent on something else. Many of us have lead poisoning. That's what they call it."

As Otis continues his conversation with Edith, he is pleased that she is so willing to open up to him. Maybe she's lonely. Could be no one takes the time to listen. He takes a risk and says, "I'm putting together a photo album of people I meet during my travels. Would you like to be included?"

"Me? In a picture? Nah. My picture taking days are over and done with. This old lady isn't what she used to be."

"You seem like a spring chicken to me. I'll bet you've got a good book inside of you," says Otis. "I've been talking to people ever since I left Maine. Some of their stories are tragic, but just as many are uplifting. Inspiring, even."

Otis now thinks about Lloyd at Whispering Pines. He had a good story. The man had worked hard over the years to keep his campground going. A few good decisions, including focusing on excellent customer service, had led him to be as successful as his father. Fewer people were camping, Lloyd had told him, but he had persevered. "I'm not too worried," Lloyd had told Otis while they were playing cribbage. "Worse comes to worst, I can always retire and sell the place. My son will make his way in the world, campground or no campground."

Yes, Lloyd's story had been inspiring. And then there was John Penewait. The man is a hero in Otis's eyes.

"You by yourself?"

Edith's words bring Otis back to the moment.

"I'm sorry. You caught me daydreaming."

"I asked if you were traveling alone."

"Just me and my dog. That would be Sadie." He thinks of her now, hopes she's okay. "Forgot to lower the window for her. Be right back."

Otis leaves Edith standing at the end of the check-out lane while he goes to the truck. When he returns, he finds that Edith is no longer there. Moments later, he finds her in aisle four stocking the shelves with canned soup.

"The boss is always finding things for me to do," she says.

"How long have you worked here?" Otis asks.

"Thirty-one years. Ever since Roy died. That'd be my husband. Lots of folks come to Duncan Purdy Williams for a job when they need extra money," she says, whispering. "Roy warned me about Mr. Williams. Told me he was a mean son of a gun. But I wouldn't listen. The truth is, I had no choice. Roy suffered a long and painful illness before he died, and I needed money to pay the bills. One day I asked Mr. Williams if he needed help, and he put me right to work. Been at it all these years."

Otis recalls his own experience with a sick spouse and sympathizes with Edith. He thinks for a moment and hopes he isn't about to offend her. "Forgive me for saying, but you're well past retirement age. Where do you get the energy?"

"Energy? It's a matter of wanting to eat or not. Like I said, I have no choice. I've got arthritis in my hip so bad it keeps me awake at night. Needs to be replaced, but I can't take time off from work. What can I do? Gotta eat and keep a roof over my head. Don't want to rely on my kids."

Otis is quiet for a long moment before speaking again. He wonders if he might be able to help Edith. Maybe. Maybe not. But he's going to hang around long enough to find out.

"There a campground around here?"

"Twin Hills is a mile or so down the road on the right. Mr. Williams owns that, too. Fact is, not much here in Palmerton that he doesn't own. You might say DPW owns just about everything in these parts. All except for the bank and town hall and I guess the fire and police stations, too. Other than that, he's got his fingers in just about every pie."

Otis thinks about Duncan Purdy Williams, wonders how he keeps track of all the pies he's got his fingers in. Good thing he's not one to discriminate based on age. Poor Edith might go hungry if she didn't have a pay check coming in.

He also thinks about the difficulties in the old woman's life and wonders why some people seem to have all the money while others barely scrape by. He hopes that one day he'll find out. That day might come when he joins Fern in the grave.

He doesn't like to think about it, but the thought comes to his mind occasionally. He wonders how it will all end. Will his own death be quick? Will he have a lingering illness like Fern and Edith's husband? Will he be killed during a tragic accident or, God forbid, murdered?

He shakes his head to clear his mind and reminds himself that he is on this trip to help people, not dwell on his own life or what might or might not happen in the future. He allows himself one final thought—that, like it or not, everyone alive has a fatal illness, and that fatal illness is life itself.

Otis wraps up his conversation with Edith and says he'll probably stop in again for groceries.

"Have a good time while you're here," she says. "Nice talking to you."

Chapter Twenty-Five

After paying for his food and water, Otis joins Sadie in the truck and arrives at Twin Hills a few minutes later. When he pulls off the road, he gets into a long line of RVs. There are pop-up campers, too, and some people have kayaks and canoes loaded onto the back or top of their vehicles, along with bicycles and lawn chairs secured with bungee cords. It reminds him of Whispering Pines except it's busier here. He waits a good twenty minutes before his turn at the guard shack. When the driver ahead of him continues on his way, he lowers the window and comes face to face with a girl young enough to be his granddaughter. Otis takes note of her short, dark hair with the bright pink stripe hanging down on the side. He also notices her nose ring, tattoo of a star on her forearm and the name printed on her badge—Roxie.

"Hello, there. Do you have a reservation?" she asks.

"No, I don't. Thought I'd take a chance. See if you have any space."

"An hour from now you'd probably be out of luck, but right now I still have a few open spots. How long you planning to stay?"

Otis has no idea. He thinks about Edith. Roxie might know her.

"Probably no longer than a week, maybe less," he says. "Say, Roxie, do you know a woman named Edith? She works at the grocery store."

"Edith Kulp? Sure do. She's everyone's grannie. And a champion knitter. She's made hats and mittens for all the kids in Palmerton for years. Makes them from old sweaters she gets at the thrift shop. I've still got the pair of red mittens she made for me when I was five. I love Edith. Everyone does."

"Sounds like a special lady," says Otis. "I'm on a bit of a mission to meet people like her. Love hearing their stories." John Penewait springs into Otis's mind again, and he wonders if the bursar at the University of Maine has contacted him. Later in the week, he'll give Lloyd a call and wait for an opening to ask about John. Maybe he'll have some good news.

"You can have Lot 5 over by the lake. It's a nice spot. Quiet. Not as many kids," Roxie says. "There's a nice walking trail for dog-walking, too."

Fine with Otis. He hands Roxie his credit card.

"I'll only charge you for one night now. If you stay longer, I'll get you on the way out. Here's a map of the area. I'm not putting a plug in for the cinder bank, but a lot of people want to see it. News reporters come here all the time to write about it, and no wonder. It's the worst abuse of land I've ever heard tell of. And here I am, living right in the thick of it."

"Today isn't forever. One day, you might find yourself living in a big city or in a cottage by the sea," Otis says.

"I wish. My dad owns this campground. He expects my brother and me to take over when he retires." So she's Duncan Purdy Williams's daughter, Otis realizes as he connects the dots.

He thinks of Lloyd and recalls what he said about his son taking over Whispering Pines someday.

"Well, that'd be up to you, right?"

"Ha! You don't know my Dad. Oh, look, the line just got longer. I'm sorry. Gotta ask you to move along. Here's your receipt. Enjoy your stay."

And then Otis is off to find Lot 5. Roxie is right. According to the campground map, it is right near a lake small enough to be classified as a pond. At water's edge, he sees a dock where five outboard motor boats are lined up in a row. When he reads the pamphlet about the campground, Otis learns that the boats are available for rent by the hour. Later on, he'll take Sadie out on the water, but right now she needs to go for a walk.

While at Twin Hills, Otis meets people from New York, New Jersey, Ohio and West Virginia. There are also three couples from California traveling in a convoy. He has found everyone friendly and willing to share all kinds of stories and information about the Trail.

Most of the campers near his site are his age or older. Otis has found them to be down to earth, and everyone agrees that road tripping beats every other kind of travel. Henry Marshall, a man renting an RV on Lot 20, told Otis he likes the freedom of coming and going as he pleases and staying in one place for as long as he wants before moving on to somewhere else. Henry wonders aloud why people put up with noisy hotel guests who allow their children to slam doors and run up and down corridors at midnight. The other campers have told him this kind of behavior is common and they want no part of it.

More and more, Otis is convinced that he made the right decision to buy the F-150. Now, he's thinking about future road trips that will take him to places like the Great Lakes and Niagara Falls. He'd like to see the Mississippi River, too, and maybe the Pacific Ocean. He thinks about the beauty of the Rangeley Lakes region and the brilliant blue of the water and sky. He knows that what he has seen so far is just a single gem in a long, winding belt that circles the globe and he is hungry for more.

One night while sitting with the other campers in the dining hall, Otis learns about an incident that happened the week before at a campground outside of Ellijay, Georgia.

"A man got a campfire going and gave his grandkids sticks for roasting marshmallows," says Ray Manning, a retired New Yorker staying on Lot 6 with his wife, Janet. "One of the kids got too close to the flames and set his shirt on fire. Suffered third degree burns to his arms, face and chest. Last I heard, the boy was still in the hospital fighting for his life," Ray says. "Sixty percent of his body was burned."

"That poor kid. And imagine how the grandfather feels . . . and his parents," says Otis, shaking his head and clicking his tongue.

"To add insult to injury, there's no health insurance," Ray continues. "The bills are going to be astronomical. A fund's been set up, but any donations will only cover so much. They've got a long road ahead of them."

"Goes to show that this country is behind the times," says another camper whose name is Marty Collins. "We need some kind of national health coverage. Countries in Europe have it. Canada has it. We should, too."

While listening, Otis remembers all the medical bills from Fern's illness. He's glad he paid them off before he left Maine.

"Ha! Canada? My sister and brother-in-law live in Ontario," says Ray. "They have a friend who was diagnosed with breast cancer. Took six months to get the poor woman into surgery. By then, it had spread. She died within a year."

"Sorry to hear this," says Marty. "I sure do feel sorry for that little boy, too . . . the one who was burned." Ray nods his head in agreement.

Otis thinks there must be a story online about the boy. After he cleans up and settles in for the night, he looks on the Internet to see what he can find out. He scrolls through the listings and there it is. The headline reads: Boy, 9, suffers major burns at campfire. The dateline is Ellijay, Ga.

Otis wonders if the family lives near to where the tragedy took place or whether they had traveled to Georgia from somewhere else. He reads the story for more information and learns that the boy and his grandparents were traveling by RV along the Trail and considered the trip a geography and social studies lesson for their three grandkids. The doctor in charge was quoted as saying that the boy faces numerous surgeries, including plastic surgery for facial injuries he sustained in the fire. The piece ends with a tagline stating that donations for the boy can be mailed to a post office box in Ellijay.

Otis writes down the name and address of the bank handling the donations. He will send a generous check. $25,000 Sounds just about right. $50,000 Sounds even better. So does $100,000.

After mailing a cashier's check, Otis spends the next two days gazing at what looks like a barren, low rise mountain known as the cinder bank. He hopes that someday the government will do something about the toxic waste dump so the residents of Palmerton won't have to live with those awful toxins.

The scenery and friendly campers at Whispering Pines have brought peace to Otis's grieving heart and, thanks to Lloyd MacNeill, knowing that he has paved the way for John Penewait to continue his education has sent his spirit soaring. Otis feels like his broken heart is finally beginning to heal.

A week has passed since Otis arrived in Palmerton, and now he knows his way around town. On a rainy afternoon he stops at the Cup o' Joe Diner just beyond the town limits and sits on a stool at the counter. Out in the parking lot, a woman half of Otis's age is heading toward the door.

As he watches her approach, he is reminded of Fern when she was that age. When she walks through the door, he smiles and comments about the rainy weather.

"A good day to stay inside and read a good book," she says with a little laugh. She sits on a stool near the cash register and places her white purse on the counter. A moment later, a waitress comes through a pair of saloon doors separating the dining area and kitchen.

"Hi, Janine. No work today?" says the waitress.

"I went in early this morning so I could have the afternoon off. Thought I'd stop by for one of your famous cups of coffee and a tuna sandwich," she says.

"I'll put on a pot. Just for you."

"Thanks, Dottie. You're the best."

The waitress then turns to Otis and asks if he's made up his mind. "I'll have what she's having," he says, joking. The two women laugh when they recall the line from *When Harry Met Sally*.

When Dottie leaves to place their order, Otis is the first to speak. "I took my wife to see that movie," he says. "We laughed all the way through."

"So did I," says Janine. "One of the best comedies ever. I love Billy Crystal. Meg Ryan, too." She pauses, then comments about Tom Hanks and Brad Pitt. "I loved Tom in *Cast Away*."

"Didn't see that one," says Otis. "Someday."

Janine then asks if Otis lives in the area, and he tells her about his trip.

"Really? Where did you start?"

"Maine. A little town near Bangor."

"Hmmm. You're a long way from home."

"And when I get to Springer Mountain in Georgia, I'll be an even longer way from home," he says, pausing. "You know, as long as we're both in the mood to chat, would you like to share a booth with me?"

Janine thinks a moment, then says, "Sure. No plans this afternoon. I'd like to hear about your trip."

And Otis would like to pick her brain about someone in Palmerton who might be desperate for help.

After settling in a booth, Janine asks Otis where he's staying, and he tells her about Twin Hills.

"Oh, you're camping, then. Twin Hills is a nice place. Duncan Purdy Williams sees to that. One of the saving graces of this godforsaken place."

"You know Mr. Purdy?"

"Everyone knows him. He owns just about everything in Palmerton, including Twin Hills."

"And then there's the cinder bank." Otis is interested in hearing what she has to say about the monstrous toxic dumping ground.

"The cinder bank. Oh, yes. We're known for that."

"I take it you've lived here for a long time?"

"Born and bred," Janine says. "Haven't left yet. Maybe someday."

Before Otis can ask another question, Dottie arrives with their coffee and sandwiches. "Can I get you anything else?" she asks.

"All's well, Dottie. Thanks," says Janine.

Otis is trying to figure out a way to bring up Edith's name in a casual way. An idea suddenly pops into his mind.

"You know, I've been thinking about people who live along the Appalachian Trail. I read somewhere that there's a lot of poverty. Is it true?"

Janine takes a sip of coffee before answering. "There are poor people everywhere, but the ones who live along the Trail seem to be even worse off because of the remote areas they live in. In other words, no jobs. Coal mining dominates everything, and you probably know about the hazards of that job. Why do you ask?"

"Just interested in people and their stories. That's all." Otis then skirts around the topic of money before zeroing in on Edith. "While I was on the way here, I listened to a radio call-in show. The host asked people to call the station to tell him what they'd do if they found $1 million." There he goes again. Another lie. Otis is disgusted with himself. "I thought about it a lot while I was driving. So, now I'll ask you. What would you do if you found that kind of money?"

"Me? With $1 million to spend?" Janine asks.

"You with $1 million. What would you do with it?"

Janine turns the tables on Otis. "Well, what would YOU do?"

"I asked you first."

Janine laughs and says, "First, I'd pay off my bills. Then I'd help people in my family."

"I'd probably do the same thing," Otis agrees. "Then I'd have a lot of fun with it."

"Yeah, me, too," says Janine.

He pauses, looks out the window and says, "This morning I stopped in to get a few groceries at DPW. Met an interesting lady. Edith. Do you know her?"

"Edith Kulp? Sure, I know Edith. In this town everyone knows everyone. Don't tell me she got your ear."

"I think it was more like I got hers," he jokes.

Janine laughs. "And speaking of people to help . . . she'd be at the top of my list."

"Really? Why's that?"

"It's a long story, but if you want to hear it I've got the time."

"I'd love to hear it. No plans today."

Chapter Twenty-Six

Janine sighs deeply before she starts telling Otis Edith's story. "Where do you want me to start?" she says.

"How about the beginning?"

Janine suggests that they refill their coffee mugs. "We'll probably be here a while."

After Dottie pours their second cup, Janine launches in. "Edith was born during the Great Depression. She was one of thirteen children."

"Wow. I guessed right, then. She's somewhere in her eighties," Otis says.

"Yes, eighty-four."

"And she's still working?"

"Edith has always worked. Keeps her young, I suppose. And it occupies her mind so she isn't sitting around thinking about her tragic past. She grew up on a farm. Her parents never got along and her father eventually found a girlfriend and brought her to live in the same house with Edith's mother and all the kids. Eventually, her mother laid down the law and told him the girlfriend had to leave. Then the farm got sold, and the children had to be fostered out—except for Edith."

Janine continues. "The woman who lived next door thought Edith could help her work in the garden and do some household chores. She couldn't have children of her own, so she talked her husband into taking her in. But that was the start of even more trouble for Edith."

"Hmm. Go on."

"The Shaws—they're both dead so it's okay to tell you about them—Mrs. Shaw was nice enough, but Mr. Shaw was a terrible man. When Edith was a teenager, he'd make up some story about her being sassy or accuse her of stealing something and take her out to the wood shed for a 'beating.' When they were out there, what he did had nothing to do with discipline. He'd lock the door and have his way with her."

Otis knows men like this exist. Monsters.

"That poor girl," he says. His thoughts turn to the elderly Edith and tries not to envision her in such a horrible situation.

"That's not all. She ended up pregnant by Mr. Shaw, and when Mrs. Shaw found out about it, she took her out to the wood shed—this time for a real beating. Her backside was so bloodied she couldn't sit for weeks, poor thing. She soon lost the baby and that turned out to be a blessing."

Otis shakes his head sadly. "Did Edith tell Mrs. Shaw that her husband was the father?"

"No. He threatened to kill her if she ever told. But eventually he got what was coming to him."

"Always happens," says Otis. "What goes around comes around."

"The Shaws sold their old place and bought a small farm. They had a few dairy cows and four or five sheep. At the time, there was a no-good in Palmerton. Larry Owen. Homely as a hedge fence is what I'm told. Couldn't get a woman to give him a second look. So, late at night he paid visits to the Shaws' farm."

Janine stops, looks down at her plate and then back at Otis. "It was the sheep he was after," she says. "Some men have been known to take advantage of these sweet and beautiful animals . . . in an unnatural way."

"So I've heard," says Otis. He almost wishes he hadn't asked Janine to tell him Edith's story.

"One night, Mr. Shaw heard one of the sheep bleating. It was way past midnight when things should have been quiet. He went out to investigate and found Larry Owen . . . well . . . I don't want to be graphic. Mr. Shaw didn't let on that he had seen Larry Owen and went back inside the house to get his shotgun. When he came outside again, he caught Larry . . . in the act. There was shouting and then a scuffle. Then, Larry Owen somehow got the shotgun away from Mr. Shaw and killed him."

Otis shakes his head and buries his face in his hands. He and Janine sit in silence for a few moments before Otis says anything.

"You were right, Janine. He did get what was coming to him."

"I think so. And there's another chapter to Edith's story."

"What's that?"

"When she turned eighteen, she left Mrs. Shaw and married Oswald Kulp, but what she did was swap one bad situation for another."

"Why is that?"

"Because Ozzie liked his tea too much."

"Tea?"

"Booze. He was a mean drunk. By the time Edith was twenty-five they had three kids. One year, on St. Patrick's Day, Ozzie took the day off from work and went to a bar. When he got home around suppertime, he was three sheets to the wind. Edith tried to put him to bed, but he was in the mood for a fight. There they were, on the second floor of their rental cottage when he pushed her toward the staircase. When she turned to get away, he shoved her hard and she fell down every one of those stairs all the way to the bottom."

Otis clicks his tongue. He can hardly believe what Janine is telling him.

"That's not the end of it. A few broken ribs later, Edith crawled to the living room couch and tried to rest in spite of the pain. Meanwhile, Ozzie was upstairs in bed and smoking up a storm. He must have fallen asleep because the bed caught fire. By then, Ozzie was awake and there were flames everywhere. Edith heard screams coming from upstairs. Then, she saw smoke in the hallway. She got out, but Ozzie didn't, and he took everything with him. There was nothing left of that house but a big pile of ashes."

"You said Edith had three kids. Where were they?"

"That's the only good part of the story. Edith had been trying to get Ozzie off the booze, and my grandmother offered to take them for a few nights. They were with her."

"So, your grandmother and Edith knew each other?"

"I'd say they knew each other quite well and still do."

"You seem to know a lot about Edith's life," says Otis. "How do you know all the details?"

Janine looks Otis in the eye and says, "Because Edith is my great aunt. My grandmother's older sister. If my cousins had been home that night, they might not be alive today."

"I'm sorry. I shouldn't have burdened you. I don't know why I told you all that about Edith. I mean, I don't *know* you. I don't even know your name. I feel terrible—I just betrayed poor Aunt Edith."

Otis looks into her eyes and sees that tears have formed. "I don't know anyone in your family," he tells her. "Edith's secrets are safe with me."

"Well, I can't believe I opened my mouth. I've never told another soul. I feel so sorry for her."

"Believe me, you've done her a favor," Otis says without thinking.

"What do you mean?"

Otis tells Janine that he misspoke. He meant that Janine has done herself a favor and that burdens are never meant to be carried alone. He could tell her about the plans to help Edith that are taking shape in his mind, but he won't—not if he wants her to witness a miracle.

"So, what *is* your name?" Janine asks.

"It doesn't matter. You'll probably never see me again. Just passing through. I'll be moving along soon."

Janine stares at Otis, but he refuses to meet her gaze. If he tells her his name, she might put two and two together later and know that it was him who helped her Aunt Edith. She might even try to track him down.

"Just tell me your first name. Please. So I can at least thank you . . . for listening."

Otis racks his brain to remember what Fern had told him about Andrew Carnegie. She had read him a quote . . . something he had said about being rich. What was it? He wishes his memory had a reset button. Then, with clarity, he recalls the quote. "No man can become rich without himself enriching others. The man who dies rich dies disgraced."

"All right, Janine. My name is Andrew." This is one lie Otis thinks he'll be able to live with.

Otis has trouble falling asleep that night. The story Janine told him about Edith is keeping him awake. The following morning, he stays in bed and doesn't get up until after nine o'clock.

Later that morning, Otis goes to DPW Grocery on the pretense that he needs to buy bread and milk. He wanders the aisles, compares prices, puts items back on the shelves, goes to the next aisle and repeats the process. After half an hour of browsing, he finally finds what, or whom, he's been looking for. Edith is in the produce department placing bags of apples in fruit bins. When she finishes, she heads to the back of the store and disappears behind a set of swinging doors. Five minutes later she comes back, and this time a man is pulling a pallet of bagged onions behind her. He then leaves and returns to the rear of the store. Otis watches while she places the onions in another bin, and Otis feels tired just from watching her. When she finishes, she looks up and sees Otis at the apple bin looking over the fruit.

"Nothing like fresh," she says as she approaches. She mops her forehead with a handkerchief. "Aren't you the traveling man with the truck?"

Otis laughs. "Can't say I disagree about the fruit," says Otis, embarrassed. He hopes she didn't catch him watching her. "Yes, I'm the traveling man."

"Well, good to see you again. Been out to the cinder bank yet?"

"Sure have. What an awful sight that is."

"Can't argue with that. Well, I best get back to work. One load of peaches, and I'm done for the day."

"Looks like it'll be a nice afternoon. Bright and sunny out there," says Otis.

"Looking forward to sitting on the porch when I get home."

"I'll be on my way, then. See you again sometime." Otis heads for the pet food aisle. He might as well buy Sadie a treat of some kind.

After he pays the cashier, he heads toward his truck but doesn't get inside. Instead, he opens the door and gives Sadie her treat before he lets her out. He then attaches the leash to her collar and walks her around the parking lot, hoping that Edith will be out soon. Five minutes later, he sees her coming through the store's front door. When she steps outside, Otis moves into her line of vision.

"Well, fancy that. Didn't think I'd run into you again so soon," Edith says when she gets closer to Otis. "Who's this handsome lad?"

"Lass," Otis corrects her. "Sadie's a girl. She's been cooped up all morning. Figured she'd like a little exercise before we hit the road."

"Well, hello there, Sadie." Edith gives the dog a pat on the head.

Otis doesn't want to let an opportunity slip through his fingers. This is his chance to find out even more about Edith Kulp.

"There's a McDonald's next door," he says, pointing to the iconic Golden Arches. "Would you like some lunch?"

"Oh, now that's very nice of you, but I really can't."

"Got a date with someone?"

Edith raises her eyebrows and smiles. "My dating days are long over," she says.

"Tell you what . . . I'd love some company. Let me buy you some lunch. We can eat outside."

Edith pauses and then looks at Otis's kind face. "Okay. I haven't had one of their strawberry shakes in a long time. And a burger. I'd be lying if I said I wasn't hungry."

They walk across the parking lot to the restaurant and Edith sits at a picnic table while Otis goes inside to place an order. He returns a few minutes later with a tray loaded with food.

"That's right nice of you," says Edith. "Right nice. Thank you."

"It's nothing. Sadie's been great to travel with, but all she can do is bark. It'll be nice to have someone to talk to. You live close by?"

"Half a mile down the road. Big yellow house just before you get to Twin Hills. On the right."

Otis knows the building. A lemon yellow three-story house. Looks like a giant rectangular box with windows. He has seen elderly people sitting on the front porch.

"I'll have to move soon," she continues. "The owner is selling the place."

"Hmm. Any idea where you'll go?"

"No. Senior housing is all filled up. But something will come my way. Always does. Anyway, wherever I end up will be better than living in a rooming house."

Otis nods, says it must be tough. He knows he can do nothing about her past, but he can make sure she lives the rest of her days in comfort. The scars on her heart and soul are another matter. There's nothing he can do about that.

For the next hour, Otis listens to Edith's stories, and he tells her about his life in Hopewell and that he decided to drive the Trail after Fern died. He says nothing about meeting Janine. When they finish eating, he offers to drive her home, but she says she'd rather walk.

"Need the exercise to keep going," Edith tells him.

Chapter Twenty-Seven

That afternoon Otis takes a drive around town with one purpose in mind—to look for a property that's for sale by owner. He has already Googled the median price for homes in the area and knows what to expect. After going up and down dozens of streets, he finally finds what he's looking for. There's a small ranch style house in good condition on a corner lot just up ahead, and it's the perfect size and location for Edith. A sign out front reads FOR SALE BY OWNER. There's a Toyota SUV in the driveway, so the owner might be home. He leaves Sadie in the truck and walks to the front door.

Seconds after Otis rings the doorbell, a man wearing jeans and T-shirt opens the door. "You here about the house?" he asks Otis.

"Yes. I saw your FOR SALE sign. Are you the owner?"

"Sure am."

"I'd be interested in having a look around. Would you mind showing me the inside?"

"It's not in the best shape right now," he says, "but if you don't mind a bit of dust and dirty dishes you're welcome to come in. The name's Richard Anderson."

"Mike Newhall," Otis says, extending his hand. "Pleased to meet you." Andrew? Mike Newhall? What next—Horatio Hornblower? He tells Mr. Anderson his own place is plenty dusty so it won't bother him a bit. When Mr. Anderson opens the storm door wider, Otis steps inside the living room and sees that it's quite lived in. There's a stack of newspapers on the coffee table, and from where he's standing, he can see into the kitchen where unwashed dishes are sitting on the countertop next to the sink. Right away, he can envision Edith sitting in a recliner while watching TV.

The living room has a bay window and there's a fireplace on the side wall. The kitchen and bath have been updated and there are two bedrooms and a screened porch at the back of the house. Beyond the porch are mature plantings in a small yard. A washer and dryer are in a utility room off the kitchen.

"Where you from?" Mr. Anderson asks.

"Vermont. Just outside of Burlington." This time, Otis doesn't feel bad about not telling the truth.

"You planning to move to Palmerton?"

"No. Just looking to invest in some real estate. What's your price?"

"There's no sales commission, so I think $105,000 is fair."

"And the taxes?"

"$760 a year."

"I can give you $100,000 in cash."

"Cash?"

"Cash."

"As in dollars and cents?"

Otis nods his head.

"Can I think about it and call you tonight?"

Otis pulls a small notebook and pencil from his pants pocket and writes down his phone number. "Sure. Give me a call when you decide." He tears the page out of the notebook and hands it to Mr. Anderson.

"I'll do that. Thanks for stopping by."

"You live here by yourself?" Otis asks before he leaves.

"For the past six months I have. My wife died last November, and I've decided to move to Florida. I've had it with the cold northern winters."

That night when Richard Anderson counteroffers one hundred three thousand, Otis offers one hundred two thousand and a deal is made. The next day, Otis drives to Allentown where he sets up three bank accounts and establishes a blind trust for Edith. There's enough money in the trust to provide a monthly stipend for her food, clothing and utilities for the next five years.

The only possible fly in the ointment might be Janine if she becomes suspicious. But she has no idea who Otis is or where to find him unless she does some serious Internet digging.

On his way back from Allentown, he thinks about Janine and hopes he doesn't run into her again. He'll keep a low profile for the rest of his time in Palmerton and head into town only when he needs food. Better yet, he'll take a drive to find another grocery store. DPW's isn't the only game in town.

Chapter Twenty-Eight

As soon as Otis finishes taking care of Edith's needs, he leaves Palmerton and sets out for Damascus, Virginia. On the way, he decides to stop in Washington, D.C. to tour the nation's capital. When he arrives, he finds a hotel that allows pets and buys a ticket for a nighttime double-decker bus tour to see the monuments.

It is now noontime and the tour doesn't start until seven, so he takes Sadie for a long walk with two destinations in mind. The first is on Pennsylvania Avenue, the second is on 9th Street NW.

Just as he did at the Fort Knox site in Maine, Otis asks a stranger to take his photo on Pennsylvania Avenue, and when he arrives at his destination on 9th Street NW, a man sitting on a bench volunteers to take a photo of him and Sadie.

When he returns to Hopewell, he'll have all three photos matted and framed. The first will be of Otis and Sadie standing in front of the U.S. Mint, the second will show them in front of the U.S. Treasury and the third, Fort Knox in Maine.

The three photos, grouped together and hung on a wall—maybe in the bathroom so he can look at them while he's sitting on the pot—will bring a smile to his face when he recalls his trip along the Trail. He only wishes he could have included The Vault.

When he hears a small voice in his head telling him he's thinking too much about money, he tells it to shut up and leave him alone.

Otis has only seen the national monuments on TV and in magazines and can hardly wait to see them in person. In a few more hours, the bus will pass by the White House, Capitol Building, Lincoln Memorial, Washington Monument, U.S. Marine Corps War Memorial, National Mall, Vietnam Wall, Holocaust Museum and a few other famous sites.

Tomorrow, Otis plans to visit the National Museum of American History where Archie Bunker's chair, Dorothy's ruby slippers, Thomas Jefferson's desk and Abraham Lincoln's top hat are on display. He also wants to spend a full day in Gettysburg. Maybe he'll spend a night or two in Philadelphia while he's at it.

One night while he's still in Washington, he walks Sadie along the National Mall to people watch. There are young parents with children. Couples holding hands. An elderly man pushing a woman in a wheel chair. A cluster of men and women wearing U.S. Navy uniforms.

Otis thinks about their lives and wonders if they are happy, sad or indifferent. Life is complicated and difficult for so many. A series of gains and losses. As he contemplates the lives of these strangers, he is overcome by a deep sense of loneliness.

When he returns to the hotel room, he sets aside his sorrow and opens his computer to learn more about Damascus. While he's there, maybe he'll rent a bicycle to ride the Creeper Trail and go to the Hiker Parade over the weekend. Every May the town hosts Trail Days, and a festival and parade are central to the celebration. Festivities include board games, zen coloring, chalk the walk and artwork exhibitions. Live music, too. And lots of food vendors.

Now Otis has something new to look forward to. He can't wait to get to Damascus.

The drive from Washington to Virginia will take more than five hours. On the way, Otis thinks about Edith. He would love to be a fly on the wall when the bank notifies her about the house he bought for her. He recalls now that John Olsen, the man who handled the blind trust, had thought Otis was joking when he told him what he wanted to do.

"You're serious." John Olsen had said.

"Dead serious."

"But why?"

"Simple. Because I can. And because I care."

"Mr. Kingston, I don't mean to be skeptical, but I can't help it. No one just up and buys a home for a total stranger, let alone establish a trust."

"Well, you're in the company of someone who has done exactly that."

The banker had placed his folded hands on his desk before looking straight into Otis's eyes. "Tell me about the strings attached," he had said.

"There are no strings. I just want to help someone in need."

Otis has a reservation to stay at a campground in Damascus called The Plantation. The weather will be just right for bike riding and going to the Hiker Parade.

He learns more about the weekend when he stops at a Waffle House and strikes up a conversation with a young man seated at the table next to his. The man has a map spread out across the table, and Otis is curious about where he's going.

The man introduces himself as Tim and tells Otis that he's on his way to Damascus and that going to the Hiker Parade is something he has done every year since his college days at Emory & Henry. "Wouldn't miss it," he tells Otis.

"I'm headed there, too. Maybe we'll run into each other," Otis says.

"It's possible, but unlikely. The place will be overrun with people this weekend, but you never know."

"You're right," says Otis. "Either way, it should be a lot of fun."

Around noontime, Otis stops at the side of the road so Sadie can relieve herself. After he feeds her, he makes himself a ham and cheese sandwich.

He fills an empty gallon container with water pouring out of a pipe at the side of the road, and when he takes a sip, he discovers that the water is delicious and ice cold, just the way he likes it. He only hopes it's clean and isn't harboring something like bear scat that will have him running to the bathroom in the middle of the night.

He takes his time eating and savors the quiet beauty of the surrounding mountains. A scenic outlook is nearby, and Otis takes his folding chair out of the truck's bed so he can sit a while and enjoy the view. An hour later he is still sitting by himself. Not one car has passed by, and there has been no sign of human life. When another wave of loneliness sweeps over him, he and Sadie get back inside the truck and continue on their way.

He arrives at The Plantation around six in the evening, and after checking in he continues to his RV rental near the dining hall. The place is full of campers with license plates from as far away as Oregon and as nearby as West Virginia. Otis fills Sadie's bowls with food and water and when she's finished, they set out for a walk around the grounds just as they always do.

Soon, he hears music coming from one of the lots. As he draws closer, the strains of old time music float through the air. A few moments later, he comes upon a campsite where people are gathered and playing guitar, mandolin, banjo, fiddle and flute. He and Sadie stop to listen, and before long Otis is tapping his foot in time with the music. He thinks about going back to his RV to get his fiddle, but it's been a long day and he's tired. Maybe tomorrow night if they're playing again.

In the morning, Otis sets out early to take in the sights. For the first time in his life, he goes horseback riding with four other tourists at the Mount Rogers National Recreation Area. The guide takes them on a path through a dense forest dotted with pretty lakes in several clearings, and the group stops every ten minutes to admire the exquisite scenery. When they finish at noon, the guide turns them around and everyone heads back to where they are staying.

Otis thinks this is a place he could call home. And if not home, a place he could return to again and again and not grow tired of it.

Chapter Twenty-Nine

The next day, Otis drives slowly through downtown Damascus and parks in a public lot. Sadie is sitting beside him.

"Let's go have a look around," he says to the dog, taking note that the shopping district is on Main Street not far away. Otis exits the truck and moves aside for Sadie to jump down. With leash in hand, he turns right at the first corner where, just ahead, is a barber shop. The pole out front is twirling its bright red, white and blue stripes. He realizes for the first time since his departure that he must look scruffy. He sees a "Pets Welcome" sign in the window and goes inside.

A barber is just finishing up a customer's haircut, and no one else is there so Otis takes a seat and waits. Sadie finds a sunny spot by the front window and plunks herself down. The barber turns to Otis and tells him he won't be long and invites him to help himself to coffee at the rear of the shop. He picks up a *Field & Stream* and thumbs through the magazine's pages while he waits.

The barber and his customer return to their conversation about a car crash that took place several years ago during the Hiker Parade. Otis tunes in.

"Such a shame," says the customer. "So many good people hurt. Things will never be the same."

"You got that right," says the barber. "You just never know what's around the next corner."

The customer says he agrees, and for a moment they are quiet. Then, the customer starts up again.

"What do you think? Will there be a lot of people at the Parade?"

"Probably hordes. If the weather holds, that is."

The customer says that his wife was asked by their church to make her famous ginger snaps for the occasion. "A nickel apiece. Can't see how that's going to help the church," he laughs.

"Well, every little bit helps," the barber replies while snipping away. "Even the pennies."

"I reckon."

"There now, you're looking pretty spiffy, if I do say so myself," says the barber. He twirls the chair around so the customer can see the back of his head in a handheld mirror.

"Flo will be real happy to see her old man looking like a young pup again," the customer jokes.

"Hope so. That'll be $7, Don."

"That's what I like about you, Clyde. You keep your prices nice and low. Can't imagine what a haircut would cost over in Fisherville."

"And I appreciate your loyalty. Now, you have a good day and stay out of trouble." Clyde smiles and takes $8 from his customer. He places a single dollar bill inside his tip jar on the shelf in front of the mirror and motions for Otis to sit in his chair. The customer says so long and goes out the door.

Otis soon finds out that Clyde is the only barber for miles around. It's not like the men can go anywhere else for haircuts unless their wives put a bowl on their husbands' heads and take up a pair of scissors. What a mess that would be.

"What can I do for y'all?" Clyde says.

Otis asks him to take a little off the top and clean up the back and around his ears.

"You're not from around here, are you?" Clyde says.

"Must be my accent." He tells Clyde he's from New England.

"That right? What are you doing around these parts?" Clyde picks up his scissors and starts snipping.

Otis tells Clyde about his trip along the Trail but says nothing about his mission, only that so far he's met some interesting people and that a pig roast will be held at The Plantation over the coming weekend. Otis also tells Clyde about the little band of musicians at The Plantation and how fun it will be for him to join in. "I hope they don't mind," he says. "If they don't want me buttin' in, I'll just stick around and listen."

Clyde nods his head and says that folks around Damascus are known for their music and anyone can play along and often do. "Wait till you hear the music coming from the Front Porch tomorrow," he says. "Anyone can join in."

"Can't wait," says Otis. "I heard you talking about a car crash. What happened?"

Clyde tells Otis about the Hiker Parade disaster in 2013 when an elderly driver crashed his Cadillac into a group of pedestrians, leaving many critically injured.

"Not sure what caused the accident," Clyde says, shaking his head. "An old man was driving the Cadillac. He may have had some kind of medical emergency when he plowed right into the middle of the crowd and hit people marching. Bystanders, too."

"That right? No one killed, I hope."

"Thank the Lord, no, but three people had to be rushed to the hospital over in Abingdon. It was an afternoon I'll never forget. Happened just a stone's throw away from this very spot. One person was pinned underneath the old man's car. There was blood everywhere. What a sight."

Otis says he can only imagine, and Clyde goes back to his work.

"What made you pick this area?" Clyde finally asks.

"I heard about the Hiker Parade and didn't want to miss it. My wife died last year. We never did any traveling, and I thought it was high time one of us did. I guess that would be me."

"How're you gettin' around?"

"Truck. Bought a new Ford F-150 last fall. Got a good deal. Planned the trip all winter and left Maine on May 1."

"And you brought your dog with you."

"Got Sadie from a shelter. She's been good company." Otis glances at the dog, still curled up in front of the window.

Clyde finishes cutting Otis's hair and uses a small brush to sweep away the stray hairs around his collar. "There you be. What a handsome dude you are." Otis thinks Clyde must say that to all his customers. Even so, he looks in the mirror and sees what Clyde sees. "Not too bad for an old geezer," he laughs.

"Not bad at all," says Clyde. "And by the way, you're no geezer. The ladies around here will think you're a stud."

Otis smiles into the mirror and is suddenly glad he had his teeth fixed before leaving Hopewell.

"Well, you have yourself a grand time, and stop in if you come this way again. How far you going, by the way—if you don't mind my asking?" Clyde says.

"To the end of the Trail—Springer Mountain. In Georgia."

"That right. Sounds like the adventure of a lifetime."

"You have no idea."

"I'll bet."

Otis pushes a $100 bill in Clyde's hand and tells him to keep the change. When he starts for the door, he hears Clyde gasp. The barber starts to tell Otis he overpaid him, but Otis cuts him off. "That was no mistake," he says, smiling. Never in his life did he think that being generous could be so much fun.

Outside the barber shop, something sweet is permeating the air. Otis looks for the source and discovers honeysuckle climbing a nearby fence.

As he walks along with Sadie, he breathes in the cool, refreshing mountain air, not unlike the air back home. He has avoided stopping in big cities except for Washington, D.C. and knows he would never want to live in a big place like that.

Chapter Thirty

People in Damascus like dogs, he has noticed, and not one of them has been on a leash. They just seem to wander around on their own. A sweet little beagle eyes Sadie as they wait to cross the street. The beagle lets out a little yip and, in response, Sadie sniffs at him and wags her tail. Shop owners, Otis also notices, are outside sweeping their sidewalks, likely in preparation for the parade.

Up ahead is an unoccupied park bench, a good place to sit and watch the world go by—or at least a small piece of it. For a little town, there are quite a few people out and about.

While seated on the bench, Sadie at his feet, he watches an old man crossing the street. In his right hand is a cane; in his left, a shopping bag. Otis wonders what's in the bag. Maybe a quart of milk or tub of ice cream. Or maybe a bottle of Jack Daniel's. You never could tell about people. Some of the most innocent looking ones were the worst sinners. Thinking this reminds Otis that he's no saint, either, and hasn't been to church in a long while. Right in downtown Damascus there's a Presbyterian church, but he would rather go to a Baptist service so he can tell Pastor Wright and Colleen about it when he gets back to Hopewell. Maybe there's a church that has a Gospel choir. He'd love to go to a service where people are speaking in tongues, waving their hands in the air and fainting in the aisles after being slain in the Spirit.

For a time, Otis sits alone and studies his hands. It is now the third week in May, but it seems like only yesterday that he left Hopewell.

His thoughts turn to Fern. He is still wearing the ring she put on his finger the day they were married. Their wedding had been a simple affair held at the Baptist church in Aurora where his mother had taken him and his brother when they were children. They had invited family and a few close friends, and after their "I do's" everyone headed to fellowship hall for coffee, tea, cookies and little triangle sandwiches with the crusts cut off. There was also the cake his mother made for the occasion—a white cake with pink frosting to match the color of Fern's dress. She had made it herself and wore it with a pair of pumps she bought on sale at The Shoe Box in downtown Bangor. Practical to the core, Fern had worn the dress for special occasions throughout the years. She had told Otis that the classic look would never go out of style, and she was right. In fact, Fern was buried in the dress she wore on their wedding day. She had taken pride in the fact that she had not gained weight over the years and, until the time of her illness, had kept her youthful figure. Then, as cancer took over her body, she lost so much weight that she was nothing more than skin and bones when she died.

While contemplating his life with Fern, loneliness begins to creep in again like an uninvited guest. Otis sighs. He wonders if he will always feel this way. Missing Fern. Missing the way things were between them before she got sick. He regrets that he had never planned a trip like this to entice her. He should have put his foot down. Should have refused to take no for an answer. Fern had missed out on so much. What kind of man was he, anyway? Why had he allowed Fern to rule the roost? He knows why. Because he loved her. But why had he not insisted that she seek the opinion of doctors in Boston or even Portland? Why did she have to die?

Otis's train of thought now leads him to think about The Vault. From where he is sitting, he can see the F-150 parked in the lot where he left it and can imagine the money hiding there in secret. He's hardly put a dent in the more than $4 million he found in that ditch back home.

He now knows what it feels like to have millions of dollars in his hands, and he knows the power of that money. He can have anything his heart desires. Anything at all. Except for Fern. No amount of money will ever bring her back. She is gone, and he will never again see her in this life. His faith reassures him he will see her in the next life, but how does anyone know if heaven is a real place? No one—except maybe for those who claim to have gone through a near-death experience. For all he knows, people who say they saw the light of Jesus at the end of a long tunnel might not be telling the truth. Or, maybe some kind of brain activity at the end of life causes dying people to hallucinate. Otis has no idea if there is an afterlife. He hopes there is, but where is the guarantee? He had asked Pastor Wright about it one time, and even he could not say for certain that life would continue after death, though he was 99.9 percent sure that it would.

The more Otis thinks about this, the more gripped he is by sorrow. He needs to get outside of himself. He needs to perk up and get back to living. He had thought that giving money to strangers in need would lift his spirits and in a sense it has, but he is still a long way from feeling any kind of peace and happiness. Soon after Fern's death, Pastor Wright had suggested that Otis join a group for grieving widows and widowers, but he didn't want to do that. Maybe he should have. Maybe he will when he gets home.

He looks toward the sky and sees that the sun is now covered over by dark clouds. He hopes there's no rain in the weather forecast. Bad weather would put a damper on the parade. He smiles when he realizes he just came up with a pun.

People seem to be revved up about the parade, and signs are everywhere announcing the town's signature event. There's even a banner hanging across the middle of downtown encouraging everyone to come. Otis plans to stay in Damascus for at least the weekend, but he thinks he will move on to his next destination early next week. He hasn't met anyone in serious financial need, but that could change at any moment. Fern had been a great one for telling him that change is only a heartbeat away. And he has come to believe it himself. There was the time, for instance, when he lost his part-time job pumping gas when he and Fern were first married. The job loss had discouraged him, made him think he was worthless. But then there was Fern, telling him that something better would come along, and it had. Not long after, a job opened up at the paper mill and he had worked there for most of his life. And then, of course, there was the fact that he had gone out for a walk to clear his head and had come upon all that money, more than he would ever need, more than he could ever spend. He knows now that money will never make him happy. What will? To share his life with someone else? Maybe, but that someone else will never be Fern.

Otis stands up and looks around. He feels a raindrop fall on his forehead, then another on his hand.

"Come on, Sadie," he says. "I think rain is coming."

Back inside the truck, Otis considers his options. Take a drive? Go shopping? Find a book store?

He sighs. Not having a plan for the day depresses him. All of a sudden he feels homesick. He has all the money in the world to put himself up in a fancy hotel, but the little bungalow back in Hopewell is where he feels most at home. And he misses it. He wonders if he should call it quits and head home. He could always put the money back in the ditch where he found it. He still has the duffel bags. Sooner or later, someone would find them and turn the money over to the police. Or keep it. That's what he should have done in the first place, he now realizes. Turn in the money. What was he thinking, buying such an expensive truck and going on the road to play Robin Hood? While he sits there feeling sorry for himself, the sun breaks through the clouds. Maybe it's a sign.

Otis gives Sadie a little scratch on the head. "Let's go find a waterfall. There must be one around here somewhere."

Chapter Thirty-One

A gas station attendant tells Otis that Gentry Creek Falls is a forty-five-minute drive from Damascus. To get there, he'll cross the state line into Tennessee and travel south on Route 91 before the road takes a turn north. When he gets to the falls, he'll park in the lot and walk the trail with Sadie.

The sky is now clear, and Otis finds the cool mountain air invigorating as he drives along with the windows open. The region's flora is a beautiful mix of Virginia bluebell, spiderwort and snowdrops along with various ferns, bracken, black and yellow birch, white pine and hemlock. As he continues along the road, he notices a river running along the side.

Otis stops the truck and he and Sadie make their way through the grassy embankment to water's edge. He takes off his shoes and socks and rolls up his pants before stepping into the icy, crystalline water. He then bends down, scoops water into his hands and drinks. He and Sadie stand there listening to the water tumble over rocks and to Otis it sounds like its own kind of music. He looks around and sees that he's alone, so he strips off all his clothes and wades into deeper water, taking Sadie with him. When he emerges, he lies on the grassy embankment and idly picks leaves off a winding vine. The sun dries him in no time, and soon Otis and Sadie are back on the road. They continue to the twin waterfalls and Otis is struck with wonder when he sees that they are sixty feet high. He sits on a bench with Sadie at his feet and moves over when a man with a camera hanging from his neck approaches. The man gives Otis a friendly nod.

"Pretty nice, isn't it?" he says.

"Sure is," Otis replies.

The two men sit in silence for a while, then Otis asks him where he's from.

"Canada. My wife's back at the hotel having a spa treatment."

"Which province?"

"New Brunswick. A town near Moncton."

"Thought so. I can hear it in your voice."

The man asks about Otis, and he tells him about being from Maine and that he's staying at a campground in Damascus.

"We're staying in Damascus, too. The Old Mill Inn. Beautiful place. We're celebrating our fortieth anniversary."

"Happy anniversary," says Otis.

"You traveling with anyone?"

"Just me and Sadie here. My wife died last year. Decided it was time for a change of scenery. And here I am."

"Sorry to hear. Must be tough."

"It is. More than you know."

"Well, best be getting back to the hotel. Don't want to worry my wife."

"Understandable. You have a good trip. Name's Otis, by the way."

"Phil."

The two men shake hands.

"Going to the parade tomorrow?" Otis asks.

"Wouldn't miss it."

"Might see you there."

"Maybe. Have a good day."

A few minutes later, Otis drives back to The Plantation feeling uplifted by the magnificence of the scenery he has seen and his brief encounter with Phil. Maybe he'll run into him and his wife at the parade tomorrow.

~~>>>>>   <<<<<~~

Later that night, Otis is roused out of sleep by a constant itch. He has been scratching in his sleep, and when he turns on the light next to the bed, he sees why. Both of his hands and forearms are covered with a rash. He knows right away what it is. Poison ivy. The itch is driving him insane, and the more he scratches, the worse it gets. About the only thing he didn't pack for the trip is calamine lotion.

Otis fills the sink with water and immerses his hands and arms to the elbow. He washes with soap and water but that doesn't help much. He opens his first aid kit to see what's in there, hoping he'll find some kind of lotion. There are Band-Aids, bacitracin, aspirin, tweezers, alcohol wipes, an ice pack, Q-tips and a few other odds and ends but nothing that will help the itch. While he's looking at his hands, his entire back starts to itch, too, and he realizes he never should have laid in that grass on the embankment.

Otis knows he needs medical attention, but where can he get it at this hour of the night? He opens his computer, goes to Google and types HOSPITALS DAMASCUS VIRGINIA. He waits a moment and then a site for Johnston Memorial Hospital in Abingdon pops up. A twenty-minute drive from The Plantation. He looks at the time. Twenty minutes past midnight. Maybe the emergency room will be empty.

＞＞＞＞ ＜＜＜＜

When Otis and Sadie get into the truck, he enters the hospital's address into the navigation system and off they go. As he drives along in the dark, the itching intensifies.

After arriving at the hospital, he follows a sign that points the way to the emergency room at the rear of the building. He parks the truck, lowers the passenger side window enough so Sadie will have fresh air, locks the doors and hurries to the entrance. Once inside, he sees a reception desk straight ahead and a doctor in scrubs talking to a woman sitting in front of a computer. Both turn to Otis when he reaches the desk.

"I've got a big problem, and I hope you can help me," Otis says, showing the doctor his hands and arms.

"Looks like you had a run-in with poison ivy," the doctor says.

After Otis gives the receptionist his name and date of birth, she places a plastic band around his wrist. "Do you have insurance?" she asks.

"Self-insured," he says, adding that he'll pay the bill on the way out.

"Okay. Follow Dr. Maxwell," she says. "He'll take good care of you.

The doctor leads Otis to a cubicle and asks him to sit on the medical bed. After he draws the curtain, Otis tells him about lying in the grass. The doctor puts on Latex gloves and looks at Otis's rash. He confirms that he has a nasty case of poison ivy.

"It's not just my hands and arms," says Otis, pointing to his backside.

Dr. Maxwell takes a look and shakes his head. "That happened to me one time, and I never went near the woods again. Couldn't sit in comfort for more than two weeks."

He tells Otis that nurse Julie Charlton is working that night. "I'll ask her to get you a bottle of calamine lotion and a few Benadryl and I'll order a prescription for a cortisone-based product," he says. "That should take care of it. If you start having problems with your breathing, get back in here right away."

Otis says he will, and Dr. Maxwell leaves the cubicle. Otis then hears the doctor talking to a woman beyond the drawn curtain. A few moments later, the curtain is pulled back and in walks Julie Charlton.

"Otis Kingston?"

He tries to open his mouth to say something but words won't come. Standing there, right in front of him, is a piece of art worthy of Botticelli. Julie Charlton is even prettier than Fern. She has light brown hair that tumbles in waves to her shoulders, blue eyes and a Cupid mouth. Her skin is flawless, and when she smiles he feels like he's in the presence of an angel.

She repeats his name, and he nods his head. "Yes, Otis Kingston," he croaks.

"Yes, I see that in Dr. Maxwell's notes. He tells me you had a collision with poison ivy. Mind if I have a look?"

Otis stretches out his arms so she can examine the rash. "It's starting to blister," she says while looking at it closely. "Would you mind if I put calamine lotion on the affected areas?"

Would he mind? Absolutely not. In fact, she can rub it on all night if she wants to. When he finds his voice again, he asks for her name. Anything to start a conversation with this woman.

"Julie Charlton," she says. "See here? It's on my pin."

"Oh, yes, now I see. I like that name. Julie. What does LPN mean?" he asks, as if he doesn't know.

"Licensed practical nurse. One step away from being a registered nurse. Where are you from, Otis?"

"Maine. I've been traveling. Staying a few nights at The Plantation in Damascus."

"I know the place. Good people own it."

"You know them?"

"Oh, yes. Jacob Fanning. He's the owner. Nice family, the Fannings are."

Otis has to think of a way to see her again. The parade. Maybe she plans to be there.

"The Hiker Parade is tomorrow," he says. "Will you be going?"

"So you heard about it. Wouldn't miss it. Are you?"

"Wouldn't miss it, either. I hear it's the event of the year."

"It sure is. An entire day of fun."

"I heard about the accident."

Julie's facial expression changes when Otis mentions it. "Ouch," he says. "I'm sorry I brought it up."

"It's okay. I just have terrible memories of that day. I had to work, and many of the injured people came through our emergency room. I'm afraid I was traumatized by what I saw."

Otis likes Julie Charlton. Not only is she a pleasure to look at, she has a good heart, too. He tries to see if there's anything on her ring finger, but she has on Latex gloves, making it hard to tell.

"Well, I hope something like that never happens again," Otis says.

"I hope not."

Julie moves the curtain aside and tells Otis she will get some calamine lotion, Benadryl and prescription. Otis watches as she walks away. She is limping slightly, but he tells himself the reason is none of his business even though he's curious.

Julie returns a few minutes later, and she spreads calamine lotion over his hands and arms. Even through the gloves, her touch is tantalizing, and he never wants her to stop. When she finishes, she places the lotion and pills inside a plastic bag and hands it to Otis. "Oh . . . I forgot your back . . . would you like me to spread some calamine . . .? That area will be hard to reach."

Otis is mortified. His hands and arms are one thing, but his entire back right down to his near end? "Not to worry," he says. "I'll find a way."

"Okay. Use the lotion twice a day," she says. "That should give you relief. Take cool showers, too. As cool as you can stand. No baths, though. It should quiet down. The tablets will help you sleep and relieve the itch."

"I hope so. I want to be at that parade tomorrow." To himself he says that he wants her to be there, too.

Before Otis leaves the hospital, he asks about charges for services rendered. He then writes a check for twice the amount. The woman seated in the reception area tries to get his attention when she looks at the check, but Otis is already out the door.

Chapter Thirty-Two

Otis feels buoyant the next morning, as if he is floating on a big puffy white cloud, and it has nothing to do with the medications Julie gave him.

He has been thinking about her since he woke up this morning. Even the sound of her name pleases him. He is curious about her and hopes to see her at the parade today.

A river of guilt floods his mind because of Fern and he tries to dismiss the feeling but finds that he cannot. He knows that she would not want him to become trapped in the past because she had died before him. She had told him to continue living after she was gone. Besides, he's getting to the age of . . . what would he call it? Well, he's getting to the age where romance isn't the most important thing in life. But female companionship *is* important to him, and he misses it more than he ever thought possible.

Just as Julie had advised, he has taken two cool showers since returning to The Plantation. He has also checked The Vault to make sure it's still secure. By nine o'clock, he's ready to go to the parade, but instead he sits in his folding chair and lets his mind wander. He thinks of Fern first and starts a one-way conversation with her inside his head. He tells her that he will always love her, that he will never again feel the love he had for her with anyone else. He tells her, too, that he's lonely and needs permission to start living again. As if in response, a little breeze passes through the campground, as if Fern's approval were floating on the air. He thinks about the money stashed away and wonders what Julie's reaction would be if she knew about it. Maybe he'll stick around Damascus for a while and not leave next week after all.

With only a few hours of sleep the night before, he is tired this morning. While sitting there, he closes his eyes, nods off and dreams. Fern is there with him, and she is asking him to help her plant flowers. He uses his hoe to make a nice even row, and she drops seeds into the soil four inches apart. She tells Otis that the flowers she is planting are for him. Something to remember her by, she says. And in the next moment, flowers begin sprouting and they grow taller and taller. Soon, the blossoms are as big as hula hoops. And then the image fades and Otis finds himself inside the Church of the Blinding Light. He is crying and pleading with Pastor Wright to raise Fern from the dead. But the minister only shakes his head sadly. "Nothing can bring her back, Otis. Nothing."

"But Jesus raised Lazarus from the dead. Can't you try?"

"Otis," says Pastor Wright kindly. "I am not God. Only Jesus could do that."

When Otis wakes up a moment later, he realizes he cannot grieve forever. He thinks about Julie again and wonders if she is thinking about him, too. He remembers the compassion in her smile, the lilt in her voice when she spoke his name. He thinks she might be a special kind of person, someone like Fern. The more he thinks about Julie, the more he wants to get to know her and will not leave Damascus until he does. But in the next moment he has second thoughts. People can be deceiving. For all he knows, she might have a mean streak or throw tantrums. She might be a shopaholic. Maybe a two-timer. Who knows what lurks in the heart of Julie Charlton. For all he knows, she might even be married.

Before Otis leaves for the parade, he pops in a *Spanky and Our Gang* CD. Oddly enough, the first cut is *Like to Get to Know You*. He sings along with Lefty Baker's mellow voice and the other members of the band:

"But I'd like to get to know you (yes I would)

"But I'd like to get to know you (if I could)

"But I'd like to get to know you, know you, know . . . you"

He opens Google on his cell phone and on the search line types JULIE CHARLTON DAMASCUS VIRGINIA. Her name pops up, but there is nothing beyond that. No mention of her age or employment. No marital status or information about family members. Nothing. A blank slate.

Around noontime, Otis drives to downtown Damascus. The streets are blocked off from traffic and there are swarms of people milling around. He also notices there are police officers on patrol. While in a line of traffic, he looks to his left and spots Julie coming around a corner. She is with a woman about her age and is carrying what looks like a musical instrument case. They are also lugging folding chairs. He watches while they set up right in front of Clyde's barber shop. His heart is doing cartwheels.

Otis pulls into a public parking lot and exits the truck. "Come on, Sadie. Let's go say hello to the ladies."

After locking up and checking The Vault, he takes his chair from the bed and gives his keys a toss in the air before putting them in his pocket. That cloud he's been walking on is becoming softer and softer. As he draws closer to Julie and her companion, she sees him approaching. Otis gives a little wave and she waves back.

"Hello, there. Are you feeling better?" she says when he's standing in front of her. "How's the calamine lotion working?"

"Much better. I don't know how to thank you."

Julie turns to her friend and explains that she met Otis the night before in the emergency room. She then introduces Otis to Carolyn Baxter.

"Had an encounter with poison ivy yesterday," Otis tells Carolyn. He shows her his hands and arms to confirm what happened while at the river's edge. "Your friend here helped me out. Sadie, say hello to Julie and Carolyn." The dog shakes her head and looks up at Otis.

When Julie invites Otis to join them, he doesn't hesitate. After unfolding his chair and filling Sadie's water bowl, he and the two women talk about the parade and entertainment planned for the afternoon. He eyes the wooden case at Julie's feet. Judging from the shape and size, he guesses a mandolin might be inside. He waits for the right time and then asks.

"Mind if I ask what's in the case, Julie?"

"My mandolin. I'll be playing on the porch later."

"Porch?"

"Oh, you probably don't know. 'Pickin 'n Grinnin' on the Front Porch' is a really fun music event. Anyone who plays an instrument can join in. In the past, we've had about ten people on that porch all at one time." Julie points to a packed area down the street where people are sitting in front of a house with a farmer's porch.

"Bluegrass?"

"Oh, yeah. All the oldies but goodies."

"How about you, Carolyn? Do you play, too?"

"My hands. I clap," she laughs. "Never miss a beat."

Otis wants to tell Julie about his fiddle but holds off. While she's playing with the others, he'll go back to his truck, get his fiddle and surprise her when he steps onto the porch.

"Big crowd today," Otis says, sweeping his eyes across the town.

"There'll probably be more coming. It's early yet." Julie pauses, then asks about Sadie.

"Best dog ever," Otis says.

"You sure are a pretty girl," she says, ruffling the dog's fur.

And to himself, Otis says, "So are you, Julie Charlton." He tells her about the rescue center in Bangor and that it was as if he and Sadie were meant to be.

"Just you and the dog?" Julie asks.

Otis nods, then tells her about Fern's death and his interest in exploring the Appalachian Trail. "Springer Mountain will be my final stop."

"When my husband died nine years ago, I took a trip to Mexico to clear my head," says Carolyn in a southern drawl. "Thought I could get over it easier if I wasn't home, but it turned out that the geographical cure wasn't any cure at all. Time is what heals."

Julie nods her head in agreement, as if she can relate.

"Are you a widow, too, Julie?"

"No," she says. "I never married. I guess I've been married to my job."

"Hmm," Otis says, wondering whether she really means it. Maybe she likes things the way they are.

Otis says no more, and neither does Julie. Seconds later, there's a rumble of drums from the opposite end of the street. The parade is about to start any minute. When it's over, he'll offer to buy Julie and Carolyn lunch. On his way downtown, he had seen signs for fried chicken and black-eyed peas, burgers and fries, country ham, biscuits, Brunswick stew, BBQ, huckleberry and chess pie and a whole lot more.

Otis's stomach growls when he remembers that hours have gone by since breakfast. His heart is hungry, too. Hungry for love.

Chapter Thirty-Three

Otis runs his eyes over the people gathered in downtown Damascus. Hundreds of men and women, boys and girls, young couples holding hands, babies in strollers, teenagers and old people are making their way through the crowd. He tries to picture what it must have been like on the day of the accident. So many people injured. He wonders if any of them are here today. Maybe they're still too traumatized to attend.

While Julie and Carolyn are talking, Otis chimes in when there's a break in the conversation. He starts with Carolyn.

"Are you a nurse, too?" he asks her, assuming she has a job.

"No. I work at the library. Started as a part-timer in high school. After graduation, I went full time. I love being around books."

"I do, too. Books, magazines, cereal box labels," Julie says with a little laugh. "I'll read just about anything."

"Any book recommendations?" Otis asks.

"I'd have to think about it. What's your favorite? Mysteries? Historical fiction? Non-fiction?"

"All of the above," he says, before being interrupted by the sound of blaring trumpets. No sooner does Otis get his words out than the parade starts with the marching band coming down the street playing John Phillip Sousa's *The Stars and Stripes Forever*. Otis sits up straighter in his chair and cranes his neck to watch. He'll have to wait and ask about books later.

"Such great music," he says loud enough that the women can hear him. "Reminds me of the Fourth of July back home. Bangor puts on a parade every year, and there's always a marching band."

When the song ends with a flourish, Julie asks Otis if he misses his home.

"Not as much as I thought I would," he replies, raising his voice above the applause.

"What do you think of Damascus so far?"

Otis pauses a few seconds and then says, "It's a beautiful little town. I was thinking just the other day that it's the kind of place I wouldn't mind visiting again."

"Well, the world is full of beautiful places," says Julie. "I've never traveled much myself but sure would like to one of these days. Have to save my pennies, though. Being on the go like that must cost a bundle."

"If you plan it the right way, you can go on the cheap pretty much," says Otis. He then tells her about the campgrounds where he has stayed and some of the people he's met.

The marching band starts up again, drowning out any chance for further conversation, and he and the two women, along with hundreds of other people, fall silent as they listen to patriotic songs. When the band starts playing music from the Big Band era, people rise to their feet and start dancing.

Otis surprises himself when he asks Julie if she likes to dance.

"I do. But I can't be up long," she says. "My hip tells me when I need to sit down."

So, there's something wrong with her hip. He wants to ask about it but decides it's not the time or place. Besides, it's none of his business. Fern taught him well.

"Wanna give it a try?" Otis asks.

"Sure. Why not?" Julie says without hesitating.

Before long, he and Julie are swinging their arms and moving their feet in time with the music. Otis can't remember the last time he had so much fun. They return to their chairs when the music ends.

"Ooh, I think I overdid it," says Julie, clearly out of breath.

"You okay?" Otis asks.

"I'll be fine."

"How about you, Carolyn? Do you like to dance?" Otis hopes not. He'd rather dance with Julie.

"I have two left feet," says Carolyn. "You're off the hook. Go ahead, Julie. Dance with Otis."

"Are you up for it, Julie?" Otis then notices the grimace that sweeps across her face.

"I'd like to, but I think I should wait a while."

Carolyn gives Julie a sympathetic look and places her hand on her shoulder, giving it a little squeeze.

"Say, is anyone hungry?" Otis asks after the marching band takes a break.

"I sure am," says Carolyn. "Think I'll get a pulled pork sandwich. Anyone else? My treat."

Otis holds out his hand like a stop sign. "Stay right where you are. I'll do the honors. Now, what would you like with that sandwich?"

In spite of Carolyn's protests, Otis won't take no for an answer. He then looks at Julie. "And you, miss, what would you like? It's my pleasure to treat you both today."

Julie shakes her head, also in protest, but Otis insists. "It's not every day that I come across two lovely ladies. Please. It'll make my day to buy you lunch."

A few minutes later, Otis is moving through the crowd to a food vendor and returns carrying two plastic trays loaded with food and drinks. On the way, he had seen signs for corn hole, board games and a whittling demonstration along with arrows pointing to an area where handcrafted goods are being admired and sold.

Just when they finish eating, Otis hears the Front Porch musicians tuning their instruments. He takes a swig of root beer and thinks about his fiddle locked inside the truck.

"That's my cue," says Julie. "See you a little later." She picks up her mandolin and goes off to join the other musicians.

Otis gives Sadie a pat on the head and asks Carolyn to keep an eye on her. He tells her he needs something from his truck and will be right back. While getting his fiddle, he'll check on The Vault and apply more calamine lotion to his hands, arms and rear end.

By the time he returns, five people have gathered on the Front Porch. Carolyn looks at him with a question on her face.

"Got my fiddle," he says, holding it up. "Do you mind watching Sadie for a while?"

"Not at all. Go on ahead. Julie sure will be surprised. I certainly am."

As soon as Otis gets to the Front Porch, he is surprised to see Clyde the barber wearing denim overalls and holding a guitar. A young man wearing a "Gospel Truth" T-shirt has a banjo. There's a woman wearing a pink flowered dirndl skirt. She has a squeezebox. A teenage boy wearing jeans with holes in the knees has a harmonica. And Julie? She's wearing a flowery sundress with a full skirt. While she was dancing with Otis, the skirt would flare out, and he got a good glimpse of her shapely legs. Now she's up there on the Front Porch tuning her mandolin. Otis's fiddle will round out the group nicely. A look of surprise crosses Julie's face when she sees Otis standing there with a fiddle tucked under his arm.

"Otis, you're a dark horse," she calls out to him. "Who taught you?"

"Self-taught. Started when I was a boy."

The five musicians and Otis ready their instruments and soon are playing a full force rendition of *Blackberry Blossom,* an old bluegrass piece, one of the first Otis taught himself. The crowd quiets as the music continues, and they switch over to *Cripple Creek.* Soon, a couple in their twenties get up to dance, and that gives way to more people getting onto their feet. There's a chorus of voices singing along, too.

For the next half hour, the musicians play on. Then, the man in denim overalls puts up his hand. "Time for a little break," he says. "Back in ten minutes."

Julie turns to Otis. "You play really well."

"Well, I love bluegrass. In fact, I love *all* music," he replies while thinking they'd make beautiful music together.

When Clyde returns to the porch, the group resumes playing. Otis watches Julie when she plays a solo. She is not only a pretty woman but a talented one, too. He thinks that before the end of the day, he'll ask her to show him around the Blue Ridge Mountains.

When the Front Porch musicians take a longer break, Otis and Julie go back to their chairs. As soon as he has an opening, he'll ask if one of them will go for a drive with him. He hopes Julie will offer.

"I could use a tour guide," he says casually when there's a lull in conversation. "Which one of you would like to show me around this beautiful part of the country? I promise I'm not an axe murderer."

For a long moment, there is silence. Then Julie speaks. "I have Monday off. If you'd like, I could show you some real pretty places."

Otis's heart does a little flip. "How about a picnic?" he hears himself say.

"That would be right nice, Otis."

"What would you like to eat?"

"I'm not fussy. I like just about everything."

"Would ten o'clock be too early?"

"How about meeting for coffee at nine? I could map out a route when I get home later."

If she had suggested they go sky-diving over the ocean, he would not have hesitated.

"Sure. Where should we meet?"

They settle on Zazzy's, a small café in downtown Damascus across the street from Clyde's barber shop.

Chapter Thirty-Four

On Monday morning over coffee and sticky buns, Otis and Julie go over the route they'll take and where they'll stop for lunch.

When they're ready to leave, Julie buys cupcakes, and Otis settles the rest of the bill with the cashier.

"For dessert," she says, holding up a cardboard box tied with string.

Around noontime, Otis pulls into a rest area off the Blue Ridge Parkway. At Food City, he bought chicken salad, sandwich rolls, pickles, chips and orange and grape drinks. He pulls two folding chairs from the truck's bed, opens them up and puts Sadie on her leash. Otis has a special treat for the dog.

While they eat, Julie tells him about her week at work and a funny story about a shopping trip to a strip mall near Damascus. In turn, Otis tells her about jamming at the campground and a few stories about people he's met on the Trail. Their conversation is light and easy, and he is thinking he doesn't want the day to end.

When Julie rises from her chair to stretch, he sees her wince.

He feels so easy with her that he dares to ask about her obvious discomfort.

"Is it arthritis? In your hip, I mean."

"I wish it were that simple."

"If it's not arthritis, what is it?" Otis makes sure his tone is compassionate.

"It's a long story. I don't want to bore you."

"You won't bore me. Promise."

A silence follows, then she says, "Before I started my job at the hospital, I worked somewhere else."

"Oh? Where?"

"In a doctor's office."

"In Damascus?"

"Abingdon."

"I worked for Dr. Davis for nine years and loved my job. He was kind-hearted and treated his patients as if they were family. He was never in it for the money so he operated on a bare bones budget. I didn't have health insurance and couldn't afford to pay for it on my own, so I took my chances."

Otis takes a sip of his drink and waits for her to continue.

"I was taking sharps out of a container one day and accidentally stuck myself. I didn't think much about it at the time, but a few months later I came home from work so tired that I went straight to bed. As the days passed, I noticed I had no appetite. Then I started having fevers off and on." Julie pauses before continuing. "I remembered the incident with that hypodermic needle but was afraid to be tested . . . afraid of the results."

Otis glances at Julie. "The results?"

"I was afraid that I had picked up a serious illness."

Otis fears that she will tell him she has AIDS.

"But eventually you were tested?"

"Yes. And the news wasn't good."

Otis says nothing in response. He looks out to the mountains and sees the majestic scene before him. He wonders how the lovely woman sitting next to him could be sick when there is so much beauty in front of him. He wants to know what's wrong, but a big part of him doesn't. He likes Julie a little too much, and truth to tell he has wondered what it would be like to start over with a new woman. Someone like Julie. Soon, the one-year mark of Fern's death would be here. Otis reflects on their marriage now. It had not been perfect, but it had been loving. They rarely argued, and they never held grudges. They never went to bed angry, either. Their differences were always resolved before they went to sleep. Otis fears he would never be able to replace Fern, but then again why would he want to? He thinks about this for a moment before finally admitting to himself that he does not want to spend the rest of his life alone.

He hears Julie's voice. "Earth to Otis. You've been a thousand miles away. I told you my story would be boring."

"No . . . no. It wasn't. I was just thinking about what it must have been like for you, waiting for test results."

"I kind of knew. The symptoms were classic. But being in denial was so comfortable. I didn't want to face it."

"Can you tell me what it was?"

"You don't want to know."

Well, maybe he doesn't. Maybe he's better off not knowing anything more about Julie Charlton. But there's something about her that has captured his interest, something he just cannot resist.

"My body harbors a virus," says Julie. "When I stuck myself with that hypodermic needle, it had been used on someone who also had it."

"So you have a virus," Otis says. "You'll get over it, right?"

"No. Not this one. Once it's in your system, you have it for life."

"What kind of virus, then?"

Julie hesitates before answering. "Believe it or not, the only person I have ever told is Carolyn. And my doctor knows, of course."

"Why me?"

"I don't know, Otis. Maybe it's because you're passing through and will be gone soon. I feel safe talking to you."

"And what if I decide not to leave?"

"You mean, what if you decide to stay in Damascus?"

"Exactly."

"Then I probably wouldn't talk about it."

"I have a big zipper on my mouth." He smiles at her, and says, "Honest. I'm good at keeping things to myself."

Julie pauses for a moment and looks out toward the mountains.

"Hepatitis C," she says.

"Hepatitis C? What is it? Is there a cure?"

"It's a virus, like I said, and it affects everyone in different ways," Julia explains. "Some people have vomiting. Some have fatigue. Jaundice. Fevers. I have joint pain. And sometimes fatigue. It also affects the liver."

Otis looks at Julie and says warmly, "I'm sorry to hear that."

"I've lived with it for a few years now, so I'm used to it. No need to be sorry."

"What about a cure?"

"A cure." Julie sighs deeply. "There's a vaccine, but it comes with a huge price tag."

"How huge?"

"About $84,000. A pill every day for three months. That's the cure."

"Wow."

"It's all okay, Otis. Hep C is something a lot of people live with. It's not that much different from being diabetic except for the way it affects you."

"But the doctor you were working for . . . you got the virus in his office. Wouldn't he be liable?"

"Dr. Davis? I never told him what happened. He was about to retire, and the last thing I wanted was for him to worry about my health," Julie says. "He and his wife had planned a vacation to Hawaii, and I didn't want to spoil it for him. They'd both worked so hard all their lives. Besides, it wasn't his fault I stuck myself with a needle." She pauses, then continues. "Even if I did let him in on my secret, it wouldn't have done any good. He and his wife came home from Hawaii in mid-February, and he died three weeks later."

"Oh, no," says Otis. Once again, he is reminded how unfair life can be.

"I didn't have any health coverage, so there wasn't even an insurance company I could call, and that kind of money doesn't grow on trees."

Otis considers what Julie has just said. "No, it doesn't grow on trees. But what if it did?"

"If it did, I still wouldn't spend it on a cure."

"How come?"

"I just wouldn't."

"But . . ."

"It's one of those long stories, Otis."

"Okay. I understand." He pauses then says, "How would you like to go on a picnic next Sunday?"

"Sure, if you're inviting me. I'd love that? What would you like me to bring?"

"Nothing," he says, then adds, "just your sweet self."

Julie lowers her head. "You're a kind man, Otis. How about some dessert? Those cupcakes I bought look awfully good."

Otis loves cupcakes as much as he loves turkey dinners. "Sure," he says. "I'll never refuse something sweet." He winks at Julie.

Chapter Thirty-Five

A few weeks later, Otis and Julie are having supper at The Plantation, and they are talking about what life was like when they were young. Julie tells Otis that her father was a coal miner and that he nearly lost his life twice while down in the mines.

"Daddy died of black lung," she says. "About six months later, my momma went into sudden cardiac arrest. I think she died of a broken heart. I have no family left and get by with a little help from my friends, as the song goes."

"You've never mentioned sisters or brothers. Do you have any?" Otis asks.

Julie reaches for her napkin and says, "I had a sister. She was three years younger."

"Does she live in Damascus?"

"No. She passed away."

"I'm sorry to hear."

"Me, too."

"Would you mind if I ask what happened to her?"

"It's something I don't like to talk about—the memory of her death still causes me a lot of pain—but I'll tell you."

Otis takes a sip of his drink and waits for the story to unfold.

"When Corinne died, I was five. She was two. She was such a pretty baby. She had curly dark hair, big brown eyes and a dimple in her right cheek. The face of an angel, you might say. There was a bureau in the corner of the bedroom we shared. One of her toys was on top of the bureau, and I pulled a chair over so I could get it for her." Julie pauses and lets out a deep sigh. Then comes a catch in her voice. "I couldn't reach it so I tried harder, but the bureau toppled under my weight and landed on top of Corinne. It crushed her."

Otis sits there still as a statue. He has no idea what to say other than that he is truly sorry.

"Momma heard the crash and came running. Daddy was at work, so he couldn't help. I just remember her sobbing and yelling at me. She called me careless and stupid and accused me of killing Corinne."

Otis puts his hand on top of hers. "Julie, that was shock talking," he says.

"I know that now, but at the time the impact on my child's heart was devastating. For years, I believed what my mother said—that I killed my baby sister. And this is why I would never want to cure my illness. It's my punishment for causing my sister's death. I don't deserve to be cured."

"You were a little girl when that happened. You were trying to make your sister happy."

"I know. But I took it to heart and believed my mother. I've never been able to get past that. I'll carry guilt to my grave."

Otis says nothing more because there is nothing left to say. At least for now. He places his arm around her shoulder and pulls her close. They sit for a long time without speaking.

"And that's pretty much the story of my life," says Julie. "I never married and live simply. I took Corinne's life from her so why should I have one of my own? And I took up nursing because I wanted to help people."

Rather than argue with Julie, Otis continues to remain silent. He will have to figure out a way to convince her that her sister's death was not her fault. Both of them need to start living again. They each deserve at least a little happiness.

⇝⇝⇝ ⇜⇜⇜

May has turned into June and then July and now it is the end of August. So far, the summer has been hot and humid. Otis is still at The Plantation and doesn't want to leave. He is seeing Julie whenever he can, and their relationship has blossomed into a romance. Now Otis is unsure about what to do next. Continue his trip along the Trail, stay in Damascus or go home? It's not that he's less interested in his mission but more that he doesn't want to leave Julie behind.

Since the end of May, they've cooked dinners for each other, celebrated the Fourth of July together, cycled along the Creeper Trail, cooled off in swimming holes and gone to the movies. They've also attended services at Julie's church, and she has introduced him to a few of her friends.

Otis has also told her several times that he has the money to cure her of Hepatitis C, but one night she tells him she wants to end any further discussion, that she doesn't want to be cured and that she would never accept his money, even if he had $1 million.

"What if I told you I have more than $3 million?" he asks. Julie hesitates before answering.

"Otis, you know how I feel about you, but I just can't. I wouldn't feel right. For one thing, there's poor little Corinne and, second, I could never pay you back. And $3 million? Come on. Do you really expect me to believe you're that wealthy?"

"What if I told you I am that wealthy and wouldn't want to be paid back?" he says.

"Otis, money or no money, for now I have to close the subject."

For now? That gives Otis hope. Maybe she will change her mind. He doesn't mind waiting. Julie is worth waiting a lifetime for.

One Sunday when Julie and Carolyn take in a movie and supper in Abingdon, Otis has a chance to spend some time alone. Early in the morning he goes to a gospel service at Soul's Harbor near downtown Damascus. The town has become so familiar to him it feels like a second home. As he wanders along Main Street after the service, he wonders if it should be his first home. Maybe he should sell the bungalow in Maine and buy a place here. And then what? His feelings for Julie run deep and the truth is he has fallen in love with her. He thinks she feels the same way. He also thinks they could have a future together.

In mid-afternoon, he rents a small outboard motor boat and takes it for a ride around Lake Laurel. The marina's captain tells him there's a place to swim on the other side of the lake where the water isn't deep, a perfect place for Otis and Sadie to cool off. It's a restful place, a good place to think about what he should do. Ask Julie if she would reconsider his offer to pay for the Hepatitis C cure? Just enjoy her company for now? Invite her to join him on the Trail? He'll call Julie tonight to ask about her day with Carolyn. He'll invite her to have supper at the campground next weekend and go to the music jam after they eat. He'll try to see her during the week, too.

Before Otis calls Julie, he checks in with Lloyd MacNeill at Whispering Pines. He wants to ask how his friend is doing, but he also wants to find out if Lloyd knows anything about what John Penewait has been up to.

Lloyd is happy to hear from Otis and tells him things are going well at the campground. He then asks Otis about his trip, and after Otis fills him in, there's a lull in the conversation before Lloyd says, "By the way, you'll never guess, Otis. I saw John Penewait at the grocery store last week. He's gone back to school so he can finish his last year of college."

"No kidding! Good for him!" says Otis.

"The thing is, no one knows where he got the money."

"Loans, maybe?" says Otis.

"Huh. Don't know. Something else odd happened after you left," says Lloyd.

"What's that?"

"Someone sent me a new coffeemaker for the dining hall. Makes a hundred cups at a time. And that's not all. Got a big popcorn machine, too."

"Well, it sounds like good things are happening in Rangeley."

A long moment follows before Lloyd says, "Did you have anything to do with this, Otis? Did you pay for John's education, and did you buy these things for me?"

"Why would you think that?" Otis replies. "I'm not made of money."

"Well, you sure seemed interested in John when you were here. Just seems strange. First he goes back to school, and then I get a new coffeemaker. You told me I needed a new one. Remember? And then there's the popcorn machine."

"No harm in showing a bit of interest in John. I just wanted to meet him and take pictures of his family. For my photo album. And it wasn't me who bought you those things."

"Ay-uh."

"Sounds like you don't believe me."

"Well, something else peculiar happened," Lloyd says.

"What?"

"Two painters showed up and said they'd been hired to paint the guard shack and dining hall. When I asked who hired them, they said they didn't know, only that they'd been paid well to do the job and they also had all the paint and brushes and drop cloths. Who would have hired them and paid for the job?"

"Maybe Santa Claus?" Otis says, joking.

"Yeah, or maybe the tooth fairy," replies Lloyd. He pauses, then says, "Come on, Otis. Do you know anything about this?"

"The tooth fairy? Got a penny apiece for every tooth I lost when I was a kid," he laughs.

"I'm serious," says Lloyd. "Who would have sent me a coffeemaker and popcorn machine and arranged for a painter? And where did John get the money for school?"

"Well, someone must like you a lot, Lloyd. Maybe a woman's got her eye on you—and John, too."

"Ha! Unlikely. Haven't looked at a woman in years. I'm seventy-eight, you know."

"Didn't know. But why should that stop you?"

"Well, a fella . . . oh, Otis, I don't have to spell it out for you, do I? I'm not gonna start takin' those pills."

Otis gives a little chuckle, says nothing else, and the two men spend the rest of their conversation talking about the campers who've stayed at Whispering Pines since Otis left.

"Having a good season so far," says Lloyd. "Hope it keeps up. And have you met any other interesting people?"

"A few," says Otis. His thoughts turn to Edith Kulp and Julie.

"On my way back to Maine, I'll stop in to see you and stay a few days. I wanna try out that new coffeemaker."

"That'd be grand," says Lloyd. "Just grand."

They end the call when a new camper arrives at the guard shack. "Gotta run. See you on your way back north," Lloyd says.

Otis promises that he will.

Chapter Thirty-Six

After he ends his call with Lloyd, he calls Twin Hills and talks to Roxie, Duncan Purdy Williams's daughter.

"Good to hear from you, Mr. Kingston. How's your trip going?" she says.

"Great. Couldn't be better. And how are you?"

"I'm good. You'll never guess what happened."

"What's that?"

"Someone bought me an electric bike."

"Really? Who?"

"I don't know, but I love it. I go all over the place on it. I don't know who to thank."

"Well, just be careful and don't fall off."

"I won't. The strangest thing is, I've wanted one for a couple of years."

"Maybe a gift from someone?"

"Don't know, but I'm having a blast."

Otis smiles. He would have loved driving around on an electric bike when he was Roxie's age. Now that he knows it arrived safely from Amazon, he smiles to himself and tells her he's glad to hear she's having fun.

His final call is to Julie to ask if she had a good time with Carolyn. She tells him they had seen the movie *Whiplash*, a story about a young student drummer and his perfectionist, abusive professor and that they had supper at Alfonso's.

"Spaghetti and meatballs?" says Otis.

"No. It's not Italian. It's a new Mexican place. We had burritos," Julie says.

The mention of "Mexican" reminds Otis of the cartel. They must still be out looking for the money Otis has in The Vault.

"I didn't know you like Mexican food," Otis says.

"Neither did I."

Something in Julie's voice sounds off, as if she's in a hurry to get off the phone. "Is everything okay?"

"Everything is fine," she says, but Otis is not convinced.

"It's still early. Why don't I take a drive by?"

"I don't know . . ."

"Julie, is something wrong?"

"No. Nothing's wrong."

"Well, I'd like to stop by."

"Okay, but I have work tomorrow and need to make it an early night."

Otis tells her he'll be there in half an hour. On the drive to her house, he worries. She has never told him she would have to make it an early night before. He wonders what's up.

When he pulls into the driveway with Sadie, Julie is not on the front porch as she usually is. This causes Otis even more concern, and he wonders if he or Carolyn might have said something that upset her.

He knocks on the screen door and calls her name before opening it and stepping into the front hall. There's a rattling of dishes and water running, and Otis realizes she's at the kitchen sink. He calls out to her again instead of scaring her half to death by just showing up in the kitchen.

He hears the water turn off and a moment later Julie is standing in the doorway with a dish towel in her hands.

"Hi Otis," she says.

"Hi."

She stands there without saying another word. Finally, Otis asks her if he has interrupted something she was in the middle of. He notices that she is not her usual smiling self. Something is definitely wrong.

"What's the matter, Julie?"

She looks away from him and goes to the couch. "I guess we need to talk," she says after sitting down.

When Otis hears this, he is reminded of the days when Fern would say the same thing. And what she had to say was never good. Now Julie is using the same words. What did he do to cause this?

He goes to her, but she moves to the far end of the couch. "Will you please tell me what's wrong? What did I do?"

"You didn't do anything, Otis. It's me. It's us. We can't go on like this. The summer has been wonderful, but now fall is coming and you'll be on your way soon."

"But I don't want to leave . . . at least not without you."

"I can't leave. I have a job. And you have the Trail to finish. And then you'll end your trip and go back to Maine."

"But Julie . . ."

"But nothing. I've been thinking about this for a while, and our time together is . . . I'm sorry, Otis. I have to end things . . . and tonight is the night. I will not change my mind."

"Julie, please . . ."

"No. I've made up my mind."

"Can I at least call you while I'm on the Trail?"

"What for?"

"To make sure you're okay. I won't call often. Just once in a while. And tell me the truth . . . did Carolyn say something about us today that got you all stirred up?"

When Julie is silent, Otis knows that Carolyn did say something.

"Have a good time on the Trail, Otis, and take care of yourself." She rises from the couch and heads toward the door. Otis follows.

On the way back to the campground, tears fall from his eyes. There was no sense in arguing with Julie. He knows she meant what she said. He has fallen in love with a woman he cannot have, no matter how much he wants her.

Back at the campground, Otis is tempted to call Julie but decides against it. The abrupt change in her has caused him intense anguish. First Fern. Now her. If there had been a fight or even a minor argument between them, he might understand why she broke things off. But they had always got along so well, and Julie's announcement had come out of left field. Maybe time and distance will make her heart grow fonder. He hopes so.

Already, he is missing Julie. Her presence in his life was like a healing balm and such a comfort. How could she just turn away from him the way she did?

The following morning, Otis packs up and leaves Damascus. His next stop will be Gatlinburg, Tennessee, a two-and-a-half hour drive away.

When he arrives, he'll stay a night and then continue on. He has lost interest in his mission now and wants to get to Springer Mountain and then go home to Maine.

In spite of his upset over the break-up with Julie, Otis has enjoyed everything about Gatlinburg and has stayed longer than he expected. Like other spots he's visited, the music alone has made it all worthwhile. Every night he has stopped in at Ole Smokey Moonshine's music jam to play his fiddle with the other musicians. He also saw the 350 species of sea creatures at Ripley's Aquarium and overcame his fear of heights when he rode the aerial tramway. One night he thought about going to Pucker Up, a strip club in Knoxville, but when Julie came to mind he decided not to go. He hates to leave the town after spending a week, but he might as well continue on to Springer Mountain and complete the Trail.

He hasn't spoken to Julie since he left Damascus and thinks it's time to give her a call. While driving along Route 441 southeast and heading to a campground called The Bluff in Cullowhee, North Carolina, he admires the mountains, winding roads and walls of forested land on either side. Once he gets to the campground and eats a little supper he'll give Julie a call.

About ten miles outside of Cullowhee he glances at his gas gauge and sees that he's running on empty. He kicks himself for not filling up before leaving Gatlinburg, but Julie has been dominating his thoughts since early morning and his attention has been on her, not the gas tank.

When the red light comes on to alert Otis that he is dangerously low on fuel, he worries that he won't make it to the next station. He continues on for eight miles while holding his breath before he sees up ahead a one-pump station with a Mini Mart behind it. Otis thanks God for the gift and pulls in next to the pump. He turns off the engine, gets out of the truck and goes inside the store to pay for the gas. He finds it eerily quiet inside, as if no one is there. Then, he hears a thumping sound and loud voices coming from the back of the store.

Otis walks toward the cash register at the end of the center aisle, sets his key fob on the counter and rings the call bell sitting next to a gumball machine. He feels uneasy as he waits.

"Anyone home?" he calls out, certain that he can now hear two voices.

As soon as the words are out of his mouth, two men come out from a back room. An older, scruffy looking man is holding a gun to the head of a younger man. Otis knows right away that he has interrupted an armed robbery.

In a split second, the gunman orders Otis to lie face down on the floor, arms extended over his head. "Make a move, and I'll blow both your heads off," the gunman says. "Now empty that cash register. And you—on the floor—toss your wallet over here."

Otis's heart is hammering against his ribs as he does what the robber orders and hears the cash register drawer open. He can see from the corner of his eye the gunman taking a fistful of money out of the till. He then grabs Otis's key fob and backs away toward the front door, his weapon held high. When the younger man tries to move out from behind the counter, the gunman pulls the trigger. The man pitches backward and falls to the floor while the gunman runs out the door and heads for Otis's truck.

In an instant, Otis is on his feet. He wants to help the young man and hopes the bullet hit his shoulder and not his heart, but first he has to stop the gunman from stealing his truck. Once outside, Otis hears the engine turn over and watches as the gunman takes off from the station. Otis starts running and manages to grab hold of the tailgate. He hangs on as tightly as he can, nearly losing his grip twice as he is dragged a quarter mile before the truck's engine dies. No sooner does this happen than a woman driving a white SUV approaches from the opposite direction. The gunman jumps out of Otis's truck and runs into her lane. In turn, she slams on the brakes to avoid hitting him.

"Out of the car!" the gunman shouts at the woman behind the wheel. From behind the truck, Otis can see that the gunman is now pointing the gun at her head. He is so terrified that he doesn't dare draw a breath. The woman exits her vehicle and the gunman jumps inside, pulls a doughnut and speeds away. Otis is still behind the truck, shaking in disbelief. As soon as the SUV is out of sight, he comes out from behind his truck and runs to the woman.

"Are you okay?" he shouts.

Through sobs, she nods her head. "We need to call Carl. My husband. He's the sheriff." Her shaking hands prevent her from pressing the numbers on her phone.

"There was a shooting inside the Mini Mart back there," Otis says, heading for the truck. He finds his wallet on the seat, takes his cell phone from the glove box and checks to make sure The Vault is secure before returning to the woman and heading back to the Mini Mart. On the way, he tells her what he witnessed.

Otis's shoes had fallen off while he was being dragged and his knees are bleeding. As he limps along with Sadie at his side, he sees his sneakers lying in the road and picks them up. He also calls the sheriff after the woman gives him the number and tells him about the shooting. Minutes later, the sheriff pulls up to the Mini Mart just as Otis and the woman arrive on foot.

"I've got a posse out looking for the car. What happened here, Joan?" The sheriff is looking at his wife, but she's too distraught to answer.

"A man's been shot. He's inside the store. Not sure how bad he is," says Otis. "My truck is a quarter mile away. It's out of gas. The guy hijacked your car." He says nothing about The Vault.

Chapter Thirty-Seven

The sheriff tells his wife and Otis to stay put while he goes inside the store to have a look. He finds the victim lying in a pool of blood on the floor behind the counter.

"He didn't stand a chance," the sheriff tells his wife and Otis when he comes back outside. "What am I gonna tell his family? We know them." To his wife, he says with a tremor in his voice, "It was Josh Randall."

Otis and Joan, who is sobbing uncontrollably, get inside the cruiser while the sheriff radios for a tow. He tells Otis the truck will be taken to The Bluff. Otis worries about The Vault being discovered but has no choice but to go along with the plan.

"I'll need to get a statement from you," he says. "You can bring your dog with you to the station."

A moment later, the sound of sirens are heard wailing through the air. Patrol officers arrive at the scene and step out of their cruisers. As soon as medics remove the body of Joshua Randall and place him in a waiting ambulance, yellow crime scene tape goes up around the perimeter of the pump station and store. The sheriff's wife is so overcome with emotion she cannot stop crying.

Otis is beginning to realize that if he has to give a statement, he'll probably have to stick around for a while. And then he'll have to be present months down the road to testify in court if the killer is found.

"I didn't properly introduce myself," the sheriff tells Otis when he returns to the cruiser. "I'm Carl Bixby. The victim's name is Joshua Randall. A truly decent man. He had a wife and two kids." He sighs and shakes his head. "We'll gas up your truck for you. Don't worry. It's safe in our hands."

But Otis does worry. Will the truck be impounded and searched? He asks Sheriff Bixby about it in a casual way.

"No," says the sheriff. "That won't be necessary. The suspect only used it to get from this point to a quarter mile up the road. My wife's car is another matter." Otis breathes a sigh of relief.

A few hours later, after Otis has given his statement at police headquarters, Sheriff Bixby tells him he is free to leave but is asked to remain in the area for a few days.

"We'll call you when we get our man, and you can bet we will. We'll need you for the lineup."

A patrol officer drives Otis back to The Bluff. After he calms down, he calls Julie, hoping she'll be at home.

He is about to hang up after four rings when he finally hears her voice. "Julie, it's me. Otis."

"Hi, Otis." A long silence follows before she says anything else. "Well, how are things going?"

Otis takes a deep breath before answering. "I'm at a campground in Cullowhee. It's been a horrible day."

"You're in North Carolina? What happened?"

Otis wastes no time coming straight to the point. "I walked in on an armed robbery at a Mini Mart. A man working there was shot and killed. About forty years old. The guy who killed him got away."

He hears Julie suck in her breath. "What? You could have been killed, too. Are you all right?"

"I'm fine. My feet and knees got roughed up, though." Otis then tells Julie about holding on to the truck's tailgate and being dragged before meeting up with the sheriff's wife. "My shoes fell off while I was hanging off the back of the truck."

"Have they arrested anyone?"

"Not that I know of. I had to give a statement this afternoon. Police said I'd be getting a call when they have him in custody."

"Oh, Otis. I'm so sorry. Sounds like you were in the wrong place at the wrong time. That poor man."

"Well, it happened. I think I'm in shock. How are you?"

Julie tells Otis about a storm that cut a path through Damascus and left some downed trees. Then she whispers into the phone that she has missed him.

Her words are music to his ears. "I miss you, too. Have you given any thought . . .?"

Julie sighs. "Yes, Otis, I have. I think we need to talk again if you're willing to come this way on your way back to Maine."

"You bet I will. But I have to stick around here a while. There'll be a lineup when they catch the killer."

"Just be careful. Watch your back." Julie pauses before she asks Otis if he wants her to come to Cullowhee.

"No. Stay where you are. I'll call you with updates."

"Okay, but if you change your mind . . ."

They wish each other a good night's sleep and end the call. For the first time in more than a week Otis is hopeful.

"You're sure now."

"Never more in my life. Second one from the right."

Otis is at the police station in Sylva two days after the robbery and murder, this time sitting behind a big one-way window. Beyond the window, six men are in a lineup. Otis's job is to pick the man who allegedly robbed and killed Joshua Randall. The man Otis has identified is Arlen Wade, and his rap sheet is nine pages long. Until now, his crimes have been unarmed robbery, assault and battery, driving under the influence of alcohol, possession and distribution of Class A drugs, domestic violence and a handful of other crimes. Now, Wade has been charged with armed robbery, theft of a motor vehicle, hijacking and second degree murder. He is being held on $1 million cash bail.

Wade is a short, stocky man and his expression is set in a scowl. His hair and eyes are dark, and so are the clothes he is wearing. Otis knows it's him. He memorized Wade's thick neck, forehead wrinkles, bushy eyebrows and widow's peak when Wade was backing up inside the store. His height and body size are a match, too.

"It's him. Definitely."

Sheriff Bixby and Detective Tony Martinez, along with Wade's court-appointed attorney, are seated behind the one-way window with Otis.

"You're absolutely sure."

"Not a doubt in my mind."

After identifying the gunman, Otis leaves the police station and drives back to The Bluff. On the way, he stops at a store to pick up a copy of the *Smoky Mountain News*. Right there, on the front page above the fold, is a news story about the armed robbery and Joshua Randall's murder plus details about Arlen Wade's arrest. Next to the story, there's a photo of the one-pump gas station and the Mini Mart where the crimes took place. Otis pays for the paper and takes it back to the campground to read the story.

First, he makes himself a cup of coffee, then he sits in his chair to read. The lead story jumps to page 5 and again to page 14. Otis is mentioned in the news report not by name but only as an eye witness.

He goes back to the front page and skims other news. As he turns the pages, he looks at the headlines and photos and reads the captions. In the second half of the paper, he comes to the obituary section and there, at the top of page 17, he sees a photo of himself at a younger age. What in the world is his picture doing there? Where did the newspaper get it and how could they have made such a terrible mistake? Otis thinks it has to be some kind of weird mix-up. He begins reading the obituary under the photo:

CULLOWHEE—Joshua P. Randall, age 41, of Cullowhee, died suddenly on Tuesday, Aug. 28, after suffering a gunshot wound to the chest by an armed robber while working at the Mini Mart on Rte. 441, according to the Sylva County Medical Examiner-Coroner's report.

Josh, as most people knew him, was born in Hopewell, Maine and was adopted at birth by his parents Earle Randall and Elaine Randall of Sylva. They loved him dearly.

Joshua enjoyed puttering around the house, helping his wife Bonnie in the garden and fishing at local lakes. He was an adoring father and loved spending time with his two children Will and Madelyn. He attended services at Saving Grace Baptist Church where he worked part-time as a custodian. He also worked part-time at the Mini Mart on 441 in addition to his full-time job at Cobb Paper Manufacturing Company in Sylva.

Josh played violin during church services and often sang in the choir. He also enjoyed volunteering at the church's food pantry.

In addition to his parents and his loving wife Bonnie, he is survived by his son Will and daughter Madelyn, all of Cullowhee. Joshua also leaves his mother-in-law Cynthia McPhee, father-in-law Raymond McPhee and brother-in-law Paul McPhee, all of Sylva. In addition, he leaves many friends. He was predeceased by both sets of grandparents.

Visiting hours will be held Friday from 6 to 8 p.m. at Jackson Chapel on Main Street, Cullowhee. A funeral service will be at the Saving Grace Baptist Church at 10 a.m. Saturday with Pastor David Madison officiating. In lieu of flowers, contributions to the Randall Family Living Trust will be greatly appreciated. Mailing address: Randall Trust, 462 Covington Rd., Cullowhee, NC 28723.

Chapter Thirty-Eight

It's not possible. Born in Hopewell? Adopted at birth? Otis looks at the picture of Joshua Randall again, and what does he see but an exact likeness of himself at about forty years old. When he was inside the store on the day of the robbery, Otis had only caught a glimpse of Joshua Randall. Now, here he is, staring up at him from page 17 of the Smoky Mountain News. Could this man be his son? His very own flesh and blood? The son he and Fern gave up so many years ago? What would be the odds? He wonders if he has entered some kind of alternate reality.

Otis reads the obituary again. Josh Randall had a wife and two children. If this man is his son, then Bonnie is his daughter-in-law and the two children are his grandchildren. He reads the obituary for the third time, trying to make sense of the words, the names, the place of Josh's birth and his adoption.

Otis rubs his eyes. Pulls at his face. Runs his hands through his hair. He needs to know who Joshua Randall was. He needs to find out if this young man was his biological son.

He wants to call Julie to tell her the news but holds off. First, he'll try Pastor Wright. He'll know what to do.

He pulls out his cell phone and presses the number.

"Church of the Blinding Light. Colleen speaking."

"Hi, Colleen. It's Otis Kingston. Is Pastor Wright there?"

"Well, hi there, Otis! He just walked through the door. You can bring me up to date while he gets settled. How's your trip going? Where are you now?"

Otis tells Colleen that something terrible has happened and he needs to talk to Pastor Wright right away. He'll tell her about the trip later.

Colleen pauses, then says, "Okay, Otis. We can talk another time. I just want to tell you one thing, though."

"What's that?"

"A new Mexican restaurant is coming to Hopewell. Can't wait to try it."

A Mexican restaurant in little Hopewell? There's a diner and one small restaurant in the town's center. Why would a Mexican place open up? Otis doesn't like the sound of it.

"What's it called?"

"Miguel's Cantina."

"Who are the owners?"

"People are saying they're from Mexico. A couple of men opened it about a week ago."

"Huh."

Otis then hears Pastor Wright's voice in the background. A moment later, he picks up the phone.

"Well, now, Otis. Been thinking about you. How's everything going?"

For now, Otis puts all thoughts about Miguel's Cantina aside. "I've got quite a story to tell you, and I need your help."

"Oh? Well don't keep me in suspense. What's this all about?"

Otis then launches into the story about his truck running out of gas and how he stopped at a one-pump station, only to interrupt an armed robbery.

"A man was killed," says Otis. "And the man might be my son."

For a long moment, Pastor Wright is silent on the other end of the line. "Otis, what on earth are you talking about?" he finally says.

Otis repeats his story, more slowly this time, and tells him about the baby he and Fern gave up for adoption, the armed robbery and murder and the story and obituary in the newspaper. He ends by telling Pastor Wright that it's possible Josh Randall's children are his grandchildren. "What do you think I should do?"

Again, Pastor Wright is silent, then says, "You've just dropped a bomb in my lap, Otis. I need to think about this. Meanwhile, I don't want you to do anything rash. The man's family is reeling from his death. Any revelations need to be well thought out. If your suspicions are true, they don't need another shock. And remember . . . this is just speculation on your part."

Otis says he agrees, and Pastor Wright asks Otis to call him again at home that night.

As an afterthought, Otis asks if Pastor Wright will use the house key he gave Colleen to go inside and find a few photos of himself.

"You can send them to an address I'll give you. I'll use what you send to compare the pictures to the one of Mr. Randall. And I'll reimburse the postage charges. I need them as soon as possible. Please use FedEx or some other overnight service. And look in the top drawer of my bureau. That's where the photos are."

"Of course, Otis. I can do that. And I'll wait for your call tonight." Pastor Wright gives Otis his home phone number and they end the call.

After his conversation with Pastor Wright, Otis goes shopping in Sylva. He needs a sports jacket, shirt and tie and decent pants. He also needs dress shoes and a pair of socks. Tonight, he will be at Joshua Randall's wake. Tonight, if Josh is who Otis thinks he is, he might meet his grandchildren for the first time. He will also come face to face with the people who raised his son and the woman who married him.

Fern would tell him to buy a navy blue jacket and white shirt, so he doesn't have to think much about what he'll wear. At a department store in Sylva, he picks out a blazer, shirt, navy blue and red striped tie and khaki pants. He prefers loafers over tie shoes, so he buys them in cordovan and picks out a pair of light-colored socks. He wants to look presentable for Josh's wake.

At five o'clock, Otis makes himself a BLT and washes it down with a glass of milk. After brushing his teeth, he heads over to Jackson Chapel and sees a line of people snaking from the front door all the way to the parking lot and around the building. Many are crying and offering comfort to one another.

Otis wonders how to introduce himself to Josh's parents, wife and children. "Hello, I'm the one who witnessed your son (or husband's) murder. And by the way, I think he's the son my wife and I gave up for adoption about forty years ago."

No. He would never say any of that. Fern was always telling him he needed to be more sensitive. But how? What words would Otis use to show genuine sympathy, all the while knowing that their dead son and husband might have his DNA?

Otis figures it will take at least an hour to get through the line, so he has plenty of time to think. This is another chapter of his life he'll have to go through alone. He can't very well talk to the people in line about it.

Maybe the best approach is to offer condolences and ask if he might visit the family sometime next week. But then the family might not want to talk to him. He witnessed Joshua's death, after all. Otis is a stranger, and they don't know him from a buffalo. On the other hand, they might want to talk with him. An idea springs into his brain. He will tell them that Josh said something before he died. They will wonder about that. They will want to know what he said. Otis might have to make something up, but what's one more lie?

The line moves slowly, and by the time Otis approaches the grieving family members it is nearly eight o'clock. He tries to see who Josh's parents are, but they are around a corner and he has to wait for two more people to move along before they come into view.

Five minutes later, he is standing in front of Josh's father, Earle. He glances down at Josh's two children. The boy is probably around twelve years old, the girl about ten. Both have tears streaming down their cheeks. Otis wonders if they should even be there and thinks it would have been better if they had been left at home instead of being exposed to their father's death. The casket is closed, so at least they don't have to look at his body.

Otis has no idea what to say. In the end, he decides to just be himself.

"I'm Otis Kingston. I'm so sorry. I witnessed your son's death," he says to Earle Randall.

"Yes, I know who you are, Mr. Kingston," Earle says, reaching out to shake Otis's hand. He then breaks down in tears. "He was our only son, our only child."

"I'm so sorry. So, so sorry."

"Thank you." He recovers enough to introduce Otis to his wife. "This is Joshua's mother, Elaine."

"I'm sorry, ma'am. It's a terrible loss you've suffered."

Elaine Randall cannot answer because she is crying so hard. "Why did it have to be him? Why him?"

Otis has no answer, and he doesn't know what else to say. He says another feeble "I'm sorry" and moves down the line until he is standing in front of a young woman with shoulder-length auburn hair. Otis notices that her eyes are red from crying. The children are now standing next to her.

"You must be Bonnie," Otis says. "And Will and Madelyn?"

"Yes. I'm Josh's wife. And our children."

Otis offers his condolences and introduces himself.

"So you witnessed what happened. I'd like to talk to you about it. Would you meet with me privately sometime next week?"

Otis breathes a sigh of relief. Now he doesn't have to make any overtures. Bonnie has saved him from that.

"I'll give you all the time you need," Otis says. "I'm visiting the area, but I have to stay in town until the police release me." Otis takes a slip of paper from his jacket pocket and writes down his cell phone number. "Please . . . call me. I'd like to talk to you, too."

Chapter Thirty-Nine

When Otis returns to the campground after Josh's wake, he changes into a pair of shorts and T-shirt. He pours himself a glass of root beer and calls Pastor Wright. He picks up on the first ring.

"Otis. How're you doing?"

"Okay. Just got back from the wake. Joshua was well liked. Must've been five hundred people there."

"Well, I've thought about your situation all day. Couldn't even concentrate on writing my sermon for Sunday."

"I'm sorry . . ."

"No. Don't be sorry. At a time like this, you need all the support you can get."

"It's just . . . it's just so unreal. All those years Fern and I wondered what happened to our son . . . and then to witness the murder of someone who might be him. It's too much."

"Even thinking he might be your son . . . you must be in shock."

"That's an understatement."

"Look, Otis, please don't jump to conclusions. It's possible that Mr. Randall isn't your son. But if he is, I'd have to say that the improbable does happen at times, doesn't it?"

Otis agrees more than 100 percent. The drug money. His new truck. Sadie. Julie. "But I swear to you, he looks just like me—at least the picture of him in the newspaper does. Especially around the eyes. And his smile. Then there's the mention of Hopewell and adoption. His age. It all adds up to the fact that Joshua Randall was my son."

Pastor Wright pauses before continuing. "I read the obituary online, Otis. His pastor was David Madison. I don't know the man, but I could call him on your behalf to see what he thinks. We have to handle this with a lot of tact and sensitivity. In fact, I'm thinking maybe I should get on a flight to North Carolina. And by the way, the photos you wanted are on the way. You should get them tomorrow."

"Thank you. And I'd appreciate it if you'd give the pastor a call. But coming to North Carolina?"

Pastor Wright says, "I think Pastor Madison, you and I need to meet to sort things out."

"The funeral will be held tomorrow. I would pay for your flight and hotel. Food, too."

"It's not necessary."

"Yes, it is. It's absolutely necessary. Would you like me to make reservations for Saturday afternoon?"

Pastor Wright sighs. "I really think the three of us should meet. So, yes. But don't spend a lot for a room. An inexpensive motel will do. I'll get someone to fill in for me on Sunday."

➤➤➤ ◄◄◄

Otis attends Joshua Randall's funeral on Saturday morning and learns that the man he thinks was his son was loved and respected by hundreds of people. He was considered humble, kind and always willing to lend a helping hand to anyone who asked. According to one friend, he had a keen sense of humor and was fond of practical jokes, especially when they were played on him. Josh's best man at his wedding said that when Josh met Bonnie, he was head over heels in love with her and the day he married her was the happiest of his life.

"Though Josh's parents are wonderful people, he was always curious about his biological parents," the best man says. "A slender thread ran through Josh that made him think he was never good enough, that he was somehow unworthy of anyone's love, that he didn't measure up."

When Otis hears this, tears spring to his eyes. He leaves the back pew and slips out of the church, unnoticed. On the front steps, he is racked with sobs that come from deep inside. He never got to know Joshua Randall. And Joshua never got to know him or Fern, his own mother.

Otis books a flight to Greenville for Pastor Wright and reserves three nights at the Grand Old Lady about ten miles outside of Cullowhee.

The flight is on time, and on the way to the hotel Otis tells Pastor Wright more about his romance with Fern when they were teenagers. The Pastor offers compassionate responses as he listens to Otis's story.

On Sunday, Pastor Wright attends the service at Saving Grace Baptist Church while Otis is at the campground. When he greets Pastor Madison on the way out, he introduces himself and asks if they could have a word in private. As soon as everyone in the congregation has left, Pastor Madison invites Pastor Wright to his office.

Pastor Madison is the first to speak. "Everyone's gone, but feel free to close the door if you like."

Pastor Wright gets up from his chair and closes the door.

"What I have to say is highly confidential," He says.

Pastor Madison nods. "I gathered that."

"I've come to Cullowhee from Hopewell, Maine," Pastor Wright begins. "I need to talk with you about a matter that concerns a member of my congregation."

"And who is that?"

"Otis Kingston. You probably wouldn't know the name. He witnessed the shooting death of Joshua Randall."

"Ah, yes. I read in the paper there was a witness. No name was mentioned, though. I think Joshua's wife and parents were the only ones who knew."

"There's more. Otis is prepared to swear on a stack of Bibles that he is Joshua Randall's father."

Pastor Madison is clearly taken aback and sits in silence as he tries to absorb what Pastor Wright has just told him. Finally, he says, "Strange things happen in this great world of ours. Nothing surprises me anymore, and I'll bet you would agree."

"I sure would. Heard it all, seen it all. Just about, anyway. Why don't you tell me about Mr. Kingston. Why does he think he's Josh Randall's father?"

Pastor Wright tells Pastor Madison about the connection to Hopewell and the adoption factor. "Mr. Randall was also the exact age as his son. They shared the same birth date."

For the next hour, the two pastors talk about Josh Randall, his family and Otis Kingston.

"What do you think should be the next step?" Pastor Wright asks.

Pastor Madison exhales loudly. "It depends."

"Depends on what?"

"On whether Mr. Kingston wants to add further misery to the Randall family. They've lost a son, a husband and a father in a violent way. If Mr. Kingston suddenly makes an announcement or requests a paternity test, it would likely only compound their grief. And what if the DNA shows there is no familial connection? It would needlessly upset the Randall family."

"I have photographs of Otis Kingston with me," says Pastor Wright. He pulls a manila envelope from his briefcase and hands it to Pastor Madison. When he takes the envelope with reluctance, Pastor Wright says, "It's okay. Go ahead and open it."

The first picture was taken at Otis's high school graduation. The second shows Otis and Fern on the day of their wedding. Three others were taken when Otis was about forty years old and won a blue ribbon for catching the biggest trout at a fishing tournament.

"Well, I'll be . . ." says Pastor Madison. "Either this is Josh's father, or he had a double. The resemblance between the two is astounding."

"I think so, too. And so does Otis."

Pastor Wright then reminds Pastor Madison about the other facts that make Otis and Josh a match.

"I don't think we're looking at a simple coincidence," says Pastor Madison. "I gave up believing in them long ago. But it does seem incredible that Otis just happened to stop at the Mini Mart to get gas and witness the death of Joshua Randall. Even so, I don't believe anything is ever an accident."

"Neither do I. I've heard of strange things happening, but this is the strangest yet. I've had my own share of experiences, and some have been doozies."

"I could tell you a few stories of my own. So, do you think Otis should let sleeping dogs lie? Somehow that doesn't seem fair to him."

Pastor Madison considers the question for a long moment. "You're right. It wouldn't seem fair. To Otis, I mean. There are the grandchildren, for one thing."

"What it boils down to is true parentage. The Randalls are Josh's parents by adoption, but Otis could be his father by birth. It would seem to me that Otis has a right to know if he's the biological father. But a revelation of this magnitude would rock the Randall family's world. As you said, twice devastated."

The two men sit in silence for a long while before Pastor Madison speaks again. "I'd like to get the sheriff's opinion. He's a level-headed man, and he knows the law inside out. If you agree, I'll give him a call. If he's not busy, he might not mind stopping by."

Pastor Wright agrees and waits while Pastor Madison makes the call. Twenty minutes later, a car door slams in the parking lot. "That must be Sheriff Bixby," says Pastor Madison. "Let's hope he has some good advice."

Chapter Forty

When the sheriff steps inside Pastor Madison's office, introductions are made and the sheriff sits in a chair next to Pastor Wright.

"We have a troubling situation here," says Pastor Madison.

"Most situations are," says the sheriff.

"We want to get your opinion on something that involves Joshua Randall."

"Oh? What about him?"

"Pastor Wright has good reason to believe that Josh was Otis Kingston's son. Mr. Kingston—the witness to Josh's murder."

"Yes, he was brought in for questioning. I know who he is." He looks at Pastor Wright. "He identified Arlen Wade in the lineup. Now that I think of it, when I first met Mr. Kingston I thought he looked a lot like Joshua."

Pastor Wright then tells Sheriff Bixby the details that led Otis to think he is Josh's father. "And these pictures more or less support his claim," says Pastor Wright. "They're of Otis Kingston."

Sheriff Bixby studies the pictures, nods his head. "I'd say I have to agree. They look enough alike to be the same person."

"The question is how does Mr. Kingston confirm this without causing more devastation?"

"Good question. Maybe he should start with Josh's wife. That is, if he pursues this."

Pastor Madison takes off his glasses and rubs his eyes. "I had a feeling you'd say that. I'll call Bonnie later today to see if she'll meet with us."

On Monday morning, Otis's cell phone rings. When he answers, he hears Pastor Wright's voice on the line.

"Bonnie Randall wants to talk to us," he says. "I hope you're available at one o'clock."

"I'm available at three in the morning at this point. Where does she want to meet?"

"Pastor Madison's office. It's at the rear of the church."

"I'll pick you up at twelve-thirty," Otis says. "That should give us enough time to get there." He hangs up; a shot of adrenaline is flooding his veins.

⟫⟫⟫ ⟪⟪⟪

Otis and Pastor Wright arrive at the church just before one o'clock. Sheriff Bixby's cruiser is already parked outside, and a silver Hyundai sits next to it. The two men use a side door that leads to the back of the church and follow a sign to Pastor Madison's office at the end of a hallway. They can hear a woman's voice. Bonnie Randall no doubt.

"Right on time," says Pastor Madison when Otis and Pastor Wright appear in the doorway. "Come in and have a seat." Bonnie tells Otis she remembers him from the wake, and Otis introduces her to Pastor Wright.

An uncomfortable silence follows until Bonnie finally says, "Well, what are we all doing here?"

Pastor Wright clears his throat. "Mrs. Randall, something has come to light, something that is of great importance to Mr. Kingston."

She looks at Otis and then glances at Pastor Wright. "What are you talking about?"

Otis takes over and says, "Mrs. Randall, I'd like you to brace yourself because I have something to say that will no doubt come as a shock."

"I don't understand. Was Josh in some kind of trouble? Am I?"

"No. Nothing like that." Otis looks at the two pastors and then Sheriff Bixby. They avoid looking at him. "There is no easy way to say this . . . but I have reason to believe that I am Joshua's biological father."

Bonnie lowers her head and does not look up. Otis hears her sniffling.

For the next hour, Otis and the two pastors take turns explaining the situation and counseling Bonnie while tears rain down her face. When she finally composes herself, she views the pictures Otis has brought with him and listens while he presents more evidence. On several occasions, Sheriff Bixby adds to the discussion. He finishes by suggesting that Otis have a paternity test. After the results are known, the elder Randalls would be notified but only if there is a DNA match.

Bonnie looks at Otis and studies his face. "I can definitely see a resemblance. I certainly can. The pictures and the facts of Josh's life do add up."

"Bonnie, how do you think the Randalls would react if, in fact, Otis Kingston is confirmed to be Josh's father?" Pastor Madison asks.

Bonnie pauses, then says, "I know they'd be shocked, maybe even deny it, but they're rational and reasonable people. And strong. Yes, Earle and Elaine are both strong. They're also loving and kind. I think over time they would come to accept it as one of those strange mysteries that sometimes happen in life."

"Would you rather tell them in your own way, Bonnie?" Pastor Madison continues.

"I could. But I'd prefer to meet like we're doing today. If there's a match, I would need support. And I think Otis would, too."

She breaks down in tears again, and great sobs emerge from deep inside. "Josh was a good man . . . too good for this world . . . I don't know how I'll go on without him. And the kids . . . he was their hero."

"It may seem impossible to go on, but you have Will and Madelyn to think about. They'll need you to be strong," says Pastor Madison.

"I was so in love with Joshua. There won't ever be anyone like him again."

"I know that, Bonnie. I also know how deep your grief is. It will take time to heal. A final gift to Josh might be to identify Otis Kingston as his biological father. In a spiritual sense, you would be helping him to connect his spirit with the father who was lost to him just after birth."

"Josh never thought much of himself. His adoption crushed him in ways no one could imagine or understand."

Otis looks down at his hands and finds himself fighting tears. He fears falling apart in front of Josh's widow. He needs to be strong, too. Strong for Bonnie and Fern.

A decision is made to meet again if there is a DNA match, and Elaine and Earle will be invited to attend.

One week later, seven people are sitting in the small conference room at Saving Grace—the two pastors, Sheriff Bixby, Bonnie Randall, Josh's parents and Otis. Pastor Madison is at the head of the table, a legal pad and pen in front of him.

"Thank you all for being here," he says. "The reason we are meeting will soon become clear. Earle and Elaine, as you can probably guess, this meeting has to do with Joshua."

"We thought it would," Earle says. He is clutching Elaine's hand as he speaks. A box of tissues is in the center of the table. Pastor Madison expects the meeting to be highly emotional.

He now turns to Bonnie and Otis. "Which of you would like to speak first?"

There is a long moment of hesitation before Otis answers. "I will," he says quietly.

All eyes are on him as he once again tells the story about running out of gas, stopping at the Mini Mart and walking in on the armed robbery and murder.

"I only glimpsed your son, Earle . . . Elaine. But then I saw his picture in the *Smoky Mountain News* and read the obituary. That's when I started to put two and two together."

Otis sees the look of confusion on both Earle and Elaine's faces. "What two and two are you talking about?" asks Earle.

Otis takes his time answering. "I think I'm Josh's father."

Elaine raises her head and looks at Otis. "You, his father? Earle is his father."

"Yes, he is. You gave him a good life. But my wife, Fern, and I were the ones who *gave* him life."

It is Earle who speaks next. "Are you saying that you think you're our son's biological father?"

"Yes. That's what I think," Otis says gently.

"And you just happened to come along in his final moments. Do you really expect us to believe that? What led you to this preposterous conclusion? Why would you come up with such absurd fiction?" Elaine looks at Otis in disbelief.

Otis then recounts the story of his and Fern's romance and the birth of their son when they were teenagers. He also tells the Randalls that they relinquished him for adoption.

"I know it sounds impossible, but life is sometimes like that. Bizarre things happen all the time. I do admit that this story is strange, but I'm not making it up."

Earle and Elaine turn to Bonnie. "If what he says is true, this means that Will and Madelyn have a biological grandfather," says Elaine.

"The only way to determine this is through a paternity test," Sheriff Bixby says. "Mr. Kingston has arranged for one through the medical examiner."

The room goes silent before Pastor Wright speaks up a moment later. "A paternity test is needed to prove or disprove Otis's claim. He deserves to know one way or the other. I think the whole family deserves to know."

Bonnie agrees and a moment later so does Elaine. Earle remains silent.

"Before we talk about this any further, I need to know what Mr. Kingston's intentions are regarding the children," says Earle. "I don't want them traumatized again. Bad enough they've lost their father."

"My intention would be to love your grandchildren," Otis says calmly. "I live in Maine so I wouldn't be knocking on your door every five minutes. I could give some financial support. I'd also like to keep in touch with them through e-mail or phone calls. Maybe both. I could visit a few times a year. Or even invite them to Maine over summer vacation. I'd like to be a friend to them. A second grandfather."

Chapter Forty-One

The days pass quickly for Otis. He has driven around Cullowhee countless times and has called Julie every night. He'll drive back to Damascus to see her, but first he wants to complete his trip by going to Springer Mountain.

It is now Friday morning, and the results of the DNA test have come in. Everyone involved in the life story of Joshua Randall except for Bonnie and the children are now seated in the Saving Grace conference room. Sheriff Bixby is holding a sealed envelope. A few minutes pass before anyone speaks. Earle goes to the window and stares out to the parking lot. Elaine is seated next to Pastor Madison. She glances toward her husband when the pastor breaks the silence. "Bonnie called this morning," he says. "She'll be here with the children in a few minutes."

Pastor Madison leans toward Pastor Wright and whispers something. A moment later, the two men rise from their chairs and Pastor Madison suggests that they all join hands in prayer.

Pastor Wright begins: *Dear Holy Father, we are gathered together in your son's name and give thanks for your guidance during this difficult time. We give thanks, also, for the life of Joshua Randall. We now ask for protection and provision for those who are mourning his loss—the entire Randall family, Otis Kingston and the rest of us. We ask, also, for your wisdom when we learn the results of the DNA test. Finally, please accept Josh into your kingdom, and find a way to bring good out of this tragedy. High praise to the Holy Trinity. Amen.*

Earlier in the week, Otis drove by Bonnie Randall's home, a two-story stucco with a wide front porch. Otis plans to buy the children something special, new bicycles maybe. He will also set up a college fund for each of them. He can hardly believe that he stumbled upon his son in such a tragic way. Of all people, he understands that no one knows what is waiting around the next corner in the most literal sense, but this story is beyond what he could have ever imagined.

"May His wonders never cease," Otis says under his breath at the close of the prayer.

Otis hears children's voices outside in the parking lot. So Bonnie has arrived with Will and Madelyn. Any moment now, he will come face to face for the second time with two children who are likely his own flesh and blood.

A few nights ago, he had called Bonnie to talk about Josh. She had told Otis that she was in the process of accepting the truth about her husband's murder.

"It all seems like a nightmare," she had said. "How could this have happened? The fact that Josh was murdered is hard enough to accept. The fact that you could be his biological father and witnessed his death is even harder."

Otis is tempted to tell her about the day he came across three duffel bags stuffed with money but knows he cannot do that. Instead, he says, "I know all of this is hard to believe, but I can tell you that over my lifetime things have happened that no one would believe, least of all me. It's been said that God works in mysterious ways, and all I can say is that He sure does."

Otis had told Bonnie about Fern and that she carried her guilt about Josh until her dying day. He tells her, too, that Fern was never able to have more children and thought she was being punished for giving away their baby. "I would tell her that God is a loving God, and he would not punish her that way, but she wouldn't believe it. She blamed herself, and I couldn't change her mind."

Bonnie had waited for Otis to continue while silence hung between them for a long moment.

"I'd like to ask you about Josh," he had finally said. "I'd love to know about him. What was he like?"

Bonnie had sighed and began to tell Otis the story of Josh's life—how Elaine and Earle had wanted children but Elaine was unable to conceive. She told him that Earle and Elaine had been living in Maine around the time of Josh's birth. A few months after they adopted Josh, Earle's company offered to promote him if he would relocate to Sylva. The job was too good for Earle to pass up, so the family moved to North Carolina.

She had told Otis about Josh's childhood—how he had loved music and had shown an early talent for violin. He also liked to sing and had been a great storyteller. Earle and Elaine had encouraged Josh to study hard so he could go to college, but he was more suited to working with his hands.

"He loved to work with wood," she had said. "He made most of the furniture in our house." As soon as Otis heard this, he thought about the bookcase he had made for Fern. He, too, loved working with wood.

Otis also learned that Josh was good-natured and funny. He rarely raised his voice and loved playing with the kids.

"He was a hard worker," Bonnie had said. "Anyone who holds three jobs would have to love to work, and he did."

She had continued by telling Otis that he worked a few hours a week at Mini Mart so the owner could spend time with his wife. "Jack King would have had to work sun-up to sundown if Josh hadn't stepped in to help him. That was Josh. Always there to fill a need."

"I wish I had known him," Otis says.

"I wish the same. As much as Josh seemed happy, there was always a part of him that he didn't let anyone see. Sometimes he would cry out in his sleep. He would always tell me he'd had a bad dream, but I wondered what could be eating at him. One time, he mentioned you—not by name, of course—but he said he wondered who his 'real' father was. He wondered about his mother, too. I think many, if not all, adopted children must wonder."

Otis nods his head. "I would think so," he says.

"He liked to write," Bonnie had said. Then she had paused, and Otis thought she might be finished telling him about his son but then she said, "He wrote you letters. Never mailed, of course. They're in one of his bureau drawers. Would you like them?"

Otis had felt his heart lurch. "I'd love to have the letters. I really would."

And Bonnie had replied, "I thought you might say that. They're yours—if the DNA results show that you are his biological father."

Before Otis turns in for the night, he opens the envelope Bonnie gave him and sorts through the letters Joshua wrote. Once he's in bed, he leans back against two big pillows and flicks the switch for the reading light. His first pick is a letter dated December 25, 1985. Joshua was nine years old. He begins to read.

Dear Mom and Dad,

Today is Christmas and I wonder where you are. Why can't I be with you? Didn't you love me when I was born? Did I do something wrong? If I did, I'm sorry. Guess what? I got Legos for Christmas. And lots of other stuff, but Legos is my favorite. I hope you have a good Christmas. Your son, Joshua

Most of the letters are like this. Short and to the point. But there are other longer ones Joshua wrote when he was older. One that was typed reads:

April 16, 2000

Dear Mom and Dad,

Today is my birthday. I'm 24 years old. Sometimes I look in the mirror and wonder who I look like. Do I look like you, Mom? Or do I look like you, Dad? I also wonder if we'll ever meet. I don't know a thing about you, but I'd like to. What do you like to do, Dad? What about you, Mom? Someday I hope my girlfriend Bonnie and I have kids. They'll be my only blood relatives. It'll seem strange, but in a lot of ways I can't wait. All my life I have wondered who I am and why you gave me away, but my kids will know who they are. My daughter. Or my son. Maybe both. Do you think of me on my birthday? Do you remember the day I was born? What was it like when you handed me over to strangers? Did you cry? Or were you glad to be rid of me? I hope you put me up for adoption because you were sick or poor and not because you didn't love me. If you didn't, it would break my heart even more. No matter what, I will always love you. Your son, Joshua

P.S. Don't get me wrong. I love my adopted parents. They've been great.

Otis tries to imagine the sound of his son's voice, his southern drawl. He is glad that he's alone with his tears. He can grieve for as long as he needs with no one around to tell him to "get a grip." He had one chance in life to be a father, and in a matter of minutes, it had been stolen. In fact, he has lost his only son twice. He remembers the day Joshua was born. April 16, 1976. Fern was in labor for fifteen hours, and she was not having an easy time of it. He was at the hospital but not allowed inside the labor room to see her through the ordeal. Instead, he walked back and forth in a waiting room and tried to read an article in *Motor Trend* while wondering what was going on beyond the maternity ward's swinging doors. His mother came by after work and suggested they go to the hospital chapel to pray. It helped some but didn't take all the pain away. Fern's mother and father came to the hospital, too, but they didn't go to the chapel. Nor did they say much to Otis and his mother. They mostly just sat in a corner in the waiting room, saying nothing and staring at the floor.

The baby, a boy, was born at five minutes past four in the afternoon. Papers were already signed, and he was taken away to an area of the hospital that was off limits to Otis and Fern and their parents. Neither Otis nor Fern ever laid eyes on their baby's face.

Chapter Forty-Two

Exhausted, Otis turns off the light and tries to sleep, but he is so distraught that he only tosses and turns. He turns on the light again and reads another letter from Josh. This one was written on his birthday a few months before he married Bonnie. He wrote:

June 17, 2002

Dear Mom and Dad,

I don't know who you are or where you live, but this is your son Joshua writing. I want you to know that I don't hold it against you for giving me up for adoption. My life has been a good one. Mom and Dad Randall have treated me real good, and I've wanted for nothing, except maybe a sister or brother. I have a few cousins my age, and we're close like siblings, so I've had them. There's something I want you to know about my girlfriend, Bonnie. She's pretty and sweet. And here's what she looks like: She has light brown hair but in the sunlight it looks like gold. She has pretty brown eyes, a face shaped like a heart and a smile that melts my soul. She is 5' 2" tall and weighs 120 pounds. I think she's the most beautiful girl I've ever seen, and the best part is that this afternoon at two o'clock, she will become my wife. She tells me I am her hero. No wonder I love her so much. I wish you could know her. I wish you could know me. Maybe someday we will meet. I hope we do. Someday. Love, Josh

Otis sets the letter aside and tries to envision the man he glimpsed at the Mini Mart as a living, breathing human being. All he has to do is look in the mirror to see what Joshua looked like, but his son had his own thoughts, his own ways and his own mannerisms and though the letters help Otis know who Joshua was, his son's entire life is like a giant unsolved jigsaw puzzle.

He decides to read one more letter before he calls it a night. This one is dated November 18, 2005.

Dear Mom and Dad,

Today is one of the best days of my life. My son, Will James Randall, was born this morning at ten minutes past eleven. He weighs seven pounds and six ounces and is twenty inches long. He came out screaming, so I already know he's going to be a handful. When I found out Bonnie was pregnant back in April, I was so happy I danced her around the kitchen. When I went to bed that night, I laid there in the dark and thought about you. Knowing what I know now, meaning knowing what it's like to know you're going to be a parent, I'm having a real hard time understanding how you could have given me away. I mean, all those months when Will was growing inside Bonnie we talked about how we would raise our baby—we hoped it would be a boy—what we would teach him and the fun we'd have watching him grow. We even joked about what he would say first, Mama or Dada. Of course, I was hoping Dada would be his first word. Maybe it will be. When you were waiting for me, what did you talk about? If you weren't married, did you want to be? Did you ever think about abortion? Are you sorry that you gave me up? I'd really like to know because I can't even IMAGINE giving up Will. He's my son, and Bonnie's son, and I don't want anyone else to have him or love him but us and his grandparents and other relatives. If you had kept me, Will would be your grandson. What would you think about that? Would you even care? I thought I had forgiven you long ago for putting me up for adoption, but now that Will is here I'm not sure if I ever will entirely. When I held him for the first time this afternoon, I thought to myself "this little bundle is my flesh and blood. I would never leave him or give him away. How could my own mother and father do that?" You probably had your reasons, and you probably thought you were doing me a favor, but the truth is that even though Earle and Elaine Randall have been good parents, what you did was no favor to me. For my entire life I've felt trapped in a strange kind of world. I feel like a young tree that was pulled out by the roots and left by the side of the road. And then some kind strangers came along and planted me in their backyard. That's how I feel. I promise you this. I will never ever do anything to hurt my son. And if I do, I will regret it until my dying day.

Maybe you're living with regrets of your own. If you are, I understand all too well. Your son, Josh

With his heart now completely shattered, Otis folds the letter and returns it to the envelope. He turns off the light and lies in the dark, sobbing.

He remembers the day he walked inside the Mini Mart. If he had stayed to help Joshua instead of running out the door to save his truck and The Vault, would his son still be alive? How had money become more important than a human life, a human life that was his son? Seconds pass and then he hears Sadie's claws scratching against the floor. Otis knows she is coming toward hm. She nudges his hand and lets out a little moan. Otis reaches out in the dark and strokes her fur. Sadie is a comfort to him, but she is no substitute for human love. "You know me well, girl. Yes, you do. You know when I'm happy and you know when I'm sad. What do you say we move along tomorrow and go to Springer Mountain. Then, we'll go back to Damascus. Someone we both love is waiting for us."

Chapter Forty-Three

In the morning, Bonnie enters the conference room with the children, and they look surprised to see Otis sitting there.

"This is Mr. Kingston," Bonnie says to Will and Madelyn.

"You were at my Dad's wake, weren't you?" Will says. "Were you his friend?"

"I never knew your Dad, but I think we might have been good friends."

"How come you didn't you know him?" A look of confusion crosses Will's face.

"Well, for one thing, I live far away. For another thing, I didn't know where he lived."

"I don't get it." Will looks at Madelyn to see if she might be able to explain.

Pastor Madison does it for her. "First, I'd like you and Madelyn to sit across from me. And Otis, you come sit right here next to me."

Once everyone is seated in their places, Pastor Madison asks the children if they remember the story of Jesus' birth.

The children nod, and the pastor says there is a part of the story that isn't always emphasized.

"What part?" Will asks.

"Well, Jesus was conceived by the Holy Spirit. This means that God the Father planted Jesus inside of Mary. He didn't have a father the way you had your father."

"So?"

"So, Jesus' father—Joseph—adopted him. You understand what adoption is, right?"

Will and Madelyn both nod their heads. "It's when a mommy can't keep her baby because she doesn't have enough money and food and gives it to someone who will take care of it," Madelyn says.

"Exactly, Madelyn, but there's more. Though Joseph wasn't Jesus' actual father, he loved him as if he were his own flesh and blood. When your Dad was born, his parents couldn't keep him because they were too young. So, another couple adopted him."

"Dad was adopted?"

"Yes, he was adopted. And in a greater sense, we are all adopted."

"Why?" asks Will.

"Because when we are born, our parents make a choice to either keep us or let us go. Most times parents choose to keep their babies, but sometimes circumstances don't allow them to. They might be too young, or they have no money to support them. They want what's best for their children, and sometimes the best is to let them go. This is an act of love like no other because doing this is a hard, hard thing. Now, we are about to find out about Mr. Kingston. Are you ready?"

The children nod and both look first at their mother, then at Otis.

Pastor Madison turns to Sheriff Bixby and asks for the envelope. When he opens it and reads the contents, he continues in a soft and gentle voice.

"Now, sometimes adopted children never find out who their birth parents are. Sometimes they do. If your Dad had lived, he would have met his birth dad when Mr. Kingston went inside the Mini Mart on the day your Dad was working."

"I still don't get it," Will says.

Pastor Madison points toward Elaine. "Who is that woman?"

"Grammie Randall," says Madelyn.

"And what about this man next to me?"

"That's Mr. Kingston."

"Right. But Mr. Kingston is also your Dad's actual father. Your Grandpa Earle is his adoptive father."

The children stare at Pastor Madison for a long moment. "Does that mean Mr. Kingston is my grandfather?" Will asks.

"Yes, and he is Madelyn's grandfather, too."

"That means we have two grandfathers again. Our other grampy died."

"That would be my father," says Bonnie in explanation.

"But we don't know Mr. Kingston. How can he be our grandfather?"

"Because he and your father share the same DNA," says Pastor Madison patiently, explaining to the children the best he can what DNA is all about. "If you'd like, you can get to know Mr. Kingston. He lives in Maine, but he says you can visit him."

Otis leans toward the children. "I could send you gifts and maybe even invite you to spend a few weeks with me during summer vacation."

"Do you have a cat?" Will asks. "I'm allergic."

"No. But I have a dog."

"What's his name?"

"Her name is Sadie. She's a girl."

"Do you have a swing?" Madelyn asks.

"No, but I have lots of trees. I could hang one for you."

"How about a swimming pool?"

"No, but there are beaches and lakes in Maine."

"And you would take us?"

"Yes, and treat you to blueberry pie and vanilla ice cream."

The children look at each other, their eyes wide. "Can we go next summer, Mama? Please . . ." says Madelyn.

Otis looks at Bonnie, and she gives a little smile.

"Maybe. But I would want to go, too."

Otis gives Bonnie a compassionate smile. "And I would put out the welcome mat for you, Bonnie. Yes, I would. And for Earle and Elaine, too."

Otis leaves the church and drives back to The Bluff, anxious to see Sadie. Walking her always calms his mind, and he thinks that whoever said a dog is man's best friend knew what they were talking about.

Around four o'clock, he drives to Sylva to have an early supper with Elaine and Earle Randall at Delilah's. Inside the restaurant, he talks to Valerie, a chatty waitress about half his age. He has requested a table where he and the Randalls can talk privately. Valerie takes him to a small room in the back that's been set aside for this purpose. Otis studies the menu while waiting for his guests to arrive. Mixed grill looks good.

A few minutes later, he hears Earle's voice and then Valerie's as she leads them to the small room where Otis is waiting. He stands to shake Earle's hand, and there's an awkward moment among the three but it soon passes. Otis asks for a pitcher of ice water when they sit down.

"Well," says Otis, his tone serious, "never in a million years did I ever think I'd be sitting here with the people who raised my son . . . your son . . . I guess our son." He folds his hands and lays them in his lap.

"We feel the same, as you can well imagine," says Earle in a barely audible voice. Elaine's eyes are downcast. She is fiddling with her napkin.

"Especially for your family. I never got to know Joshua, but . . . I'd like to get to know him . . . through you. I also want to know what I can do to help Bonnie and the children. I need to ask you . . . was there life insurance?"

"Unfortunately, no. The only plus is that we helped Josh and Bonnie buy their home, and now it's free and clear," Earle says.

Otis is beginning to realize just how much the Randalls did for their son—his son. "I am humbled to think that you did so much for him. Thank you."

"It was our joy . . ." Otis hears Earle's voice catch. "He was our joy . . . we loved him so much." Earle picks up his napkin and wipes his eyes. Elaine sniffles.

"I'm so sorry . . . if I had been at the store a few minutes earlier, I might have been able to . . . well, Joshua might be alive today." Otis waits for Earle to collect himself.

"I doubt it," says Earle. "Arlen Wade has always been a bad sort. He might have killed both of you, not just Josh. Mr. Wade will be behind bars for a long time. As for Josh, he had a strong faith. We know he's in a good place. Elaine and I raised him in the church, you see."

"Yes. Fern and I would have raised him in the church, too. She would be so pleased to know you loved him enough to do that."

"And then some," Elaine says, finally. "We loved him as if he were our own flesh and blood—well, you know."

Otis tells Earle and Elaine about his talk with Bonnie and says that he and Josh shared more than a few traits. Woodworking. Puttering around the house. A talent for music. He asks if there is anything else he should know.

Earle pauses for a moment before responding. "When Josh was about fifteen, he came to me and asked if we'd take him to Maine. He was at that age when kids start questioning things. I think he wanted to know about you and your wife . . . his mother. He didn't say it out loud, but I think he wanted to know who his biological parents were. I also think he wanted to know why he was given up."

"Did you ever talk to him about it as a family?" Otis asks.

Elaine responds this time. "I asked him one time if he had any desire to find his birth parents. He said he didn't, but deep inside I think he might have."

Otis thinks about the letters Bonnie gave him, but neither Earle nor Elaine have mentioned them so he keeps it to himself. "I suppose the grandchildren give you a lot of pleasure."

Earle and Elaine exchange looks and smile. "More than you could ever know," Earle replies. "I don't think they've been able to grasp that their father won't be coming back. Pastor Madison told us to be on the lookout for behavioral changes. He said that grieving kids almost always act out."

"I suppose they would," says Otis. "I think you should know that I'm going to set up a college fund for each of them and arrange that they have new bikes or something they need. And, of course, you know about the invitation to visit me over summer vacation. That would also include you two and Bonnie. I might like to visit North Carolina once in a while to see them, too."

"I'm sure Bonnie would appreciate that," says Earle. Elaine nods her head.

A moment later Valerie appears and asks if they are ready to order. Otis asks for the mixed grill. Earle requests beef short ribs. Elaine says she isn't hungry. "I'll pick at what's on your plate, dear. I have no appetite."

Otis and Earle glance at one another. "She hasn't eaten enough to keep a bird alive since the day of the funeral," Earle says. "And come to think of it, I haven't had much to eat, either."

When the food arrives, the two men eat in silence while Elaine sips at her water.

"When will you be heading back to Maine?" she asks Otis.

"I have one more stop in Georgia. After that, I'll be going to Virginia to see a friend. And then I'll go home."

"Would you do something for us?" says Elaine.

"Anything."

"Please stay in touch."

"You can count on it," Otis says.

Chapter Forty-Four

It is now the second week in October, and Otis thinks about the old Joni Mitchell song lyrics *I get the urge for going.*

"You've been a great guest," George Crawford tells Otis. "And Sadie, too. Come back to The Bluff anytime." Otis tells George that he hopes to do just that.

The following morning Otis packs up his truck, settles the bill and is on his way to Georgia by ten o'clock.

He gets on Route 23 toward East Franklin, which will eventually take him to Route 64 west. The unsettled area is a gorgeous display of forest and distant mountain scenery. Otis pops in a John Denver CD so he can listen to *Rocky Mountain High* and sing along. He will stay inside the Chattahoochee National Forest tonight at a campground right on a lake. He thinks it would be a good place to take Will and Madelyn camping someday. There's plenty of swimming, hiking, fishing, games and stargazing to keep kids busy for weeks on end. They could bring their bikes and maybe even a few of their friends. When he gets settled later today, he will set aside some time to read more letters from Josh. There must be fifty or more in the big envelope Bonnie gave him.

While driving along, he mulls over in his mind what he will say to Julie when he sees her. A few days from now he will leave for Damascus with the hope that she will agree to be treated for her illness. Otis has prayed for divine intervention; maybe his prayers will be answered.

When he arrives at the campground, he checks in and finds that he has a spot near the dining hall. Fine with him. He hopes there'll be people he can talk to. Otis knows this is not a good time to be by himself. Having a little company will help get his mind off of what happened in Cullowhee.

Later, when he takes Sadie for a walk, he stops at the canteen and picks up a can of root beer and a copy of the *Times-Courier,* a newspaper published in Ellijay, Georgia. He goes back to his site, settles in and begins to read. There are the usual political stories on the front page, police and fire reports and the goings-on at City Hall. When he turns to the Lifestyle page, he sees a black and white photograph of a young boy with a bike at his side. Otis reads the cutline and discovers that the boy, Ben Prescott, is recovering from burns he suffered at a campfire in Ellijay. When Otis reads the accompanying story, he discovers that Ben is the son of Henry and Thelma Prescott. The father is a construction worker, and the mother stays home to take care of a younger son who has cerebral palsy. An older daughter is prone to epileptic seizures, according to the story. Some people have more than their share, thinks Otis, shaking his head. When he comes to the end of the story, he reads:

"I don't know what we would have done if folks hadn't helped us out," said John Prescott. "Someone we don't even know sent $100,000. That money helped pay the medical bills. Who would just hand over $100,000? I ask you. Who? I'd like to meet that person someday."

Otis knows the answer. Oh yes, he knows who gave the Prescott family that money. But he will never let on. "Don't let your right hand know what your left hand is doing." That's what Pastor Wright has always preached.

On the morning of October 11, before he leaves for Georgia, Otis calls Bonnie, Earle and Elaine to see how they're doing and to say so long for now.

Will and Madelyn have new bicycles. A red one for Will, purple for Madelyn. Otis has also arranged for Bonnie to buy the children school supplies at Walmart and clothes at Old Navy and The Gap as they are needed. A gift card to Sav-Mor will pay for a year of groceries.

The drive on Route 64 west will take him to Springer Mountain alongside the Blue Ridge Mountains. Otis shakes his head when he recalls that he had estimated he'd be back in Hopewell by Labor Day. Five months later, here he is on the last leg of his journey. He now thinks he'll be home before the end of October.

As he continues his drive with Sadie by his side, he pops in a Ricky Nelson CD and hears the strains of *Travelin' Man*. Otis sings, *"I'm a travelin' man, made a lot of stops..."*

And he has. But unlike the man in the song he has met only one woman, and her name is Julie. He thinks about her now and asks Fern to forgive him for having feelings for someone other than her. He recalls the night they were watching a sad movie on television about a woman whose husband had died suddenly, and Fern had turned to Otis. "If anything ever happens to me," she'd said, "I want you to go on living. We'll be together again in the hereafter so what will it matter?" At the time, Otis had brushed off what she said, but maybe Fern had known somehow that she would die before him. She was telling him that she would want him to never forget her but to go on and love again.

His plan now is to drive the more than two hours to the end of the Trail and call it a day. He hopes there's a sign for Springer Mountain along the way because he'd like to have a picture of himself and Sadie near the sign to show they had traveled the entire distance.

Julie already knows about what happened in Cullowhee, so he won't have to explain it to her again, though she might press for more details. She is a tender-hearted woman, and if there's anyone on the face of the earth who can help him heal, it will be her. He thinks about the last time he was with Julie. She had been so distant. He's sure Carolyn had something to do with it. Maybe she told Julie to forget Otis because soon he'd be on the road. Maybe she even told Julie that he was using her. By now, he hopes her heart has softened and has dismissed anything Carolyn might have said. Otis can only hope.

The day is bright and sunny, and the fine autumn weather lifts his spirits. He thinks about Joshua and wonders if he will see him in the hereafter, too. The more he thinks about the past five months, the more he has realized that each person's life is a book and each chapter is filled with adventures, ups and downs, joys and sorrows, harmony and discord and every emotion under the sun. Or maybe it's like a giant jigsaw puzzle, and as each puzzle piece is put into its rightful place, the picture of a man or woman's life begins to emerge. The final piece to be placed, of course, would be the lowering into the grave.

Otis is surprised to find himself thinking of such things. Maybe he's getting old or he's becoming philosophical. Whatever the case, he is enjoying thinking about what life is all about. He wonders if God has been his invisible, silent partner and travel companion, overseeing his every thought, his every word, his every step. If He has been, Otis hopes that he has done nothing to offend Him. Seconds later he is reminded of the lies he has told since finding all that money. He turns down the volume of the music and offers an apology. "I am so sorry for my behavior, Lord. Please forgive me and help me to live a righteous life, one that will honor you." The money. Otis thinks about the day he found it lying in the ditch. It has changed him in ways he never expected. On one hand, he was able to help other people. On the other hand, he has come to worship it way too much. Is there a happy medium? Otis isn't sure about that. He has to mull it over.

He feels better, having confessed. He turns up the volume on the radio. This time, he hears Frankie Ford singing *"Oo-ee, oo-ee baby. Won't ya let me take you on a sea cruise..."*

The lyrics remind Otis that he had thought about going to the Cayman Islands and opening an account there. He'd be allowed to deposit $50,000 without the IRS knowing about it. He could invite Julie to go with him. Maybe he'd ask Fred Turnbull to watch Sadie while they were away. Or Colleen. But not Pastor Wright. He's too busy to take care of an animal. Fred and Colleen only work part-time. Then again, Julie might not like the idea of cruising. For all he knows, she might not like boats at all. He still has a lot to learn about Julie Charlton, and it'll take time. But like that old Rolling Stones song goes, time, time, time is on his side. Yes, it is.

Otis's thoughts about Colleen remind him that she had mentioned a new Mexican restaurant opening in Hopewell. Why would Mexican people open a restaurant in such a little town, unless the owners have an agenda. He wonders who these people are and worries that they might be a front for one of the drug cartels. He knows he'll have to be careful, and he definitely will not go inside the place. He won't be calling for takeout, either. He'll have to keep a low profile.

Chapter Forty-Five

Ninety minutes later, Otis pulls to the side of the road and backs into a space where an outcropping faces the summit of Springer Mountain. One other car is parked there, so he takes his camera with him when he and Sadie get out of the truck. Maybe someone will snap a picture of them next to the sign. When he moves to the front of the truck, he notices that a couple have a small table set up for a picnic. There's a platter of fried chicken, cole slaw and some kind of muffins. There's also a cake with a few candles stuck in the chocolate frosting and a pitcher of cold drink on the hood of the couple's car. A birthday celebration, then. When he approaches, the woman looks up.

"Come and join us," she says. "We have plenty to share."

"Thanks," says Otis, "but I'm just stopping by to take in the view. There is one thing you can do for me, though, if you wouldn't mind."

"What's that?" asks the man, introducing himself as Keith.

"I'm Shirley," the woman adds, extending her hand toward Otis.

"Otis. Whose birthday is it?"

"Mine," says Keith.

"Well, happy birthday. Nice way to celebrate."

"It's our tradition," says Shirley.

"I'd love to have a photo of me and Sadie here showing that we arrived at Springer Mountain safe and sound," says Otis.

"How about right over there?" Shirley says, pointing to an area about twenty feet away. "That's everyone's favorite spot."

"Sure. Thanks."

Shirley and Keith get up from their chairs and follow Otis and Sadie to a low wooden split rail fence. A sign is posted that reads "DANGER: LOOSE LEDGE" and another that reads "BEAR WARNING."

"Some tourists have ignored the warnings and have either fallen or done battle with bears," says Keith. "They're usually harmless, though. Even so, everyone should take the warnings seriously. Why don't you and your dog stand right over there . . . a little to the left."

Otis does as Keith says and smiles when he's asked. But a sudden movement catches Otis's attention, and his eyes turn toward Shirley and Keith's car.

In an instant, a scuffling sound can be heard, and Shirley and Keith have also become aware. "Don't move . . . " Keith says, his voice barely a whisper. "Rein in the dog and keep her close to you. We've got a visitor."

The look on the couple's faces tells Otis that Keith is serious. He pulls gently on Sadie's leash until she's tight to his side. She senses danger and lets out a low growl.

"Shh . . ." Otis says in a whisper. "It's all right."

Keith continues in a low voice, "Now, move very, very slowly toward your truck and be as quiet as possible. When you get to the passenger door, open it and get inside fast. We'll go to our own car."

"What is it?" Otis asks.

"Hurry! Run!" shouts Keith.

But Otis just stands there in a state of shock and confusion.

Chapter Forty-Six

"**B**ear!"

When Shirley shouts the warning, adrenalin starts racing throughout Otis's body. Sadie senses the animal's presence and starts straining at her leash. When her murmuring becomes a growl, Otis places his hand over her muzzle to quiet her.

He can now see the black hindquarters of the bear as he and Sadie move slowly toward the truck. Otis is certain that the birthday food attracted it.

The bear topples the small table, causing the pitcher of lemonade and food to crash to the pavement. Otis opens the truck's door just as the bear comes around the front end, likely having sensed Sadie. The animal lurches toward them just as they scramble to get inside the truck and, in a matter of seconds, the bear is at the passenger door trying to get inside. It stretches out its massive paw, only to get its foreleg wedged in the door when Otis can't shut it fast enough.

Otis sees up close the bear's curved four-inch claws while it bellows in pain. He has no desire to mess with the animal or hurt it, but he also doesn't want to put himself and Sadie in grave danger. His only option is to release the door so the bear can free its foreleg. But then there's the risk that the animal's rage will motivate it to force its way inside the truck. Otis has another problem. Sadie. Her nose is pressed against the window and she's barking uncontrollably. Otis tries to push the dog to the back seat, but she's too heavy and won't budge. Shoving her to the floor is his only other option. He makes a split second decision and gives her a hard whack on the rump, and Otis is then able to push her out of the way. Meanwhile, the bear's foreleg is still wedged in the door, and the bellowing is only getting worse. Otis throws caution to the wind. In an instant, he releases the door slightly, stiffens his resolve, tamps down his terror and shoves the bear's foreleg away. In that one quick moment, his right hand comes in contact with the coarse texture of its fur and long claws as they rake his forearm. He slams the door shut and watches the bear lumber off across the road and into the woods. Blood is now streaming from a six-inch gash in Otis's arm. He would not be surprised if he has a heart attack right on the spot.

Shaking, he exits the driver's side of the truck to check on Keith and Shirley. There they are, sitting inside their car and laughing at Otis, but he doesn't think what just happened is anything to laugh about. Shirley rolls down her window and Keith leans over the steering wheel so he can see Otis. "You okay?" he shouts, still laughing.

Otis looks at him and does something he has never done before in his entire life. He lifts his right hand and raises his middle finger. "I'm sorry, Lord, but they deserved that," he says before getting back in the truck. He wraps his injured arm with a pair of BVDs to stem the bleeding.

"Watch out for moose!" shouts Keith as Otis drives away. "They can be ornery, too."

He has already paid for two nights at his next lodging place or he'd pass on this one. The name—Black Bear Campground— is enough to give him convulsions.

⋙⋙⋙ ⋘⋘⋘

After supper, Otis wanders over to the dining hall with Sadie to get a mug of root beer. A few of the tables are occupied, one by a Boy Scout troop and their leader, one by a family of six and another by a young couple in their twenties.

Otis finds a table near the entrance, pulls out a chair and sets down his mug. A few minutes pass before the young couple get up from their table and walk toward him. He notices that the man has a wound about nine inches long on the outside of his right leg. The injury is uncovered and appears to have been stapled instead of stitched.

Otis gives a little wave and invites them to join him. The woman tells Otis her name is Trish and that she and her husband Jake are on their honeymoon. Otis asks about Jake's leg and they take turns telling Otis about the struggle he had with a black bear.

"They usually don't bother people, but Jake was trying to get a picture, and he got too close," says Trish. "We think it was a mother bear and she was trying to protect her cubs."

"Looks like she took a nasty swipe at your leg," Otis comments.

"Sure did. Twenty-six staples later."

"Ouch."

"I bled like a stuck pig. If it wasn't for a guy who tossed a pulled pork sandwich in front of that momma bear, I don't know what would've gone down."

Trish nods in agreement. "Scariest thing we've ever been through," she says while twirling a hank of her long dark hair.

Otis points to his own wound.

"Wow. So you had an encounter, too," says Jake. "You should probably see a doctor."

Otis nods and says he's been treating it with an anti-bacterial ointment and antibiotics prescribed by a doctor at an Urgent Care.

"Where you from?" Otis asks, noticing their deep southern accents.

"Louisiana . . . Baton Rouge."

"What's your line of work?"

"Chef. At Ragin' Cajun."

Otis nods toward Trish. "How about you?"

"I teach at LSU. Art history. We got married last Saturday. Back to work on Monday."

"Well, enjoy your life together. It goes by fast."

"Your wife with you?" asks Jake. "Or you by your lonesome?"

Otis leans back in his chair and crosses his arms. "I'm alone. But I think that's gonna have to change real soon."

"Well, enjoy the area. We plan to," says Trish.

As the pair walk away, Otis hears her say that he'll never be lonely as long he has her. Otis wants to tell her not to count her chickens before they hatch. She has no idea what the future holds. No idea at all. If Otis is sure of one thing, it's that.

A spur of the moment floats through his head. He reaches into his pocket and pulls out a packet of $100 bills. He counts out ten and follows the couple to their car. Trish activates the passenger window to the down position and asks Otis if he forgot something.

"Sure did," he says.

"Here's a little something from me to you. Best wishes on your marriage."

He drops the bills into Trish's lap and laughs at her shocked expression.

"We can't accept this," she says. And Jake agrees.

"Yes, you can. And you will. Now put it in the bank for when you have an emergency. You never know what lies ahead. Enjoy your trip now."

And then Otis is gone. When he pulls out of the parking lot, he can see that Trish and Jake are still sitting inside their car, probably talking about their unexpected windfall.

>⟫⟫⟩⟩ ⟨⟨⟨⟨

Otis's thoughts turn to the early days of his marriage to Fern. They never did have a honeymoon, not even a weekend away somewhere. But no use crying over spilled milk. What's done is done. Next time—if there ever is a next time—he would insist on some kind of getaway.

The following morning, Otis awakens to rain and strong wind gusts. There's a hurricane headed for the East Coast, and the weather is forecast to be like this all week, so now he thinks it's time to high tail it to Damascus. There's no sense in hanging around if he can't go swimming or take a long walk with Sadie. There's zip-lining, but Otis would never try that. Even if he did, what fun would it be in the rain?

That night, he calls Julie and tells her he'll arrive in Damascus the day before her birthday, October 16. She says she has missed him and can hardly wait to see him again. When Otis asks about the weather, she tells him that the hurricane has gained strength and it's expected to impact the weather up and down the Atlantic coast. "The storm is aiming for North Carolina. Next stop, Virginia. Good thing Damascus is inland." Julie advises Otis to stay on Route 64 and not take any back roads due to flash flooding.

Chapter Forty-Seven

While Otis is packing up to leave the campground, he thinks about Julie and what he will say to her when they see each other again. They certainly have a lot to talk about. The drive to Damascus will take a little over five hours, giving him plenty of time to think about what he wants to say. He is in love with Julie and he's sure she feels the same way. But what do they do with their feelings? He will be cautious when he brings up the subject of her illness since he doesn't want to pressure her in any way. Otis only wants what is best for her, and he's not sure what that is. He hopes she's had a chance to think things over and has come to her senses about accepting his offer for curing her illness. How he can convince her to come around to his way of thinking is a hurdle he'd like to jump with flying colors. He just doesn't know the way.

If Fern were alive, she would suggest that Otis go on his knees and pray that Julie will accept his offer. But if his will and Julie's aren't the same, what then? Otis has no answer so he just prays that God will change Julie's heart. Then the problem will be in His hands, not his own.

After settling his account with Black Bear Campground owner Dan Franklin, he leaves for Damascus. Dan also suggests that Otis stay on Route 64 due to bad weather.

He pops a country western CD into the player and sings along to Willie Nelson's *On the Road Again*. The rain is coming down in torrents now and as he drives away, he is in such deep thought that he misses the sign for Route 64.

Forty-five minutes later he has to pull over to the side of the road until the downpour subsides. The windshield wipers are set at the highest speed, but the rain is so heavy they can't keep up. He sees signs for Fontana Lake and Almond and discovers that he is way off track when he consults his road map. The country road is filling up quickly with rain water, and Otis fears that the lake will soon overflow and spill across the embankment. He needs to find his way, but the truck's navigation system isn't working in this remote area and he has nothing to rely on but his wits and the Rand McNally. He has his compass, too, and prayer. All four should be enough to get Sadie and himself out of the middle of nowhere.

Chapter Forty-Eight

According to the Rand McNally maps of Georgia and Virginia, Otis needs to find I-26 west, a direct route from Almond to Damascus at a more than 190-mile distance. He notices that the sky has darkened to a purple-black, the clouds are swirling and the wind is now gale force. The sound of cracking tree branches as they fall to the ground reverberates, and many smaller ones are now strewn across the roadway.

Sadie is whimpering and pacing in back of Otis from one end of the seat to the other. Up ahead, Otis sees something in the sky he has never seen before. A huge tan-colored cloud, wide at the top and narrow at the bottom, is heading toward the truck. Suddenly, the wind dies down, hail hits the hood and roof and Sadie starts barking wildly.

He then recalls a TV documentary about a tornado that tore through Udall, Kansas in the 1950s and a movie about a storm chaser who followed tornadoes. Otis lets out a soft curse when he realizes he's in trouble. If a tornado is coming, the best place to be, the chaser had said, is in a culvert or ditch but never below an overpass. Otis thinks it's safest to stay inside the truck with the windows up. He knows he and Sadie would be swept up in an instant if they were in the tornado's path, but there's nothing he can do but pray and wait it out. Otis moves to the bench seat with Sadie and snuggles close to her. Then the waiting begins.

The wind becomes violent again, and this time it causes the truck to shake so hard it's as if the earth has opened below. Otis sucks in his breath, holds Sadie tightly and braces for the worst. Seconds later comes the sound of a tremendous boom that doesn't let up. Never before has Otis been filled with such raw terror. The sound is so loud it feels as if he and Sadie have climbed inside a jet engine at full throttle. While lying in the back seat with her, memories of his entire life flash through his brain, as if he were watching slides being rapidly projected onto a screen, one after the other. The wind worsens by the second, and though it is daytime the inside of the truck has darkened. When Otis feels the front of the truck lift, he screams and holds on to Sadie for dear life. The force of the wind slams them against the back of the seat, and now he can feel the truck listing toward the passenger side. Any second now Otis expects it to tip over or be sucked into a monstrous vortex. If that happens, he'll never get to Damascus. The bear encounter seems like a kid's birthday party compared to this. Otis's heart is hammering against his rib cage as he calls out to God to save them. Sadie is whimpering, and her body is shaking. A moment later there is calm.

Otis and Sadie lie there, breathing heavily. He prays that the twister has passed. If it has, he will get on his knees and thank God that his life has been spared. And Sadie's, too. Now, as never before, he can't wait to be back in Hopewell where, except for the cold and snow, the weather is rarely extreme. Suddenly, he hears Fern's voice: Remember what Pastor Wright said about trusting God? Trust him and He will give you the desires of your heart. "I trust you, Lord. I trust you—please help us get out of here!" Otis calls out, tears streaming down his face.

⟫⟫⟫⟶ ⟵⟪⟪⟪

It is after midnight when Otis arrives in Damascus. After the tornado passed and he was able to drive the truck, he witnessed nothing but destruction. Trees had been torn out of the ground by their roots. Roofs on houses had been ripped off. Debris was scattered everywhere. While driving along a river, Otis saw furniture, appliances and other household items floating along with the current. Work crews were out cleaning up the mess and rerouting traffic due to flash flooding in five or six areas. After checking in at The Plantation, Otis goes to bed exhausted and sleeps for the next twelve hours.

Around one o'clock in the afternoon he drives downtown and orders a dozen red roses for pick-up at five o'clock. He will deliver them to Julie himself.

He calls her when he knows she's on break. "I'm here and in one piece," he tells her, adding that for most of the trip phone service had been down. "We have a lot to talk about, honey," he says.

Julie sighs when she hears Otis's voice. "I was worried sick," she says. "That tornado. You were right near it. I'll be home by five o'clock. Come by then. And Otis? I missed you."

"I missed you, too. I'll bring us supper."

During the day, Otis buys Julie a birthday card at the gift store next to Clyde's barber shop and then heads to Walmart to look for a few gifts. He knows just what to buy.

When Otis pulls into Julie's driveway late in the afternoon, her car is already there. On his way he stopped by the florist to buy the roses and ordered two takeout meals from a restaurant downtown: country baked ham, mashed potatoes, peas and a salad. He also has two chocolate cupcakes tucked inside a box from Sweet Tooth Bakery. He takes a quick look in the rear view mirror and notices the intense expression in his eyes and face. He knows he's been grinding his teeth in his sleep because when he wakes up his jaw aches. It comes as no surprise that his recent emotional stress has had a terrible effect on him.

Julie opens her front door before Otis has a chance to knock. In a matter of seconds, they are standing on the porch locked in an embrace.

"For you," says Otis, handing her the flowers when they break away. "I figured we could celebrate a day early."

"Oh, Otis. You didn't have to . . ."

"You're right. I didn't. But I wanted to."

A moment later Sadie gives out a loud woof.

They both turn toward the truck and laugh.

"Gotta give my girlfriend a hug, too," she tells Otis. He follows her to the truck.

After letting Sadie out, Otis suggests they go inside. "I'm hungry, and you probably are, too," he says.

While in the kitchen, Julie arranges the roses in a glass vase and sets them on the table. They eat mostly in silence, only pausing between bites to talk about trivial matters. The weightier topics will come later.

After she clears the table, she takes Otis by the hand and leads him to the living room. They sit on the couch together and hold each other for a long time before either of them says a word.

Otis finally says, "It's been just awful in recent days. I couldn't wait to see you."

"I know, Otis. I've thought about you every day."

Otis then tells her more about Joshua, the bear encounter and tornado, and Julie tells him he's lucky to be alive.

"Well, quite a lot has happened in the last few weeks. I'm going to be summonsed to appear in court when Arlen Wade's trial starts." He pauses for a long moment. "He killed my son. I was right there when it happened. I had no idea. No idea at all. Not until I saw Joshua's picture in the paper."

Julie takes his hand in her own. "It must have been a devastating shock. I'm so sorry you had to face that alone," she says.

"There wasn't anything anyone could do. It's something I had to go through by myself, I guess. My son . . ." The tears come then and continue for a long while. Otis heaves great sobs until there is nothing left inside. "I never got to know my own son. He wrote me letters. To Fern, too. When we let him go, we sealed his fate. No one would ever understand the guilt I feel."

Julie moves away from Otis and faces him. "I hope that doesn't include me. Of all people, I would understand. I have my own burden of guilt, and it started when I was just five years old."

"I'm sorry. Please forgive me for saying that. I know you feel guilt. But you were just a child. Fern and I were nearly adults when Joshua was born. And we gave him away. He never knew why. He never had the chance to know his own parents."

"But the people who adopted him . . . they gave him a good life. They loved him as their own. That's what you told me. They said that, Otis. Don't you remember?"

"Yes, I remember."

"You know, while you were gone, I gave a lot of thought to what happened the day Corinne died and decided to make an appointment with Pastor Wilson. You met him when we went to church those few times."

Otis nods his head. "What did he say?"

"We had six meetings, and during the last one he quoted something out of the New Testament, something I have not forgotten. 'If our hearts do not condemn us, we have confidence before God.' Pastor Wilson told me that it is not our business to carry guilt. The cross took care of that. God wants us to cast all our cares—and that includes guilt—upon Him because His yoke is easy and His burden is light. He grieves when we carry our guilt alone and won't let it go."

"That's a tall order," says Otis. His tears have subsided, and he blows his nose.

"It is, but when I thought about it I realized that I wasn't making Him happy by carrying all that guilt. Pastor Wilson prayed with me, and I was finally able to release some of it. And since that day, I've been releasing it more and more."

"And you're telling me that's what I should do."

"Yes. That's what I'm telling you."

"It'll take time."

"Of course it will. It did for me. Letting go of guilt doesn't happen overnight."

"I keep reliving Joshua's final moments. If only I had been there a few minutes earlier."

"All the 'if onlys' will not bring Joshua back, Otis. There might be a perfectly good reason for why this happened, and we won't know until we leave this life. We have to trust that there was a greater purpose at work."

"Pastor Wright said that when he spoke at Fern's funeral."

"I'm not surprised. He must be a wise man."

"I believe he is."

Otis spends the rest of the night with Julie, and in the morning he gets up early and makes breakfast for her before she goes to work. He sets the table and places a gift bag next to her plate so she will have a surprise when she comes into the kitchen.

"Happy birthday to you!" Otis sings when she appears in the doorway.

Julie goes to him and gives him a kiss. He pulls out a rectangular box from the gift bag.

"This one first," he says.

Julie tears away the paper gently and discovers a child's slate under the wrapping.

"A blank slate," Julie says. "Aren't you the clever one."

Otis smiles. "A blank slate for both of us," he replies. "Now this one."

Again, Julie tears away the wrapping gently. "A journal," she says. *A New Beginning* is written in script on the cover.

Finally, Otis hands her the smallest package. When she opens it, she finds chalk and a pen inside.

"It's up to you to write our story. Would you like to join me in a new beginning?"

Julie pauses, then says, "Yes, I think I would."

"Then you start writing and I'll join in. I love you, Julie Charlton."

"And I love you, too, Otis. Yes, I do."

Chapter Forty-Nine

In the coming days, Otis and Julie continue to talk about Joshua's death and the drug that will make her well. She is now more willing to accept Otis's offer to pay for it. The only drawback, she tells Otis, is that she will be paying him back for the rest of her life.

He tells her not to worry about it, that he is a man of great means. What he does not tell her is how those means came to him. He knows she would not believe him if he told her he had earned it while working at the paper mill. She *might* believe him if he said he had inherited money, but if he intends to build a life with Julie he doesn't want to start off with a lie. In fact, his lying days are over. From now on, whatever comes out of his mouth will be the truth.

He knows at some point he'll have to tell her. He just doesn't know when that will be. The opportunity finally comes one night while they are on Julie's living room couch, Sadie lying at their feet. Something unexpected pops out of his mouth. "Neither of us . . . well, we aren't getting any younger," he says. "We'd better get started writing our story."

"How do you want it to begin?" Julie pulls away from him and looks into his eyes.

"How about marriage?"

"Marriage? But you live in Maine. I live here. How would that work?"

"Well, we could rent your house and live in Maine until we're old enough to retire. Then we could live summers in Maine and winters here. Or we could sell both and move to Timbuktu." Julie laughs at his joke.

"It isn't that simple, Otis. Nothing ever is, and we both know that. For one thing, I have my job . . ."

Otis kisses her hand. "There are hospitals in Maine, Julie. We would have the best of both worlds. Lobster and blueberry pie in the summer and southern fried chicken and hummingbird pie in the winter."

Julie laughs again, and Otis is glad she appreciates his sense of humor. "When you put it that way, how can a lady refuse?"

"She can't, Julie. So I'm assuming you just said yes."

In her canine way, Sadie says it for her with a sweet little woof.

⟫⟫⟫ ⟪⟪⟪

Julie has been in treatment for her illness for the past five weeks and is doing well. By the new year, she and Otis hope to be married, but he has one more hurdle to cross. He has to tell Julie about The Vault.

He decides to do that on the night he takes her to the Old Mill Inn. It is Thanksgiving weekend, and Otis thinks having supper at a nice restaurant will be romantic and the right place to tell her. On the way to the inn, Julie tells him about Henry Mock and General Imboden and their connection to the surrounding land. It is thick with rhododendrons, mountain laurel, white oak, poplar and hemlock trees. Originally a house, the Inn overlooks a pretty waterfall, and Otis has reserved a table where they can watch it tumble over the rocks below.

"And speaking of mock, that reminds me of a dish I want to make for you sometime. Mock duck. Maybe it originated with Henry Mock."

"What is it?"

"A hamburger dish. You flatten hamburger into a square, put stuffing mix on top of the meat, fold up the sides and cook it in the oven. Tomato soup is the final ingredient. You pour it on top of the hamburger like a gravy for a few minutes before you take it out of the oven."

"An unusual recipe," Julie says.

"And delicious. Trust me." Otis doesn't mention that it was one of Fern's specialties.

When they are seated by a college-age waitress, Otis gives her their order (The Old Smokey for Julie, The Virginian for him). He asks that they not be disturbed during their meal. What he has to tell Julie is too important. He doesn't want any interruptions.

He begins by telling her that she looks beautiful in her simple black dress. She is wearing a turquoise necklace for a pop of color. She is also wearing her hair in a new style, and Otis compliments her on that, too.

He begins by telling her he has something important to discuss, and that something is money. He tells her about losing his job and his grief and depression following Fern's death and the medical and funeral expenses left over from her illness. He tells her, also, about the day Pastor Wright came to visit and the custodian job he left after only two weeks. Julie sits quietly while she listens to Otis tell his story.

He then tells her about his walk along SR92, his visit to Fern's grave, the state police cars speeding past him, what he found lying in the ditch and, finally, the shooting deaths of the two drug runners.

Julie's eyes grow wider with every revelation, and when he tells her how much money he found, she stares at him for a long moment.

"You're pulling my leg, Otis. Do you really expect me to believe that story?"

"It's the gospel truth."

"I don't believe it."

"Why would I lie?" Otis asks. "I expect you to believe me because it's what happened."

"But if this is all true, that money isn't yours to keep."

"There's a finders-keepers law."

"But that money came from drug sales."

"Yes. But it really doesn't matter where it came from."

"Yes, it does. It matters a lot!"

"Why?"

Julie looks at Otis in exasperation. "Because it came from evil people. It's tainted! Cursed!"

Otis considers this for a moment and says, "I never planned to keep it all."

"Then what did you plan to do?" A look of horror sweeps across her face. "Does this mean that the medical treatments I've been having are being paid for by drug money? And what about that truck you drive? Otis . . . tell me you didn't . . . please tell me. You have to get rid of that money."

"Who would I give it to? Besides, I can't. At least not all of it."

"Why?"

Otis is slow to answer. "Because I've been giving it away."

He then tells Julie about how he came up with a plan to travel along the Trail and help the poor. Julie smiles then and says, "Now *that* part I *can* believe. Who did you give money to?"

Otis tells her the stories about John Penewait, Edith Kulp, Lloyd at Whispering Pines, the boy in Ellijay who suffered terrible burns, the couple from Louisiana. Bonnie and his grandchildren and now her.

"You care about other people, Otis," she says. "It's one of the reasons why I love you. But it's still not right to keep all that money. And drug sales are paying for my cure? How could you?"

Otis doesn't know what to say in response so he lowers his head and says nothing.

In the next breath Julie says, "I can't marry you until you let go of that crime-laced money and get rid of the truck. And that's my final word."

Neither of them speak again until she adds, "And another thing, Otis. Where have you been keeping all that money?"

Otis looks at his plate of beef covered in gravy, mashed potatoes, fresh string beans and biscuit. "Some is in the truck. In a secret compartment. Some of it is in bank accounts in Maine and a few other places."

She looks at the man she has agreed to marry and says, "Either you've been telling me stories all night or you're insane. Come on, Otis. You can do better than that."

"No, I can't. It's the truth."

"Well, that takes the cake. Now I've heard everything." She bursts out laughing while Otis sits there in mental anguish.

He knows Julie is right. He has to give the money back. And he has to get rid of the truck. But all of it has given him such a great sense of freedom and pleasure that he doesn't want to give up any of it. He also knows he'll have to make a hard choice—the woman he loves or wealth—but he already knows what it will be.

Chapter Fifty

"You win," he tells Julie the following day.

"Win what?"

"I'll hand the money over to the police. And I'll get rid of the truck."

"Don't do it because of me."

"It's not because of you. I've given it a lot of thought. You're right. How about going to Maine for Christmas. We can get married on New Year's Eve if you'll have this poor old sinner."

The look on Julie's face tells Otis that she would like nothing better.

"On the way to Maine, we can make stops to see how Edith Kulp and the others are getting along."

"And you promise to hand over the money and sell the truck when we get to Maine?"

"Promise. I'll work out something we can both live with. But will you do one thing for me?"

"What?"

"Finish your treatments."

Julie turns away from Otis. "All right. But that's all I'll do. And I'll give my notice at work."

Two weeks before Christmas, Otis and Julie return to the Old Mill Inn, this time with Carolyn. Julie wants one last evening with her best friend before she leaves for Maine, and Otis wants to hear what Carolyn has to say about their engagement, but all she offers is her sincere best wishes.

Otis now thinks maybe he was wrong to think Carolyn had anything to do with Julie ending their relationship.

Before leaving Damascus, Otis calls Colleen to say he has some exciting news to tell her but first asks to speak to Pastor Wright. When the Pastor hears the news about Julie, he doesn't seem too surprised. He knows that many men remarry in the first year or so after the death of their wives. He agrees to officiate at their wedding during the afternoon of New Year's Eve and promises to keep it a secret from Colleen. Otis wants to tell her himself. He'll also ask her to stand up for Julie. He thinks the two women will become good friends. As for a best man, Otis will ask Aubrey Keane from the hardware store.

꘎꘎꘎ ꘎꘎꘎

While driving back to Hopewell, Otis fulfills his promise to take Julie to all the places he had visited while heading south. Until now, Julie has never been anywhere outside of Virginia, and she seems to be having the time of her life. She has been especially interested in the zinc mining that left Palmerton in such a horrid state, and she's been curious about the western part of Massachusetts. When they arrive in the Berkshires he pops the *Alice's Restaurant* CD into the player. She has never heard it before and laughs at all the right parts.

While on the road, Otis has learned that Edith Kulp is happy in her new home and is doing well. Tomorrow, they'll go to Rangeley to check on Lloyd MacNeill and John Penewait.

When they reach Kittery, Otis pulls in to Turkey Lurkey's parking lot. "I think you'll like it here," he tells Julia, hoping that the chef has done away with spinach and Brussels sprouts and is back to cooking butternut squash.

This time, he parks as close to the restaurant as possible and hopes no tour buses arrive while he and Julie are eating. He thinks about Mr. Auto Body and wonders what he would say if he saw Julie with him. "What'd you do, see your doctor and ask his nurse for a date?" he might say, recalling that Otis had told him he was off to a doctor's appointment.

When they step inside the restaurant, Otis sees the same waiter with the red shirt and black bow tie. He hopes he and Julie are seated in his section so he can be extra nice this time. Maybe he'll ask the hostess for one of his tables.

A few minutes later, she calls Otis's name and he asks to be seated in Mr. Bow Tie's section. "Sure, right this way," she says.

Otis and Julie study Turkey Lurkey's menu while seated at a table overlooking the parking lot. A few minutes pass before Mr. Bow Tie approaches. He looks at Otis and says, "Two turkey dinners?"

Yes, exactly. They had missed Thanksgiving dinner entirely because Julie had had to work that day and Otis will never win any awards for cooking.

"But no spinach or Brussels sprouts, right?"

"You remembered?"

"How could I forget? I told the chef to go back to butternut squash . . . and string beans."

"Well, thanks. You have butternut squash then?"

"Yes, sir."

The waiter gives Otis a little smile. "In all the years I've been waiting tables, I've had very few customers dislike spinach as much as you do. And never at the Ritz."

That nails it. Now Otis knows for sure that the man came up from Boston or maybe New York City. His job at the Ritz confirms it.

"Must have been quite an experience, serving meals to all those rich people," he says.

The waiter gives Otis a puzzled look. "Oh, not *that* Ritz. I meant the one in Skowhegan. It's a vegan place."

So he was wrong. Hadn't Fern always chastised him for making assumptions? Yes, she had.

"Might I get you something from the bar?"

"Just ice water, thanks," says Otis.

"With lemon, please," adds Julie.

"Very well." The waiter gives Otis a derisive look out of the corner of his eye and smiles. Otis smiles back. This time the waiter will be getting a big tip.

"What was that all about?" Julie asks when the waiter leaves to place their orders.

"Nothing. He waited on me when I was here last spring. He's so hoity-toity I thought he must be up from Boston or New York."

Julie looks at Otis with a raised eyebrow but says nothing more.

After they finish eating and the bill arrives, Otis takes five $100 bills from his wallet and slides them under his plate. Won't Mr. Bow Tie be surprised.

Otis recalls leaving his bungalow clean last May but hopes that Julie won't give it the white glove test. He finds that his concerns are unfounded when he opens the front door and looks around. When he steps into the living room, he sees that someone has given the place a good scouring. Maybe that someone was none other than Colleen. If she did all the cleaning, her husband is one fortunate man to have a wife like her, he thinks.

A pile of mail is sitting in a neat stack on the kitchen table. On top is a letter from Logger-Heads. He'll open it later. His old boss has probably written to let him know he won't be called back to work. Maybe he can collect unemployment benefits a while longer. Maybe the company will be sold or is closing for good.

Julie tells Otis that the house is cozy and sweet, her kind of place.

"But I think we might want a home of our own eventually," she says. "Something we can buy together. You know, Otis . . . a *blank slate,* a *new beginning?* We'll also need an extra bedroom for Will and Madelyn when they come to visit. And one for Bonnie, too. And the Randalls."

He sees her point and nods his head. "Good idea. We could wait until spring to have a look around. See what's out there."

No sooner do they agree than they hear someone knocking on the door. Otis looks out the window after moving the curtain aside. He sees a stranger holding a big manila envelope standing on the front porch.

"Huh. A dude probably looking for a donation to some charity."

When Otis opens the door, a tall, bald-headed man asks if he is Otis Kingston.

"Yes. I'm Otis Kingston."

Without another word, the constable hands Otis the envelope, return address Jackson County Courthouse, Sylva, North Carolina. After the constable leaves, Otis opens the envelope and finds a subpoena. The State of North Carolina vs. Arlen Wade. He has to appear in court on March 2. Otis will have to give his eye witness testimony concerning the murder of his son.

"I'll go with you," says Julie when Otis tells her. "We can check on the Damascus house while we're at it."

After the eleven o'clock news, Otis opens the letter from Logger-Heads. It reads:

Dear Mr. Kingston:

We have been trying to reach you without success. We are writing to offer you re-employment at Logger-Heads. The company recently signed a contract with an international paper products conglomerate that will take us well into the 21st century and beyond.

If you are interested, please call Charlotte Mitchell at 207-486-2900 Ext. 21 in the Human Resources office no later than Friday, January 3.

Sincerely, Thomas L. Webber, Director of Human Resources

Julie is already asleep. He'll have to wait until breakfast to tell her the good news.

Chapter Fifty-One

Christmas is a small celebration, just the two of them inside Otis's bungalow. The fireplace is lit, and a small tree he cut down in the woods is decorated with a few strings of popcorn, cranberries and colored lights. Several wrapped gifts are under the tree. One is set aside for Sadie—a new red collar imprinted with her name.

While ham and scalloped potatoes are cooking in the oven, they open their gifts. Julie has given Otis a humorous book titled "A Walk in the Woods" by Bill Bryson. The author walked the Appalachian Trail with a friend and wrote about their experiences. She also bought him a photo box to store pictures from his trip through Appalachia. One photo is already in place—a picture of himself, Julie and Sadie in front of the sign for Whispering Pines. He thanks her and hands her a small package.

"Otis, you didn't."

"Open it."

"I hope you didn't . . ."

"Just open it."

Julie peels back the gift wrapping and sees the name of a store she recognizes on the little box. *Happy Trails*—the little gift shop across from Clyde's barber shop in Damascus.

She removes the lid and looks inside. A pin. It is inscribed *Hiker Parade-Trail Days-May 2016.*

"Pull up the piece of cardboard."

When she hesitates, he says, "Go ahead. Take a look."

Julie gives the cardboard a little tug. Beneath is a sparkling gold ring with three tiny diamonds.

"And a partridge in a pear tree," Otis sings, right on key. "Merry Christmas, sweetheart."

"Merry Christmas, Otis."

They hear a little woof behind them and turn to see the dog standing there. "Come here, Sadie," says Julie.

All three join in a group hug, eager and ready to start their new beginning. Their wedding is only a few days away.

Chapter Fifty-Two

It is New Year's Day when Otis and Julie leave their driveway and turn right onto SR92.

They continue half a mile down the road before Otis passes through the wrought iron cemetery gates where Fern is buried. He parks his 2012 Chevy Cruze at the bottom of the hill and asks Julie to wait for him. He'll only be a few minutes. Otis wants to make sure that the spelling of Fern's name and dates of birth and death on her new headstone are accurate. When he arrives at the top of the knoll, he walks the short distance to her gravesite. Yes, everything is as it should be. His own name and date of birth are also written on the stone. The date of his death will come later—much later, he hopes.

Once again, he kneels and thanks Fern for all the love and care she gave him over the years and tells her about Joshua and his death. He doesn't mention Julie.

Back in the car, Otis continues driving along the road at a slow a crawl. He is looking for a certain wooded area and finds it a few minutes later, just up ahead. He pulls onto the shoulder and puts the vehicle in park. He wishes he could have kept the F-150, but Julie had insisted that he turn it in. The Bishop was surprised but happy to show Otis used cars on the dealership's lot, including the Chevy Cruze. Though in no way does it rival the truck, it has low mileage and runs well.

Julie and Sadie wait inside the car while he removes the three duffel bags from the trunk—the first is blue, the second is black, the third army green. He places them in the ditch six or seven feet apart and returns to the car.

Their next stop is the police station. When they arrive, Otis takes two envelopes from Julie—a white No. 10 and a manila eight by ten—crosses the road and finds a path that will take him into the woods. He leaves the eight by ten leaning against a tree in back of the building and slides the No. 10 through a mail slot out front. He will call the police from his Walmart track phone to let them know about the envelopes.

Their final stop will be the Church of the Blinding Light. Another No. 10 envelope is lying on Julie's lap. Pastor Wright's name is written on the front and beneath his name in big black letters is the word CONFIDEN-TIAL. Won't Pastor Wright be surprised when he opens the envelope and reads the letter Otis wrote but did not sign. He will be even more surprised when he finds the cashier's check inside. Otis is looking forward to seeing the church's exterior and interior painted, new hymnals and Bibles in each pew and soft cushions to sit on. The rest of the money will keep the church going for years. There's one more envelope sitting on Julie's lap. This one is for Colleen. She, too, will be surprised to find a cashier's check made payable to her.

If he were to admit the truth, Otis would have to be honest and say that a burden has been lifted from his shoulders. Being wealthy, even for a short season, gave him a feeling of security but he now knows that genuine security comes from knowing God.

After dropping off the envelopes at the church, Otis reverses direction and drives along SR92 toward home. New Year's Day is always quiet along this stretch of road, but today about 500 feet away he sees someone walking along the opposite side.

"I wonder who that is," Otis says more to himself than to Julie. "Dude doesn't look familiar."

Julie has been admiring her new ring, and when she looks up she also sees the man. He is wearing a black hooded jacket and hat, black pants and dark sunglasses. They watch as he stops every ten or fifteen feet and peers into the ditch. Otis pulls onto the shoulder and pretends to be looking at something on his lap so when the man gets closer he won't think he's being watched. He asks Julie to do the same.

"That's no hitchhiker," Otis says. "He's looking for something."

"The money?" Julie says.

"I'll bet."

When the man gets to the area where Otis left the duffel bags, he stops and looks around. Otis and Julie continue to watch him in secret as he goes into the ditch and squats A few seconds later he stands up and pulls something from his pocket.

"A cell phone," Otis whispers. "He's calling someone."

"We should go," Julie says.

"Not yet. I want to see what happens."

"We shouldn't get involved."

Knowing that Julie is right, he starts driving away but after a short distance he turns onto an old logging road where they can observe what is happening on SR92.

Ten minutes pass before the driver of a black Ford Mustang rental bearing Texas license plates stops where the man is waiting. Three other men, all wearing similar black jackets, get out and talk to the man who placed the call. Otis and Julie continue to watch as the men go into the ditch and toss the bags onto the side of the road. One of the men unzips the bags and checks the contents. He then tosses each one into the trunk of the Mustang before the men pile inside the car and drive away. Otis waits a few seconds before pulling onto the road. He and Julie then follow a quarter mile behind the Mustang all the way to Hopewell's center. While parked in a bank's lot near Aubrey Keane's hardware store, Otis and Julie watch as the men enter Miguel's Cantina. When they come out, the man in the dark clothing spots Otis's car and signals to the other men. All four jump into their car and drive toward the hardware store's parking lot, aiming straight for Otis and Julie.

"Hey, you! Get out of that car!" the man in the passenger seat shouts out the window. Otis can see that the man has a gun and is pointing it at him. He starts the engine and speeds off toward Route 9. A chase ensues, and Otis and Julie pray that the driver of the Mustang will lose interest. But the driver continues to close in on them. Suddenly, a shot is fired followed by another and another. In one quick spin of the steering wheel, Otis pivots and speeds across a suspended bridge.

"Call the cops, Julie! Call the cops!"

"I don't know the number, Otis. Those men are going to kills us!"

Gripped by fear, Otis accelerates to 70 mph while crossing the bridge.

"Dial 9-1-1! Oh, Good Lord. Hurry, Julie! And get down on the floor!" Otis dares to look in the rearview mirror, only to see the Mustang gaining ground. "They're gonna get us! Hurry!"

Otis starts to pray and begs God to help them. He drives off the bridge and continues to a traffic light, only to see that it has turned red. "I can't stop! I can't stop! I have to run the light. Did the call go through?" Otis shouts.

Julie hands the phone to Otis with trembling hands. Finally, Otis hears a voice at the other end of the line.

"Police dispatch. Sergeant Pinkney speaking."

"We need help!" Otis shouts. "Send a cruiser to the light at the beginning of Route 9!"

"Who is this?"

"Never mind that. My wife and I are being chased by drug runners!"

"Please calm down. How do you know that?"

"Drug runners were killed at the Canadian border a year ago September. Remember that?" Otis cries out in desperation.

"I remember. What about it?"

"Four men are after us. They're driving a black Ford Mustang. Texas license plate. I think they're the owners of that new Mexican restaurant in Hopewell." When the officer fails to respond, Otis tries again.

"Please help us! They have the drug money. Hurry! Please hurry!"

"How do you know they have the money?"

"Trust me. It's in the trunk of that Mustang. I know what I'm talking about. Those guys have the money, and they're connected to a Mexican drug cartel. Did you hear that gunshot? They're after us!"

"Okay. Calm down. I'm sending two officers."

A moment later, he and Julie hear police sirens slice through the afternoon air. The driver of the Mustang pulls to the side of the road, and two of the men jump out and throw the duffel bags down an embankment while Otis takes off at a high rate of speed.

He disconnects the call and heads for the Church of the Blinding Light to drop off the envelopes for Pastor Wright and Colleen before heading home. They no longer have The Vault at their disposal, but they have each other, a blank slate and a new beginning. Otis and Julie Kingston both agree that what they have is all they'll ever need.

Made in the USA
Middletown, DE
29 October 2023

41493757R00155